PRINCE OF PERSUASION

SINS AND SCOUNDRELS BOOK 2

SCARLETT SCOTT

Happily Ever After Books

Prince of Persuasion

Sins and Scoundrels Book 2

Now welcome, somer, with thy sonne softe,
That hast this wintres wedres overshake,
And driven away the longe nyghtes blake!
~The Parlement of Fowls
Geoffrey Chaucer

CHAPTER 1

LONDON, 1812

*H*e noticed the fellow's arse first.

The fall of the gent's navy coat—an odd cut, too bulky by half, and did nothing to disguise the firm, high roundness. Nor the wide swell of the hips. Duncan sipped his illicit whisky—smuggled, forbidden, and perfectly delicious —and allowed his gaze to trail down the mysterious fellow's buff breeches. These, unlike the ill-fitting coat, proudly displayed two knees and well-turned calves like a second, wicked skin. Slim ankles stole his attention next. So fine and…dainty beneath the stockings.

His prick twitched to life.

Bloody hell. As the owner and proprietor of The Duke's Bastard, the most fashionable and notorious gambling hell in London, Duncan catered to all manner of vices for his loyal patrons. But though he had engaged in a varied array of libidinous delights and depravities, he had yet to derive a cockstand from another man.

He swallowed another healthy gulp of whisky, relishing the burn. Damn fine swizzle, the latest batch he had been able to procure. Not strong enough to temper his lust, unfortunately, which only increased when the woman seated on his lap moved her bottom in a teasing motion over his growing problem.

"Mr. Kirkwood," she whispered throatily, her arms locked around his neck. Her mouth was so near, her lips grazed his ear as she spoke. "We could make use of one of your special chambers. Only tell me what you prefer, and I shall do anything you wish."

Her offer ought to stir him, but the stranger hovering by the hazard tables transfixed him. He had not removed his hat, perhaps because he was so newly arrived. But he held himself at a stiff angle, as though prepared for flight. Who was this interloper with the unusually feminine form, and why the devil did Duncan find himself so strangely drawn to him?

"Would that please you, Mr. Kirkwood?" Tabitha's hand swept over his burgeoning cock when he failed to answer. Apparently, the fine art of subtlety eluded her. Either his patrons were boors who did not notice such a thing, or she required some stern advice from one of his more seasoned ladies.

Tabitha was new to The Duke's Bastard, and she had yet to realize no matter how much time she spent teasing him, sidling about, casting him longing glances, and flaunting her lovely body, he would not tup her. He did not bed any of the ladies in his employ, as it muddied the waters.

Duncan preferred his waters clear and calm. He wanted the waters to line his pockets with gold more than he wanted them to satisfy his baser urges. There was a time, a place, and a woman for slaking his needs. But not here. Never within The Duke's Bastard. And not her.

"Tabitha," he cautioned, passing his hand along her thigh. Her dress was deuced thin and damp, designed to entice.

"You are tasked with entertaining my patrons. Scamper along and perform your duty."

Her tongue, which had been engaged in licking his throat above his cravat, left his skin. She shifted in his lap, her face blocking his view of the trespasser he found so damned intriguing. Wide, honey-brown eyes met his. There was no denying Tabitha's loveliness. He had hired her for it.

"I thought you might...you are ready, sir, and I only wished to please you," she said.

You are not the one responsible for this cursed state. Good Lord, he could not admit to her the true reason for the evidence of his desire she had skillfully detected. He could not even admit it to himself. Though he had to acknowledge a life of excess and sin that only heightened as the years passed, growing increasingly dissolute.

He took pity on her. "I cannot allow myself time for too much idle distraction. Thank you, however, for the offer."

"Mr. Kirkwood," she protested, pouting prettily.

He remained unmoved. Irritation cut through him, for she had not removed herself from his lap, and he was the master and commander of The Duke's Bastard. The hell was his ship, and everyone aboard it followed his orders or risked being tossed, headlong, to the waters below.

"You are dismissed," he snapped, his hands clamping on her waist and lifting her from him.

There was nowhere for the persistent Tabitha to go save elsewhere, and he suspected he had at last pierced the veil of obliviousness shrouding her. Shaking out her skirts, she offered him a tight smile. "As you prefer, Mr. Kirkwood. Enjoy your evening, sir."

He did not bother to watch her take her leave of him. His gaze had already returned to the gentleman at the hazard table, who had extracted a small ivory tablet and pencil from his voluminous coat while Tabitha had distracted Duncan. *By God.* The man had begun scribbling.

A competitor.

Duncan stood from his chair. All inconvenient leanings toward lust died a hasty death. His strides ate up the floor. His senses registered the familiar sounds of the evening: raucous laughter, epithets, and clinking dice. But inside, he was fuming.

With nothing but persistence, intelligence, and hard work, he had built The Duke's Bastard into a club even royalty begged to enter. Unlike any other club London had to offer, the Bastard was a unique blend of opulence and debauchery.

It boasted the finest French chef at two-thousand pounds per annum, and while it possessed the requisite number of diversions, the ladies he employed were not lowly street wenches. His physician performed regular examinations to make certain they did not contract or spread the pox. And for the truly depraved, there were special, private chambers catering to a broad array of proclivities. He had seen the need for such a haven, and he had created it.

He alone.

There would be no imitators or usurpers.

Others had infiltrated his ranks before, and he had reacted no less harshly than he would now. When one man reaped great rewards, a hundred others sought to follow in his footsteps by any means, fair or foul. He reached the spy, who was too caught up in his attempts to record everything he saw to notice Duncan until he stopped alongside the miscreant.

Wide, green eyes fringed with impossibly long black lashes blinked at him from behind a pair of spectacles. Shock hit him in the chest, and he could not speak for a moment as his scrambled thoughts struggled to piece themselves back into a semblance of order. The mustache affixed to the man's upper lip was false.

The spy was a female.

Thank sweet Christ for that.

But whilst relief pulsed through him, it did nothing to abate his rage. Who was she? Whose employ was she in? How had she gained entrance? Why did she have to possess the most delectable bottom he had ever seen?

He gritted his teeth, dispelling that last, errant thought. "You, sir. Come with me, if you please."

FREDERICA WOULD NOT HAVE BEEN MORE alarmed had the devil himself appeared before her. As it was, given his grim flair for dress, all black, from his cravat and breeches to his shirt and waistcoat, as if he were in a state of perpetual mourning, he resembled him well enough. The only lightness on this man was his golden hair and his bright blue eyes that roamed over her face now in a manner she could not like.

Indeed, he left her feeling…restless. Unsettled. Curious.

Who was this tall, angry, beautiful stranger?

She forced herself to speak in as gruff a tone as she could manage. "I beg your pardon, sir?"

When she had first settled upon her madcap plan, she had not imagined she would be seen. She had foolishly thought she would go as unnoticed as the wall coverings or the carpet. After all, these wicked men had so much distraction, all manner of vices. Dice. Drink. Scandalous females in dampened skirts.

She shuddered. Papa would lock her in her chamber if he learned of her disgraceful endeavors. She would be ruined. Unutterably. Ineligible for a proper marriage. She would be scorned and given the cut direct.

However, since her mother and father wished for her to marry the odious Earl of Willingham, such a fate may not prove as repulsive as one might think.

"You," the man repeated, his tone dark enough to rival his attire as he dredged her from her whirling thoughts. "Come with me."

She blinked, eyeing him over her spectacles, for she could not see through the dreadful things, and they were merely another effort to distort her appearance. "No."

He raised a lone, golden brow, observing her as a king might his lowly vassal. "You are trespassing, sir. You are not a member of my club. Indeed, you are fortunate I have not yet brought the law down upon you."

Not a member of *his* club?

Her mouth went dry.

Could it be that the man before her was the infamous Duncan Kirkwood himself? But how? He did not resemble the dark-haired, long-nosed, effeminate Earl of Willingham —his rumored half brother—in the slightest. If it was indeed Mr. Kirkwood scowling at her, none of the caricatures she had seen had done him justice. Often, he was depicted as a brute, occasionally as Beelzebub. This man was neither of those. He commanded attention, exuding an air of danger and elegance she had never before seen in another gentleman.

"I am afraid I cannot accompany you," she said past lips that had gone numb.

"And I am afraid you must." He caught her elbow then, and began hauling her through the sea of his patrons as though she were a criminal about to be cast into Newgate.

"See here, sir," she protested in as gruff and commanding a voice as she could muster, resisting his superior strength by dragging her heels and making herself a dead weight. "I am ill. I must return home at once."

Dreadful excuse, Frederica.

His attention snapped back to her, his expression cut in stone. That unnatural gaze swept over her. "You seem perfectly hale to me."

She cleared her throat. "I misspoke. My *mother* is dreadfully ill, not I. I must return home to attend her. She is suffering from the Melancholius Ague, and it will not be long until she succumbs, God have mercy upon her soul. She has no one but a gouty old manservant named Arthur for accompaniment, as our means have been substantially reduced by my love of vice."

He stared at her, and while the large chamber with its gleaming wood, sumptuous furniture, and breathtaking oil murals was laden with lords, it seemed for a moment as if they were the only two people who existed. "What manner of ague?"

Oh dear, what had she invented? This sort of thing ever landed her in trouble in her novels. On page three, the villain would be Sir Carstairs, and by page thirty, he would be Sir Carmichael.

"The Melancoholius Ague," she guessed, her mind working to save her hide by fashioning an endless fount of distraction. "The manservant also has but one leg, and he is blind. So you see, I really ought not to have left them at all. He can scarcely look after dearest Mama, but I cannot control my need for wagering and...sin."

A muscle ticked in his jaw. "Blind, you say?"

"And deaf as well," she added. "Not entirely, mind you. He can hear high-pitched noises. Kitchen mice, for instance. The squeaking, you understand. My mother's voice is quite unnaturally low for a female. The manservant cannot make out a word she says, I am afraid. You must see how dire the situation is, and if you please, I must take my leave at once."

"Indeed." His gaze roamed over her once more, seeming

to settle far too long upon her bosom, which she had painstakingly and painfully bound before donning her brother's stolen attire. "This…unfortunate creature. What is his name?"

"Who?" She blinked, her cheeks going warm at his scrutiny. He was still staring, the cad, and it made her belly quiver in a strange and unwanted fashion.

"The manservant tending your poor, dear mother, of course." He flashed her a grin that was neither pleasant nor menacing but somehow predatory instead. "What is the fellow's name? I feel certain I may know him. He sounds so familiar. There cannot be many in London who share such a tendency toward ill fortune."

"Oh, no, sir." She gulped, shaking her head. "You cannot possibly know him. His name is Arnold, but given his delicate health, he does not venture far from my mother's side."

Mr. Kirkwood's lips twitched. They were truly fine lips, she noted in spite of herself, fuller than a man's ought to be, sculpted as if by a master. Lord Willingham's lips, in contrast, were thin and wet and cold. The kiss he had pressed upon her during a ride in his phaeton had been as pleasant as she imagined setting her lips to a slimy fish would be. As had been his hard, almost punishing grip.

Surely, two men more disparate in appearance and manner did not exist. Where one was ice, the other was scorching flame.

"There is no invalid mother," Mr. Kirkwood insisted then. Correctly, drat him. "Nor is there an Arthur or an Arnold, and you will accompany me to my office. *Now.*"

Bother. Had she confused names again? It was her curse, ever plaguing her.

He did not wait for her response. He simply turned and began hauling her once more.

No. No. No.

She had to do something to halt this madness. Dressing as her brother—after pilfering the trunk-bound wardrobe he had outgrown—and sneaking away from her chamber garbed as a gentleman was scandalous enough. As was blustering her way into The Duke's Bastard, London's most infamous and exclusive club, by posing as a lord. But cloistering herself inside a chamber with the wicked establishment's equally wicked proprietor would be a social death knell.

Something inside her reminded her that perhaps a social death knell would be preferable to becoming the Countess of Willingham.

But then she banished such unworthy thoughts. After all, Duncan Kirkwood shared blood with the earl. Surely they were cut from the same cloth in more ways than not. Moreover, he was a sinner and a blackguard. A rakehell and a cad. He had built his immense fortune upon the misfortune and misguided greed of others. He had destroyed gentlemen, ruined families, and beggared lords. He was not to be trusted.

She had to fight him. Stop him. Frederica was no delicate miss. Indeed, she oft bemoaned her full hips, waist, and bosom. She would never be referred to as willowy. She was not slim. But even she was no match for the superior height and brawn of Mr. Kirkwood. She could not wrest her arm from his grasp. Nor could she stay their forward motion.

There was no means of escape, short of screaming and announcing to the assemblage of rakes and rogues that she was in fact Lady Frederica Isling, daughter to the Duke of Westlake. And as tempting as facilitating her own ruination was, it would also put an end to her aspirations of finishing her novel.

For she could not finish *The Silent Baron* if she was not able to properly conduct her research. Veracity required firsthand knowledge.

But as Mr. Kirkwood propelled her over the threshold

and into his private domain, she could not help but shiver. He released her, slanting a searching look in her direction, and closed the door, muffling the sounds of the den of vice he ruled.

She blinked, wishing she had not chosen to wear the dratted spectacles, for they forced her to peer over them if she wanted to see anything. The writer within her instantly flared with excitement. The chamber was paneled in dark wood, lit by mirrored gilt sconces crowned with lions and acanthus.

Tapers flickered, half spent. A sturdy, elaborately carved desk dominated one end of the chamber. The chair behind it was as large as a throne, depicting Hades and Persephone. The carpets were red, thick, and plush beneath her feet. The entire chamber possessed an unexpected aura of refinement. Until…

A glance at the ceiling made her gasp. Lewd and lascivious murals abounded. Nymphs cavorting. Females kissing each other. Naked breasts and bottoms. A man's long, erect…

Oh, dear Lord in heaven.

She lowered her gaze, cheeks hot, to find Mr. Kirkwood standing disturbingly near, watching her once more. She wet her lips. His office was the personification of sin. Her heart thudded. When she had dreamt up this mad scheme with Leonora, she had never imagined she would even be noticed at The Duke's Bastard. She had never imagined she would find herself alone in a chamber rife with licentious illustrations, the club's notorious, disturbingly handsome owner bearing down on her.

"Have a second look," Mr. Kirkwood invited, grinning. "The first was far too cursory."

Her face flamed hotter. He had taken note of her perusal, and her shock entertained him. The man was depraved.

She cleared her throat, forcing her voice to unnaturally

low octaves once more, for it was essential she maintain her disguise. "I do not think I shall, sir. Please, what is it you wish of me? I have already tarried here far too long as it is. My ailing mother requires me."

He had seen through her fictions. But that did not mean she was ready to surrender or admit to subterfuge. If she did not have her deceptions to cling to, she had nothing at all. For then, she was just a disgraced lady standing before the most libidinous gaming hell owner in town, with no defenses, no more excuses, and no hope of escaping this scrape with her reputation intact.

If you wish it to be intact, taunted that awful, unwanted voice.

The truth was murky. And conflicted. Ruination remained a tempting sin she had not yet entirely ruled out.

"For shame, my lord." Mr. Kirkwood cocked his head and raised his brow. "You cannot still be clinging to your lies, can you?"

"I told you no lies, sir," she denied, for she did not like to think of her fictions as lies. Rather, they were embellishments. No different than the worlds she created with her quill, ink, and paper, except they had been spoken aloud. They had been spoken to him, and with an aim to save herself from his unwanted scrutiny.

It would seem she had failed abysmally on that score.

"Truly, my lord?" Mr. Kirkwood flashed her a grin that transformed his features from strikingly handsome to breathtaking.

It was an odd thing for a man to be so beautiful, but there was no other way to describe him. Gazing upon the full effect of him now, she could not seem to find her voice. Especially since his hot gaze had once more dipped to her breasts, as though he could see the fullness of them carefully hidden beneath the trappings of civility.

Frederica blinked. *Oh dear.* What had he asked of her? One gaze into the brilliant depths of his eyes—one perusal of his full, sensual lips—and her mind was as muddled as the pages of an unbound book that had been thrown aloft. Slowly drifting to earth, but no longer in the order it had once been.

No longer the same.

Thoroughly jumbled.

She had to leave. That was the answer to this madness, this impossible conundrum facing her. She spun on her heel, desperate to flee the chamber and run from Duncan Kirkwood, his club, and the improper sensations he elicited in her all at once.

A hand gripped her elbow. Superior strength stayed her and twirled her about. The quick, forceful motions took her by surprise. Frederica lost her balance and toppled forward.

Into Mr. Kirkwood's chest.

Her splayed palms connected with his midnight superfine coat, absorbing the firm strength hidden beneath the layers of wool and linen. Her heart thudded. A queer sensation settled between her thighs. Frederica had never touched a gentleman so intimately before, and Mr. Kirkwood—well, he was surely not a gentleman. But he was of the male persuasion. And he was delightfully broad, large, and firm. Beneath her tentative hands, he was warm. He was...

"Are you feverish, my lord?" Mr. Kirkwood's deep voice, sinfully amused, interrupted her wild musings.

"Perhaps I may have a touch of my mother's ague." She swallowed, the precise name she'd given for the illness disappearing from her mind, along with most other coherent thought.

Her hands, meanwhile, required no independent guidance. She was intrigued, and she could not help herself from indulging. She could not deny herself the details she sought.

This, too, was the reason why she had taken the great risk of infiltrating his club—for research purposes. How could she write *The Silent Baron* with any degree of accuracy if she possessed no knowledge well from which to draw?

She could have guessed a man's form was firmer than her own, for instance. But she could not have known how defined and hard his muscled torso felt beneath her questing fingers. She could not have experienced the steady beat of his heart, or inhaled his delicious masculine scent of lemon, musk, and amber. She could not have noticed the tiny flecks of green in his blue eyes, or the faint brackets alongside his full lips that suggested an inclination to smile and laugh often. She would not have noted the glint of candlelight in his golden locks, which were longer than fashion and tousled.

Her liberties were unprecedented and egregious, as was being alone with him in his office, nary a chaperon to be found. In his inner sanctum at the midst of a den of iniquity. Her hands, however, had a mind of their own, traveling beneath his cutaway to his waistcoat.

What was she thinking, mauling Duncan Kirkwood's *chest*? How shocking. The trouble of it was, now she had begun, she could not seem to stop. Surely it was her curiosity propelling her. Surely it was not that she...*enjoyed* the illicit pleasure of stroking a strange gentleman's chest. Specifically, of stroking the chest belonging to one of London's most notorious men.

Nay.

He touched her forehead. Pressed the backs of his fingers to her skin for a brief moment, and the contact resonated in her core. "You do not feel feverish to me," Mr. Kirkwood said then, interrupting the heavy silence that had fallen between them. "Do you, my lord, perchance possess a fondness for testing the quality of a man's waistcoat with your hands?"

13

She swallowed again. *Caught.* How had she forgotten she was masquerading as a gentleman? She snatched her hands away from him at last, flushing. The sensation of his lean abdomen seemed imprinted upon her palms.

"No." She blinked. "Er, yes."

His lips quirked into a smile she could only describe as swoon-inducing. "Which is it, my lord? Yes, or no?"

Neither. Frederica calculated the odds of successfully fleeing the chamber once more. Perhaps if she distracted him first, or if she was somehow able to douse the flames of the wall sconces, she could detain him long enough to make good her retreat. Or better yet, perhaps she could convince him she was ill.

"Forgive me my familiarity," she said, taking care to keep her voice as gruff as possible. "I seem to have lost my balance. No doubt I have contracted the ague as well. For my dear mother, it began with her falling into things—just the furniture at first, mind you. Chairs. A *Louis Quatorze* table. Then one day, she fell atop the Duchess of Blackwater during an at home, and it was the beginning of the end. The duchess gave my mother the cut direct after that occasion. Indeed, I fear it will not be long now before death claims me as well. I ought not to be near you, sir, lest the ague be catching."

If Mr. Kirkwood did not allow her to leave after this embellishment, she knew not what would sway him.

His gaze seemed to burn into her. "This duchess…was she a friend of your mother's?"

"The Duchess of Greywater," she clarified, nodding. "Yes, of course. She and my mother were dear friends. No longer, I am afraid, and it is just as well, truly, for my mother could have infected her with the ague otherwise. I really ought to be on my way, sir. Not only does my mother require me, but I could make you ill. I would never wish for the ague to settle its curse upon you."

"Greywater or Blackwater?" he snapped.

Frederica did not follow him for a moment. Perhaps because she had been rather preoccupied by watching his mouth. His lips were so firm and supple, the loveliest shade she had ever seen on a gentleman, dusky pink, full and so well-defined. Too pretty, almost, for a man's mouth. The effect was startling and breathtaking all at once.

"I am afraid I do not understand, sir."

And she didn't. It was as if he spoke in riddles.

"The duchess your supposed mama fell atop," he elaborated, his jaw hardening and his tone deepening, resonating with anger. "Upon first reference, you called her the Duchess of Blackwater. Thereafter, you referred to her as the Duchess of Greywater. The same woman cannot be both, can she?"

Oh, how dreadful this is. The longer she remained, the more of herself she gave away. Mr. Kirkwood seemed taller in that moment. More menacing. Perhaps it was his steadfast devotion to colorlessness—his entire wardrobe was midnight black, even his cravat, and she noted for the first time the ring he wore, emblazoned with a skull.

She had never seen another man as compelling in his singular appearance—or as frightening. "I misspoke," she forced herself to say. "Do forgive me the error. It is the Duchess of Blackwater, of course."

Frederica could only hope he was not knowledgeable enough to recognize her blatant falsehood, for there was no extant Duchess of Blackwater. How could her simple foray into The Duke's Bastard have gone so miserably astray? When she and her friend and fellow wallflower Lady Leonora Forsythe had first settled upon the notion of infiltrating the gaming hell in disguise, neither of them had bargained for the madness unfolding now.

"Of course," he said smoothly.

Too smoothly.

His expression shifted, taking on a predatory harshness. He moved forward, crowding her with his tall, broad body. She forgot to breathe.

"Tell me something, will you not?" he asked before she could garner a response.

She had retreated half a dozen paces, and with the last, her back met plaster. Her shoulder grazed a painting, sending it listing to the left. Her heart thumped. Her palms were sweaty. Misgiving blossomed inside her like a triumphant summer rose.

"What is it you wish to know, sir?" she asked as his eyes burned into hers. There was nowhere else for her to go, and pinned beneath his gaze, there was nowhere else she wished to be, anyhow.

"Your name."

How dull. She could not stave off the wave of disappointment crashing down upon her. *Ninny!* She scolded herself. *What did you think? That he would ask for your hand in marriage when you are posing as a gentleman?*

There was the reminder she needed.

She straightened her shoulders, her gaze never wavering from his. "I am the Marquess of Blanden."

"Blanden?" he repeated the name she had given him—her brother's courtesy title, of course—his countenance shifting once more. Turning pensive. "Your father is the Duke of Westlake?"

She did not flinch, for her response to this question, at least, was true. "Yes, he is."

"Bloody sodding hell," he said lowly, his eyes scouring her.

It was decidedly not the response she had anticipated.

CHAPTER 2

*H*er name was Lady Frederica Isling.

And he wanted to devour her.

She was not a gentleman, *thank Christ*. Nor was she the Marquess of Blanden—*also thank Christ*, for the Marquess of Blanden was as interesting as a twig. Though she certainly did resemble him, from her raven-wing hair peeping beneath her hat to her wide green cat's eyes. Nay, unless Duncan was wrong, she was Blanden's sister.

It was his business to know every facet of the lives of the quality. He knew their sires, their friends, their sisters, and their mistresses, knew their debts and their properties and gambling habits. Knew their bedchamber preferences, knew which men were drunkards and which never drank a drop. He almost knew how many times a day they pissed.

Which was why he knew the Marquess of Blanden possessed one near spinster sister his sire was attempting to marry off. Which, in turn, meant her appearance in his club, dressed as a gentleman, in direct opposition to all decency and propriety, was providential.

Lady Frederica was everything he required. The final

ingredient necessary for vengeance upon the Duke of Amberly, a man who shared his blood but not his name. His plot could unfold according to plan thanks to the inquisitive and brash nature of one small, determined female.

And here she stood, defiant yet wary, giving herself away. She smelled of violets. Her hips were full and delicious. How he had ever mistaken her for a man—even for a moment—baffled Duncan as he looked at her now. Little wonder he had been attracted to her arse first. She was curved in all the proper places, and just thinking about her was enough to make him go rigid. He longed to pleasure her until she lost herself and her starch both.

But he could not devour her, for she was an innocent, and he was a bad man. A man she ought not to know. A man who had uses for her she could not possibly fathom.

He reined himself in. Forced himself to meet her bright, inquisitive gaze. He could gain what he wanted without debauching her. Without ruining her. She worried her lush lower lip with her teeth, biting it for just a moment as her wide eyes scanned the chamber, seemingly for a means of escape. She was a dichotomy of purity and sin—pale, creamy skin, delicious femininity, light and darkness, her hair black as a starless, midnight sky. As he studied her, all his good intentions fled, as insubstantial as unsown seeds blown away and scattered in the wind.

He could leave her entirely innocent.

But he was not going to.

"Come with me, Blanden," he said, the devil within him breaking free as he turned on his heel.

This would earn him his place in hell. But it would be worth an eternity. He had no doubt.

"I beg your pardon?" she called after him. Her attempt to keep her voice gruff and low faltered, revealing the sultry notes of her own mellifluous tone.

He stopped, sparing her a glance over his shoulder. Once again, her loveliness hit him with the force of a fist to the gut. *Christ on the cross*, she was beautiful. A few tendrils of her dark hair had escaped its confines to curl about her face.

Every instinct within him screamed to keep her here. To keep her to himself as if she were a rare treasure. He wanted to kiss the sweet fullness of her lips. To worship her limbs, from ankle to thigh. He wanted to open the fall of her breeches and set his tongue against her. To work her until she shivered and shook beneath him, finding her release with his name on her pretty lips.

But none of those things were meant to be. He would not touch her.

He flashed her one of his most charming grins instead. "Come along if you please, my lord. There is something I wish to show you."

Her brows rose. "N-no thank you, sir. I must take my leave at once."

It was time to give her games a try himself. "I understand your dear mother is in ill health, but on your last visit to my club, I was told you made a discreet inquiry. If you accompany me now, I shall take you to the secret rooms as you asked. I seek only to offer you solace in your time of trials, my lord."

She blinked, her spectacles rendering the action exaggerated. "I do not recall making such an inquiry, and I must be on my way."

"Nonsense." His grin deepened. He was enjoying himself. It had been some time since he had been intrigued by anyone. This woman, this madcap duke's daughter with her penchant for fantastical falsehoods, had somehow managed to garb herself as a man and inveigle her way into his club for reasons that currently eluded him. But he would have his answers, and she would accede to his whims. "I insist, my

19

lord. Just a few moments of your time are all I require. Then you can return to your darling mother's side. Though I must say I find it rather perplexing that the Duchess of Westlake should be attended by only a gouty, one-legged, blind manservant."

A flush tinged her cheeks. "Indeed, I fear my family has experienced a reduction of circumstance in recent years. Naturally, we prefer not to discuss our private concerns unless the situation requires it. I would appreciate your discretion."

"Of course, my lord. I am the soul of discretion whenever merited." Truer words were never spoken. He bowed. "Now, if you will accompany me?"

He could almost hear the wheels inside her mind spinning as she attempted to plot further means to deny him. What an odd, fascinating creature she was. Pity he could not do as he truly wished with her.

She swallowed. "I…perhaps I might accompany you for just a few moments, sir. But I cannot be detained much longer, I fear."

"We shan't need much time at all," he promised, feeling like a fiend and utterly unrepentant in spite of it.

He predicted she would flee within seconds of pressing her eye to the viewing hole in the scarlet chamber. Duncan strode to the hidden panel in his office that allowed him access to the secret corridor running behind the club's public pleasure rooms. His fingers found the mechanism that opened the door, and he stepped into the dimly lit hall.

In addition to providing his members with all the gambling, excellent French food, and illegal Scottish whisky they desired, he also catered to their sexual whims. The polite world thrived upon clandestine excess, and he happily indulged his wealthy patrons in every vice they could imagine. Birching, orgies, binding, two men together, two women…it mattered not. Occasionally, he watched.

Watching was the only way he would allow himself to participate, and even that was a solace for rare occasions. When the black mood struck him. When no one could slake his needs. When he looked inside himself and saw nothing but darkness where a soul should be.

"Where are you taking me, sir?"

Her hesitant voice—not even an attempt to disguise its lilting femininity now—stayed him. He turned to find hovering at the threshold, and with the light of his office at her back, she glowed. How like Persephone she was, on the brink of entering his dark underworld. But unlike Hades, he had no need of force. His inquisitive goddess would follow him because she was curious, and because she could not find another means of extricating herself from her tangled deceptions.

"Come and see," he invited. "Not every member of The Duke's Bastard is granted entrée here. It is a privilege."

She was intrigued. He could read her so easily. But she was also afraid of what she would encounter, hence the hesitation. Her sheltered mind could not possibly imagine the depths of depravity to which he could introduce her. For a moment, he imagined leading her into the sapphire room, using the silken bindings kept there to tie her to the bed. Stripping her of her masculine clothes.

Or better still, opening only the fall of her breeches so he could slide inside her. He would watch himself take her in the mirrored walls. He would make her scream his name. He would…

Bloody, bloody hell.

He would do none of those things.

"Blanden," he snapped, irritated with himself for his lack of control. A man did not reach the height to which he had scrabbled, fought, and clawed, without being as rigid and orderly as a soldier. Duncan Kirkwood did not relinquish his power over himself or others. Not for anyone. Not for any reason.

Ruthlessly, he tamped down the desire burning through his veins. He had always been aroused by the forbidden, and Lady Frederica Isling was no different. Ladies stirred his blood and his cock. Even when they wore dreadful spectacles and the ill-fitting garb of a gentleman, it would seem.

She made her decision and stepped into the corridor at last, walking with a natural sway to her hips he could not help but admire. Her thighs were shapely beneath the fluttering drape of her coat, and damn him if the sight of her in those boots did not make his prick rigid once more.

She reached him, eyes blinking behind the thick lenses, magnified and vibrant even in the low lighting. "What is it you wish to show me, sir? Let us make haste so I can return to my mother."

"The viewing you requested, my lord," he said, sliding the small door covering, the viewing hole open.

He looked first, needing to be certain what she was about to see was suitably shocking. Within the scarlet chamber, two of his ladies had a naked Viscount of Eversley tied to the bed. One was dripping hot candle wax upon his chest and the other was on her knees betwixt his spread thighs, running her tongue over the head of his erect cock.

Pity his lordship's prick was on the smaller side. It would have been much more shocking for Lady Frederica to spy a Priapus rather than a Lilliputian. But some things simply could not be helped.

Duncan stepped away from the viewing slot and gestured for her to take his place. "Here you are, my lord."

The scent of violets taunted him, perfuming the air. He slid the viewing slot closed and drew a chair forward. Some who made use of the viewing corridor preferred to be seated so they could discreetly pleasure themselves as they watched.

"Take a seat if you please, my lord," he invited.

Lady Frederica frowned up at him, but she did as he asked, gingerly seating her bottom on the edge of the chair, as if it was fashioned of live hearth coals rather than the finest upholstery, stuffing, and wood. He opened the slot before her, unable to resist drawing nearer to her.

Lust hummed through him, and it had nothing to do with the voluptuary scene unfolding on the other side of the wall and everything to do with the lady he was about to shock. Perhaps even horrify, though he hoped his inquisitorial minx would at least know a modicum of prurient interest. The moment crackled with intimacy, almost the way the air did in the midst of a lightning storm. Anticipation made his cock twitch. The mere notion of opening her eyes to the sins of the flesh aroused him in a way it ought not.

"What am I going to see, sir?" she asked, frowning at him as if she did not trust him.

Wise girl.

"An education." He reached out, plucking her spectacles from the bridge of her nose. "You may thank me later, my lord."

"Sir," she protested "I cannot see without them."

"Try," he said, tucking the spectacles inside his coat. He had no intention of returning them to her, as he was reasonably certain she did not even require the damned things to see. They were now his spoils, along with everything else that would come of her ill-fated trip to his territory. "Press your eye to the hole, my lord, and tell me what you see. If you require the spectacles, I shall return them."

A fabrication, of course. But she had laid the foundation for deception, and he was merely playing this game of chance by the rules she had established. He watched with grim satisfaction as she tentatively leaned forward and placed her eye to the small viewing hole.

He waited for a gasp.

Waited for her outrage.

And was met only with her silence and stillness.

Duncan hesitated another minute more, trying to dismiss the fresh surge of desire her rapt attention for the depravity in the scarlet chamber sent through him. Was she watching because she was intrigued? Because—*Lord help him*—the salacious scene unfolding struck a chord of desire within her? Or was it because she had been telling the truth about the spectacles and without them, she could not distinguish a cock from a chair leg? He rather hoped it was one of the formers instead of the latter. The thought of her enjoying the wickedness unfolding before her made him impossibly hard.

That simply would not do.

He cleared his throat. Attempted to clear his mind. Failed abysmally, for the only question on his lips was a wicked one. "My lord, what do you see?"

"I see a man cavorting with two women of loose morals," she announced frostily, but still she did not move. "Good heavens, that is Viscount Eversley. He courted me...er, my sister last season."

His entertainment soured at the notion of Eversley flirting with and attempting to woo Lady Frederica. Eversley was a fop, and he gambled far too deep for his pockets. Duncan liked the man even less now that he knew Eversley had been sniffing after the paradox before him. At least there was a season between them now, which meant either Lady Frederica had been wily enough to reject Eversley's suit or Eversley had searched for a larger dowry and a less distinguishing mind elsewhere.

Either way, he had not expected her to recognize Eversley, and the fact she had presented a quandary.

"Naturally, you are aware anything you witness within these walls must remain here," he was quick to remind her. The positions of far too many wealthy, important lords would be in jeopardy if their peccadilloes were ever to be made public.

Secrecy, discretion, and a healthy respect for each other were core tenets of his club. Along with debauchery, sin, and overindulgence, of course. But if even one gentleman's privacy was violated, Duncan's entire castle could crumble and fall about his feet. If the men who spent and won their fortunes in his establishment did not trust him, they would no longer frequent it. If they no longer frequented it, he would be left with a hulking, expensive St. James's Street building, a ridiculously costly French chef, hundreds of bottles of illicit whisky, the money he had amassed over the years, and not much else.

But it would appear she was not in the least inclined toward bandying gossip about, not for the moment.

"Good…oh dear, he is…oh my, she is…that is…*heavens*. I did not think it possible," she was saying to herself, her eye pressed to the viewing slot. "This is most irregular, I feel certain, Mr. Kirkwood."

Yet, she did not look away. She held herself still, as if riveted to the wicked sights before her.

It was the first time she had called him by his name, and he liked the sound of it on her tongue, delivered in her husky rasp. "Please do call me Duncan," he invited, for he longed to hear that name on her lips above all else. He wished for a drink in that moment. A whisky. A brandy. A port. *By God*, anything.

She gasped, the sound undeniably feminine. "Why is she sitting upon his face? How can he breathe? Mr. Kirkwood, you must put an end to this madness at once. I do believe that young woman is attempting to *murder* Lord Eversley.

And whilst I never liked the fellow, I cannot countenance his demise as I watch on."

He almost swallowed his own tongue. She tore her attention from the viewing window at last, her stricken gaze meeting his. And he was in a hell of a state. His initial reason for bringing her here—vengeance, pure and ugly—was all but forgotten. His instincts were at war. Part of him wanted to ravish her here and now—as long as she was willing, of course, and spent at least half a dozen times—and part of him wanted to laugh.

Hilariously.

Uproariously.

And so he did, giving in to the weakness he knew would be less dangerous to the path he had chosen for himself so many years ago. He laughed. Because she was so innocent and had no inkling of what she had just seen. He wondered if she'd even realized she'd been viewing two women and one man fornicate.

"Precious, my lord," he said, extracting a handkerchief from his coat and using it to dab his eyes when at last he'd caught his breath. "Your innocence is precious."

"You are not concerned in the slightest for the wellbeing of your patrons?" she asked, her voice high.

He slid the viewing window closed, not wanting their dialogue to carry to the occupants of the scarlet chamber and interrupt their enjoyment of each other. "The Viscount is perfectly well, Blanden. Of that you can rest assured."

"How can I?" Indignant, she rose from her chair, forgetting herself. Forgetting her ruse entirely. "It seems to me that woman was trying to do him harm. He was making all manner of horrid sounds of alarm."

Dear God. He bit his cheek, wondering how he could respond. Wondering how his plan to shock the innocent Lady Frederica Isling and use her misguided adventure against her father could have gone so awry. He counted to ten inwardly. Then fifteen before he could be assured he would not laugh again.

"My lord," he said, doing a poor job of keeping his humor at bay, "I thought you would have understood the purpose of this corridor and the private chambers here at The Duke's Bastard. Indeed, I was certain it was why you had requested access to them. But perhaps you had not realized, in your innocence, the nature of the rooms and the activities within them."

"I…" she faltered, her full lips parting as she struggled to find her words. How he longed to kiss her, then and there. To press her to the wall and fuse their mouths together.

But it was not meant to be.

She was not meant to be.

He knew this.

"These chambers are used for pleasure," he forced himself to explain. "Club members can choose a lady who appeals to them—or two or three—and bring the lady or ladies to their choice of private chambers for lovemaking."

Her face went pale. "My God," she spat, her expression a humorous commingling of horror, disgust, and something else he could not quite define. "You truly are depraved, sir. Do you abuse the privacy of all your members in such an egregious fashion?"

Of course she would think him guilty of spying upon his patrons. He clenched his jaw. "All who are watched are aware of the viewing slots. Indeed, they prefer it. They can choose which member watches, or they can decide to leave it unknown. Not knowing who is watching heightens the pleasure for some. Some members do not dabble in the sin of being watched. Thus, not every chamber possesses viewing windows."

She stared at him as if he had announced he was Hades

himself, and he was about to spirit her away into the underworld. "Lord Eversley is not in danger?"

Irritation pricked him. He disliked her protective inclinations toward the dark-haired lord. He was the antithesis of everything Duncan was, cock included. There was no need to be envious on *that* particular score. "No, the viscount is not in danger. He is being pleasured by two paramours at once. The sounds you referenced? Not alarm but pleasure, my lord. These rooms and viewing windows are dedicated to desire. Nothing more, and nothing less. Witnessing your shock, I can only suggest you leave this club and never return."

She stared at him for a beat, before her full lips pursed into a moue of displeasure. "No."

His brows snapped together. *What in the hell?* Surely, he had misheard. "I beg your pardon, my lord?"

"I wish to return," she said.

He should stop her. Put an end to this. Here was his chance. He could inform her he was not fooled by her ruse and she treaded dangerously close to ruin. But she was daring, and she was lovely, her unusual eyes sparkling with intelligence, and he was a man who could appreciate bravery above all else. He was also a man who could afford to indulge his whims.

Even when he knew he should not.

He flashed her a grin, feeling like a fox who had entered a house of plump hens with no one to stop him from feasting. "When?"

CHAPTER 3

"*I* do beg your pardon, Freddy! You simply *cannot* be planning to return to that den of iniquity. To do so would be the height of ruin."

Yes, it would. But she was not about to allow caution to curtail her quest for knowledge. Frederica chanced a surreptitious glance about the brightly lit Riverford House morning salon to ascertain their lady's maids were suitably distracted and beyond earshot before answering her best friend, Lady Leonora Forsythe. Fortunately, their mothers were otherwise occupied—Leonora's mother was abed in typical fashion, and Frederica's was on Bond Street, also in typical fashion.

She had paid a call to Leonora, as planned, following her foray into the villainous world of The Duke's Bastard the previous evening. She'd just finished her full account, neglecting to mention how attractive Mr. Duncan Kirkwood was, for her attraction to the unsuitable man was a moot point.

"Of course I am returning," she confirmed, keeping her voice low. "I must take advantage of the opportunity available to me whilst it remains. With my father gone to the country and Mother preoccupied as usual, I have unprecedented freedom of motion."

That much was true, for her father's rare absence and her mother's obsession with shopping meant Frederica was left alone most evenings. Westlake House was blessedly easy to escape from, and she had returned without anyone—neither servant nor her mother—having an inkling she'd been gone. But the convenience and occasion were not her sole motivating factors, it was true.

Duncan Kirkwood made her body perform strange, disturbing feats. His wickedness intrigued her. His darkness lured her. His masculine beauty took her breath. He made her wish for stolen kisses, sin, and freedom.

None of which she had ever experienced.

None of which she was likely to experience.

All of which she wanted to.

"It is dangerous, Freddy," Leonora warned her unnecessarily. "Was not one visit enough?"

No.

Something she had not even known existed—some improper need deep within her—would not accept one visit to The Duke's Bastard. One exchange with its enigmatic, black-clad owner. One opportunity to witness the secret side of life she had always suspected existed without knowing for certain.

She had seen it.

Yesterday. Surreal as it seemed now as she was dressed in a demure gown, paying calls as a proper lady should, a scant handful of hours ago, she had dressed as a gentleman, hired a hack, and known the terrifying, utterly freeing experience of attending a club, matching wits with Duncan Kirkwood, and witnessing the most depraved acts she could have imagined possible. She ought to be thankful she had not been discovered, that she had gone quietly and safely home with her innocence and her reputation intact.

Instead, she wanted more.

She wanted to know everything, to see Mr. Kirkwood again, to bask in his compelling presence.

"I need to conduct more research," she told her friend at length, but the words lacked conviction even to her own ears.

"You cannot do it," Leonora declared. Her white-blonde hair had, as was its wont, worked free of her coiffure to send a few stray tendrils of curls framing her lovely, heart-shaped face.

She was kindhearted, intelligent, and soft spoken. A childhood fall, and resulting broken ankle which had never properly healed, had left her bearing the cruel sobriquet Limping Leonora. Yet, she bore all with a singular grace and unparalleled sense of humor, always finding the laughter and lightness in every situation. No better friend, nobler spirit, or lovelier woman existed.

But that did not mean Frederica was going to allow her to dictate what she ought to do in this instance. Even if her friend was right.

"I must do it, Leonora," she told her softly. "I want *The Silent Baron* to be as accurate as possible. It has to resonate with readers. How can I accomplish such a feat if I do not complete my research because I am too cautious to do so?"

Again, a partial truth, her conscience nettled her. She did want her novel to be accurate. Because the baron lost his fortune in a gaming hell much like The Duke's Bastard, it would behoove her to return and conduct additional research. She had just barely scratched the surface.

But her motivations were not entirely pure, and she knew it. She wanted to see Duncan Kirkwood once more. He frightened her. He intrigued her. He inspired all manner of feelings inside her. Some of them were quite wicked indeed.

Leonora's gaze was shrewd upon hers, unflinching. "What more could you require for accuracy? You have successfully infiltrated a gentleman's club, and without discovery. You now know how the inside of one looks, sounds, and smells. Gads, I imagine it smells truly terrible. Does it?"

"Not terrible at all," she said, smiling.

And then she realized she was recalling *his* scent. Duncan Kirkwood's. Yes, indeed, he had smelled delightful. But she could not recall what the club itself smelled like, and that realization was rather vexing.

"At least," she continued, correcting herself, "not the chamber I occupied. I was not long in the public rooms, and that is yet another reason why I ought to return and take additional notes.

"You were not long in the public rooms?" Leonora's eyes narrowed. "Where were you then, Freddy?"

Frederica swallowed. *Oh, dear.* She had withheld a lengthy portion of the history of her visit. Intentionally. But her friend's clever gaze was probing hers, seeking more information now she had been teased with a glimmer. *Blast her loose tongue.*

"Just in the public rooms for a bit, and then I lost my courage and fled to a waiting hack," she lied.

But Leonora knew her. And she knew Frederica was an abysmal liar. "Where did you go?" she demanded.

"His office," Frederica admitted at last, once more checking on the preoccupation and distance of their ladies' maids. "He took me to his office."

Her friend's eyes went wide. "Good heavens, Frederica. He did not...did he? ..."

"No," she hastened to reassure her. Though she privately wished he had taken liberties. Any liberties he wished. *All* the liberties he wished. "He was a gentleman. He did not recognize me, and he initially suspected I was not a member of the club. But when I told him I was the Marquess of Blanden, he relented."

Alas, not entirely true.

But she could only imagine her friend's reaction if she confessed he had led her to a secret corridor and encouraged her to view the sinful, lustful copulation occurring within the walls of his establishment.

She had seen Eversley without a stitch of clothing, cavorting with two similarly unclothed females. Because he wished to be watched. She had witnessed his rigid...member. His maleness. And that woman had seated herself... Frederica flushed to think of what she had seen now, and her instinctive reaction to it. Part horror, part curiosity. Not for the dreadful viscount or the Cyprians with whom he romped, but rather for the notion such raw surrender to baser urges existed.

Shameful, she knew, but she could admit it to herself if no one else.

"I'm relieved no harm befell you, but my God, Freddy, even you must admit you cannot continue in this mad fashion. All it requires is one person to discover what you're about. One servant catching you up at dawn. Do not ruin yourself, my dear friend. How can a novel be worth that?"

Frederica frowned at Leonora. "My dreams are priceless. I do not know what any of the rest of it is worth. But I cannot ruin myself if I am discreet. The gambles I'm making far outweigh the potential reward. All I have ever wanted is to write a novel and see my work in print. I am so near to achieving my goal, to being taken seriously, but the plot concerning the baron must be unshakably realistic."

All this was true as well. Most young ladies aspired to marriage. Frederica had been groomed to attain the proper ladylike arts. She could sing, she could play the pianoforte, she could dance and curtsy and manage a passable effort at watercolors. She had been courted and wooed by earls and viscounts.

But all she truly wanted was to hold her book in her hands. She wanted the characters and stories rioting in her mind to come to life in ink and paper. She wanted readers to pluck her book from a shelf and share her world. It was a desire that had plagued and spurred her in equal measure from the moment she'd first held a book in her small hands as a girl. The story had captivated her, and she had known what she must do.

"I know how much you wish to finish your novel, Freddy." Leonora kept her voice hushed, but her expression was determined, jaw stubborn and hard. Her disapproval was clear. "But it is not only unwise to put yourself and your reputation in jeopardy in such a fashion, it is the height of folly. Once was bad enough. To think you wish to return…" She shuddered with dramatic flair, allowing her sentence to trail off before continuing. "You cannot think the risk of ruination is worth the reward."

"I can and I do," she insisted stubbornly. Drat her friend for being the voice of reason she did not wish to hear. She had been hoping Leonora would be as intrigued by the prospect of her return to The Duke's Bastard as she was. "I have decided being ruined may be a fate preferable to that of becoming Lady Willingham. Indeed, it holds increasing appeal by the day."

Perhaps by the hour.

Certainly since she had made the acquaintance of one Duncan Kirkwood.

What was it about the man?

Leonora gasped. "You cannot mean it, Freddy."

She raised an incredulous brow at her friend. "Would you care to be the Countess of Willingham?"

Leonora flushed and looked down at her lap. "At six-and-twenty, I suppose I should accept his suit and be grateful."

Frederica's stomach flipped, weighed down by the instant boulder of self-loathing. "Oh, Leonora, pray forgive me for my thoughtless tongue."

Frederica cursed her thoughtlessness, for no one knew better than she that her friend wished to become a wife and a mother more than she wished to take her next breath. While Frederica had never aspired to becoming a gentleman's wife, Leonora did. Her painfully shy manner around gentlemen and her limp had rendered her a wallflower. As the years went by with nary a marriage prospect—not even a dubious one like Willingham—she crept closer and closer to spinsterhood.

"You must not fret on my account." Leonora flashed her a smile of forced brightness. "I harbor no illusions about myself. How can I? Limping Leonora, with a brother who has been absent from England for years, an invalid mother, and hardly a dowry to speak of, cannot aspire to lofty prospects. It is a small mercy I have been able to gain entrée to society as I have."

"You are the daughter and sister of an earl," Frederica argued, for she hated the complacent manner in which her friend denounced herself. "Any gentleman would be fortunate to take you to wife. Indeed, there are none worthy of you. You are the kindest, most intelligent, and beautiful lady in all London."

"Pish." Leonora waved a dismissive hand through the air, as though she were discreetly shooing a bothersome fly. "I am lame as an old horse. I cannot dance. I do not flirt. I am not a great wit, and I cannot even play the pianoforte. My singing voice rivals a rooster for jarring shrillness. My family is awash in scandal, and I have no great fortune as my saving grace. Even my youth slips away with each day. I do not fool myself, Freddy. I know precisely who and what I am."

"You are perfect, and I refuse to countenance any of the things you've just said." Frederica was firm on this.

She was protective of her friend. Unlike Leonora, she had never been subject to such mockery or ridicule. They had become quick—if unlikely—friends, and Frederica was more grateful for her with each passing day. Leonora was the sister she'd never had. Each of them had one brother only, and together, they had found a mutual camaraderie borne of necessity and mutual respect.

"My darling Freddy, you are blind as ever in regard to me." Leonora pursed her lips. "It is one of the legions of reasons why I adore you. But because I love you so, I must caution you against the rash decision you have made. Indeed, I must not just caution you but advise you not to return. It is a miracle you arrived at such an establishment on your own and returned unharmed. But the thought that dreadful man had you in his office, alone, makes me long to hunt him down like the miscreant he is and lay him low."

She blinked at the vehemence in her friend's tone. Leonora was not ordinarily possessed of a violent nature. Frederica performed another cursory inspection of the chamber, making certain their maids remained otherwise occupied. Leonora's was stitching, and Freddy's appeared to have fallen asleep.

"He is not as much a villain as one would presume," she found herself defending Duncan Kirkwood.

Much to her shock.

And dismay. And shame. Great shame. But there was some part of her—some deep and previously undiscovered part of her—that felt a connection to the man. An interest. Even an attraction.

Leonora's mouth fell open. "Not as much a villain? Have you forgotten he is the illegitimate half brother to Lord Willingham, a man you detest?"

She almost had. The two men were so different that it was far too easy to forget. "He is nothing like the earl. Indeed, he is…"

Intriguing. Handsome. Magnetic.

"He is not a good man, Freddy," Leonora interrupted, saving her from making any embarrassing admissions. "Good heavens, he has beggared lords without compunction. He preys upon the weaknesses of lesser men for his own benefit. He harbors ladies of ill repute within his establishment. Scoundrels like him are the reason why you are writing *The Silent Baron.*"

"Yes." She could not deny her friend's words, for they were true. All of them. Even the last. Gambling was a sin. It was wrong. The way in which men such as Duncan Kirkwood earned their fortunes by exploiting the weaknesses of others had motivated her to write *The Silent Baron.* Her book would be a culmination of fact, fiction, intrigue, mystery, sin, and—ultimately—redemption. "I cannot argue with you, Leonora, but there is something about Mr. Kirkwood that is oddly compelling. I cannot explain it or make sense of it myself. How I wish you could accompany me."

"Accompany you?" Leonora's eyes widened. "Are you mad? What violence did he commit against you? Are you frightened of him? You can go away—join your father in the country, perhaps—if you fear for your safety."

She shook her head. "He did nothing to me."

Not true, taunted her conscience. *He took you to the viewing corridor. He allowed you to witness unspeakable acts. He showed you depravity without a hint of remorse. Indeed, he was proud of it. And you liked it. You were not shocked or thoroughly disgusted as you ought to have been. Perhaps there is something wrong with you as well. Some moral deficiency.*

Frederica ordered her conscience to muzzle itself at once. She had no wish to hear anything further on the matter. Her decision had been made, and it made her chest fill with a buoyancy she had never before felt. *Freedom. Choice.* She could be wicked if she chose. How freeing. How tempting.

"Did he take liberties?" Leonora demanded, her voice strident enough to attract the attention of their lady's maids.

Frederica pressed her lips in a firm line and forced herself to answer in an equally loud tone. "That is what the gossip sheet claimed about Lady Marigold, but I am not certain we ought to believe such scurrilous accounts."

"Just so," Leonora agreed. "How remiss of me. Idle gossip ought never to be considered."

"No," Frederica agreed quietly. "It should not. I cannot explain it, Leonora. Do not ask it of me. All I can say is there is something decidedly different about him. Something intriguing. He is not altogether bad. Certainly not good either. But he is not the devil we have suspected him of being. I feel confident of it."

"It does not signify," Leonora charged quietly. "Freddy, you cannot mean to return. You cannot even contemplate it."

But she was. And she would.

She was beginning to realize however, she would never convince her friend of the wisdom of her decision. For the first time in their lengthy friendship, Frederica decided to do the unthinkable.

She lied. "You are quite right, of course, dear friend. I shan't return. It would be dangerous, foolhardy, and ruinous. I do tend to allow my imagination to guide me, and I shall not make the same mistake in this instance. I will simply make the best of the research I was able to gather on my foray there yesterday."

Leonora's eyes narrowed into slits. Her disbelief of Frederica's abrupt change of heart was apparent. "You cannot return, Freddy. It is not an abundance of caution on my part but rather my love for you that prompts me to warn you."

Frederica sent her friend a reassuring smile. "Naturally, I shall not. Pray do not trouble yourself another moment more on my account, Leonora. I bow to your superior wisdom, as ever."

If all went according to plan, Leonora would never know.

Just one more trip into the devil's den, she promised herself. Another jaunt to The Duke's Bastard.

Once more.

That was all she wanted. All she needed. For the sake of research alone. Of course.

Leonora pinned her with a searching look she could not like. "My wisdom is superior indeed. Do not forget I warned you."

Frederica smiled. "I never required a warning, dear heart."

Perhaps you do, threatened the voice once more. *Perhaps you ought to take heed.*

She smothered it in the same fashion she buried her friend's doubts. *Down, down, down.* Until it was no longer there.

CHAPTER 4

"*S*ir, there is a visitor for you."

Bloody, bloody, misbegotten hell.

Hades and Beelzebub.

Hellfire and damnation.

Duncan threw down his quill, not caring if ink splattered on the ledger he'd been painstakingly balancing. Irritation surged within him, mingling with desire. Why the hell should his man announcing a visitor grant him a rigid—almost painful—cockstand?

Because you think the visitor is her.

Lady Frederica Isling, to be precise. She had told him she would return on the morrow.

The black-haired beauty with the emerald eyes and strange manner of conducting herself. The girl who had dared to dress as a man to infiltrate his establishment. To his knowledge, she was the only one who had ever had the gall to attempt such subterfuge in order to gain entrance to The Duke's Bastard.

Part of him admired her for it.

Part of him wanted to bed her into the next century.

Another part of him found her an irritation and a complication he did not need. Her appearance in his club had already provided him all the ammunition he required. Indeed, her usefulness to him was at an end. All he need do was pay a visit to her father, the Duke of Westlake, and vengeance would be his.

Damn.

"Who is it?" he asked Hazlitt at length.

Hazlitt, who hailed from the rookeries, and like Duncan had clawed and fought his way from seedy filth and poverty to prosperity, raised a lone brow. "He gives his name as Lord Blanden, sir."

Her.

Hazlitt's discreet disapproval left him without doubt the man did not believe Lady Frederica was her brother, the Marquess of Blanden, for a moment. Duncan did not hire fools, and Hazlitt was no exception—indeed, he was one of the cleverest men he knew. He ought to refuse her entrance. The night was early, and he had a great deal of work to accomplish before emerging on the floor. His ledgers were out of balance, and it seemed to him someone had been stealing from him.

She was nothing but trouble. If he had half the mind the Lord had bestowed upon a rooster, he would send her on her way. Forget she existed. Expunge all thoughts of wide emerald eyes framed with thick lashes, midnight hair, and full, pink lips from his mind. Visit the lovely and debauched Elise, Lady Burton, instead. The countess knew what he preferred, just how far to push the limits of his appetite for the depraved.

"You may send him in, Hazlitt." The words emerged from him in a rush. From some secret, dark recess of his mind not even he knew existed. It went against common sense, against his plans, against every damned thing to perpetuate her falsehoods. Each appearance she made at his club heightened the risk, for if anyone else suspected her or unmasked her, his carefully wrought plans for revenge against his sire would be dashed.

Hazlitt bowed and disappeared, snapping the door closed.

For a moment, Duncan was alone with his clamoring thoughts. Why the hell had he allowed her entrance? What was the purpose of delaying, of allowing her to continue with her ruse? He swallowed, raked a hand through his hair, and otherwise attempted to compose himself. Lust, he realized.

Base. Crude. Wrong.

It had felled many a great man before him. But there it was, shameful and true, a fact he could not deny. He wanted her. Last night, he had lain awake in his bed, thinking of her, hand on his cock, and he had found his release to the thought of him on his knees before her, tasting the sweet flesh between her thighs as she watched the wickedness unfolding within the scarlet chamber. How sweet her pearl would have been against his tongue. He would have sucked until—

The door opened once more, and there she stood, Hazlitt hovering over her shoulder with his piercing stare. Duncan flicked his gaze back to her, taking her in—the awkward, ill-fitting coat and waistcoat navy and gray respectively, at odds with her buff breeches. Her cravat was crooked. Her boots scuffed and clearly a discarded pair of her father or brother's. Her hair was once again stuffed beneath a hat.

He stood and willed his painfully erect prick to soften. Thank Christ for the cut of his coat, which hid his tremendous and inappropriate reaction to all thoughts relating to Lady Frederica.

He bowed. "Lord Blanden."

She bowed as well. "Mr. Kirkwood."

Her gruff attempt to disguise her voice had returned.

"Thank you, Hazlitt," he called to his hovering man, for he had no wish to perpetuate an audience. He wanted her alone so he could decide what the devil he was to do to her. *Er, with her, rather.* "That will be all."

One more dubious lift of his dark brow, and Hazlitt was gone, disappearing into the lively fabric of the club that was coming to life beyond Duncan's office. The door closed with a barely audible *snick*. He and Lady Frederica were alone.

The silence seemed suddenly ominous.

"Would you care for a whisky, Blanden?" he asked, because it was what he asked all his friends, acquaintances, and patrons of the male variety.

It occurred to him, quite belatedly, there was no means by which Lady Frederica could have ever sampled whisky, or anything stronger than ratafia or orgeat. He could only hope she did not accept.

"Of course," she said in her feigned gentleman's baritone.

Damnation.

He moved to the sideboard where he kept a decanter and glasses. Whilst he did not often imbibe, he had long ago learned that any discussion—be it friendly or decidedly the opposite—was best conducted with a bit of fire to round off the hard edges. He poured two fingers for himself, hoping to quell his ardor, and one for her before spinning on his heel.

If his eyes settled first upon her thighs, partially visible thanks to her ill-fitting coat, it could not be helped. And if they next settled upon the area where he knew her breasts hid, how could it be his fault? He could detect only the faintest swell beneath her waistcoat and shirt. Were her breasts large and full as her hips suggested they might be, or were they small and rounded? Perfect little handfuls? Did her nipples match the delicate pink of her mouth?

Lord God, he had to stop himself. He strode to her, distractedly offering the glass with two fingers of whisky in error. Before he could catch himself, she accepted the glass, her dainty fingers curling around the tumbler.

"I am honored by your presence this evening, my lord," he managed, hoping to distract her with dialogue. "To what do I owe the pleasure?"

Pink tinged her high cheekbones. "I would like admittance to the…viewing area once more, if I may, Mr. Kirkwood."

He could not have been more surprised had she punched him in the gut. Indeed, the breath fled his lungs in that moment as if she had. He raised his glass, taking a fortifying sip, measuring his response. Allowing her to view once had been reckless and foolish—a whim to sate his own wickedness. But to sanction her return, admitting her once more into the privileged world of secrecy, spoiling her innocence even further…he risked far too much.

But granting her another chance to view the revelers in the club's pleasure chambers appealed to him. It intrigued him. It made his cock stiff and painful, prodding the fall of his breeches.

"I was under the impression the viewing area left you rather shocked, my lord," he hedged, grinding his jaw.

"Shocked but intrigued, sir," she corrected, lifting her own glass to her lips and taking a ladylike sip.

She coughed, blinking, as the bite of the whisky hit her tongue for the first time. But instead of abstaining from drinking further, she shocked him by lifting the glass to her lips once more and taking a long draw. Her eyes closed, and she scarcely suppressed a shudder as she swallowed before exhaling through her mouth.

Beelzebub, this woman had audacity, raw and real and true. He had never witnessed the like. That an innocent, sheltered lady—the daughter of a duke—would dare to infiltrate his club, dressed as a gentleman, two days in a row, watch the unprincipled coupling of his patrons, and sample whisky with such daring seemed an impossibility. But here she was, brave and beautiful and brash, defying logic and reason and wisdom.

Here she was in his office, wearing breeches and ugly boots and an unbecoming hat, the most breathtaking creature he had ever seen. She frightened the ballocks off him in ways he could not begin to comprehend.

Unless...it was possible she was not as innocent as he presumed. Perhaps she had already been ruined, and her taste of the forbidden had led her here to his club. Perhaps she had been compromised by Eversley, the pompous prig with the insatiable appetite for cunny and the small cock.

If she had, *by God*, he would...

His fingers flexed at his side impotently. What was he thinking? That he would lodge his fist in Eversley's jaw to avenge Lady Frederica's honor? He was fit for Bedlam. First, he had no knowledge of whether or not the lady possessed honor, or if the viscount had indeed besmirched it. Besides, she had seemed shocked last evening, and he did not fancy her a great actress. Second, he needed more head-clearing Scottish whisky. Immediately.

"Delightful whisky, Mr. Kirkwood," she rasped in an eerie echo of his thoughts, tipping her glass back and downing the remaining contents. She gasped and coughed, bending forward, swaying on her feet. "Simply delightful. I shall have another, if you please."

Another? For all her luscious curves, she was still a lady, her frame smaller and more delicate. He could not believe she had ever sampled a spirit so strong. The effects of her first glass had yet to settle in, but they would, and when they did, he did not wish to be the man tasked with scooping her off the floor.

Even if holding her in his arms held an infinite amount of appeal.

Especially because it did.

He frowned at her. "I do not think it wise to have another glass at this early a juncture in the evening. Do you, Lord Blanden?"

Lady Frederica blinked at him. Her eyes traveled down his body in a slow, maddening perusal that somehow managed to leave him more frustrated and hungrier for her than he already was.

"Yes, I do. Of course, I do. I've never had whisky before. Er, that is to say, I have never before imbibed a whisky as delightful as this. I am loath to carry on without another glass."

Duncan tossed back the remnants of his own glass before snagging hers and taking both back to the sideboard. He poured a generous amount into each. To hell with caution. To hell with attempting to listen to his own dwindling sense of honor. If Lady Frederica wished to view the pleasure chambers once more, she would. And if she wished to get soused on his whisky, she would. Who was he to stop her?

"Here you are, my lord." He offered her the glass, their fingers brushing as she accepted it from him. The brief contact sent desire shooting through him.

She seemed similarly affected, swaying on her feet toward him. Her pupils were large and obsidian, dilated discs in the centers of such green opulence. "Thank you, Mr. Kirkwood."

Suddenly, he longed to hear his name in her husky, silken voice. "Call me Duncan, if you please, Lord Blanden."

"Duncan," she said softly, smiling. "Thank you."

For a moment, he could almost forget who and what they were. He had lived thirty years as the Duke of Amberly's bastard, knowing he would never be a lord. Knowing his sire would never acknowledge him. Understanding he had siblings who had been raised to a life of unimagined privilege, wealth, and cosseting. Siblings who would attain the respect of their peers by mere virtue of their birth, without ever having to earn it. And he had never, not once, been envious of the quality. He had never wished to be one of them.

Yet here and now, he wished—futilely and foolishly, and just for a moment—to be one of them. He wished he was a lord. He wished he was her equal instead of her inferior.

But he had learned from the time he was a lad that wishes were nonsense, and nothing he could ever do would earn him a place in the peerage. All that was left to him was making his fortune and buying his respect, and it was precisely what he had done.

He raised his glass to her in a mocking salute, taking another long draw of the liquor. "Thank me later, my lord. Come along, then. If you wish to view this evening's wickedness, I shall not detain you a minute longer."

* * *

GOOD HEAVENS.

What could she have been thinking?

Her mind and body were at war. Frederica brought the glass to her lips, trying her best not to inhale the pungent scent of the spirits Mr. Kirkwood had poured her. She swallowed, exhaling through her mouth to avoid tasting the whisky, for it was a dreadful elixir. One she would not wish to ordinarily consume save for the pleasant hum it had begun in her veins.

She felt, quite suddenly, warm. Overly warm. And relaxed. Lazy. Her pulse pounded, and her head seemed strange. Was it too large for her body? Too heavy for her neck? And why did Mr. Kirkwood—nay, Duncan—seem suddenly taller? More brooding? More handsome? Why did his chest look so broad and strong?

Why did she long to touch it once more?

"...I shall not detain you a minute longer," he was saying.

Frederica was too intent upon his lips, watching the sculpted, beautiful fullness of them moving. His chin too was lovely, a small dimple marking the tip, his jaw long and hard and dappled with the shadow of golden whiskers he must have shaved that morning. His entire countenance was not just alluring but...*arresting*. He was handsome, and yet there was more to him. He was intriguing. A bit of a mystery.

"My lord?"

His voice, steeped with a sliver of irritation, cut through her musings. She hoped she had not been staring. Why did she feel so odd? It was as if her mind was fashioned of clouds, and she could not make sense of anything or anyone. For a moment, she forgot what she was about. Forgot to keep her voice deep, to maintain the pretense she was her brother. The mustache she had affixed to her upper lip—a prop from some silly parlor game she had resurrected to assist in her disguise—itched. Her fingers longed to pluck it from her skin. When she opened her mouth to speak, the thing tickled her.

How irritating.

It had also gotten thoroughly steeped in spirits, part of it lying wetly against her skin. She wanted to say something, to answer Mr. Kirkwood, but she could not force her tongue to obey her command. It was as if she had lost all control of her body. As if she were...

Nay, it could not be. Or perhaps it could.

Was she...*soused*?

She brought the tumbler back to her lips, taking another long draught. Perhaps it would calm her. Yes, it must calm her, or at least imbue a sense of clarity. Or certainty? Which was the correct word?

"Lord Blanden?" His voice cut through her thoughts yet again, this time as demanding and sharp as a whip on her skin.

She jumped. The glass fell from her fingers, slipping to the floor. It landed on the thick carpet with a dull thud, the remainder of her whisky sloshing onto her thieved boots and the rug in equal measure. She glanced down at the mess she had unintentionally created. "Oh, dear."

At Westlake House, she never cleaned up after herself. Ladies did not do so, and the legion of staff her father employed oversaw the granting of her every whim. If she so much as upended her teacup, two maids were on hand to tidy up the spill. It was not so here at The Duke's Bastard. She knew twin, slashing stabs of guilt, for first sneaking her way into his club, and then for making a mess of his lovely carpet.

"You mustn't fret over it, Blanden. Servants will see to it."

She ignored him, her guilt overwhelming her every other sense. She sank to her knees, reaching into her jacket for a handkerchief. What a treasure that gentlemen could go about with such a convenience secreted upon their person, she thought.

And then she realized Duncan was upon his knees as well, his large hand blotting the stain with his own handkerchief, and she forgot to think about anything but him. Their eyes met. Clashed. Her heart hammered.

He was so near to her she could touch him. Could reach out and trace the bow of his upper lip. Run her thumb along the seam, cup his wide jaw. Lean forward, falling into him, their lips colliding.

Frederica meant to apologize for her startling lack of grace. For soiling his fine carpets. But instead, it was as if her body was obeying her fantasy. She lost her balance, teetering forward. There was nowhere to land but on *him*.

Her shameful descent unfolded with a hideous torpidity. Her hands flailed. Her eyes went wide. Her spectacles—a replacement pair since he had neglected to return hers yesterday evening—slid off the end of her nose. She fell into him. His hands, large and warm even through her layers, caught her about the waist, and they moved as one.

He landed on his back.

She landed atop him, colliding with his chest, her legs tangling in his. Her hat flew from her head, taking some hairpins along with it. A long, perfectly formed black curl fell across her face. She stared down at him, the evidence of her subterfuge on full display, aghast.

"My, but your hair is singularly long and lustrous for a gentleman, Blanden," he said, his bright-blue gaze burning two holes straight through her.

"It is an unusual vanity, I know," she attempted to explain, before realizing she had neglected to lower her voice. *Drat.*

"Perhaps not so unusual after all, Lady Frederica." He rolled suddenly, moving them so she was on her back on the carpet, and he was atop her instead.

She was dizzy, and it was a combination of the whisky she'd imbibed, his big body pinning hers to the floor, the scent and feeling of him invading her senses like a rampaging army, the unexpected reversal of their positions.

The sinking realization he knew who she was.

He had called her by name.

Not *Blanden*. Not *my lord*. But *Lady Frederica*.

The breath left her in a rush. Her frantic mind absorbed fragments of facts. He was atop her, settled intimately between her thighs. His arms bracketed her head. He was so near, the warmth of his breath skated over her chin like a caress. She ought to be alarmed by their position, the inappropriateness of it.

She could not have ruined herself more thoroughly if she had tried. This was disastrous. She had been caught by Duncan Kirkwood himself, deceiving him, trespassing within the hallowed walls of his club. One word from him to her father—to anyone—and all would be lost.

However, she could not seem to summon even a shred of remorse. All she felt was heat. Languorous licks of something wicked and delightful and altogether wrong, singeing her from the inside out. Beginning in her belly, sliding lower, to the forbidden place between her thighs, and radiating everywhere. Was it the spirits she had consumed? Or was it merely him?

"Have you nothing to say for yourself, my lady?" he asked softly, his voice a delicious rumble, fashioned of sin and seduction and everything she had been taught to avoid at all costs.

Everything she wanted.

She pressed her lips together, struggled to find her wits. Perhaps it would be best to make one more attempt to convince him he was mistaken. For the sake of her reputation, if nothing else. "I am the Marquess of Blanden. Would you be so kind as to remove yourself from my person, Mr. Kirkwood? I daresay this is highly irregular."

"Mmm." He flashed her a wicked grin that sent a fresh wave of need unfurling within her. "Highly irregular indeed. It is not every day that a lady, and the unmarried daughter of a duke at that, infiltrates my club by assuming the identity of her brother. What is your purpose?"

How was she meant to think or form a proper answer with his body in such distracting proximity? She had never had occasion to be in such intimate contact with a gentleman before. Not even when Willingham had forced his kiss upon her. It had been a cold, slimy peck, his lower body held away from hers, and she had been left swimming in a sea of revulsion. She had certainly not imagined how forbidden and delightful it could feel to have a gentleman atop her.

Not a gentleman, she corrected herself.

The prince of London's most infamous gaming hell. A man who ruled over his sinful kingdom with dashing aplomb. A man who was feared and revered. Duncan Kirkwood. The last man she ought to ever have known.

The only man she wished to know.

There it was, foolish but true.

She was a lady who had lived her life above reproach, who had followed all the rules, learned all the arts expected of her, who had been dutiful and good. A lady who had grown weary of balls, expectations, halfhearted suitors, and above all, propriety. Who was curious.

A lady who wanted to be debauched.

"I am conducting research," she told him at last, honestly. There seemed no further purpose in attempting to deceive him when he had already caught her out.

"Research," he repeated. He caught the curl that had worked itself free of her pins between his thumb and forefinger. Tugged it gently. "What manner of research?"

She blinked up at him, trying to comprehend his reaction. He did not seem angry. Not precisely. Rather, he seemed... intrigued. "I am writing a novel. *The Silent Baron*. The baron gambles away his entire fortune inside an establishment similar to The Duke's Bastard. I required an accurate recounting of the sights, sounds, smells, the patrons, the games, the furnishing, any and all details."

"A novel." He frowned down at her, his full lips thinning together, brow furrowing. "You are penning a novel?"

Did he think her incapable because she was female? All the naughty feelings bursting to life inside her shriveled. Her hands found his shoulders—broad, hard, delightful shoulders, drat him—and shoved. "Yes. I, a female, am writing a novel. Now if you do not mind, you are hurting my back with your hulking form, and I would greatly appreciate the removal of your person from mine."

It was a lie, of course, for he was not putting undue pressure upon her. Indeed, there was no part of his weight settled upon her, his arms bearing the brunt.

But he did not move, disagreeable fellow that he was. Rather, his eyes narrowed. "You are one of those troublesome sorts, are you? If you think for one moment, I will allow you to write maudlin drivel painting my club in a negative light, you are thoroughly wrong, my dear. Just as wrong as you were when you fancied you could flit about a gentleman's club without anyone noticing you were female."

That gave her pause. "When did you know I was a female?"

"From the first bloody moment I saw you." His lip curled. "No gentleman has an arse like that. It's unmistakable."

He rolled off her at last, gaining his feet with an effortless fluidity of motion she could not help but admire. When he offered her his hand, she took it with great reluctance, allowing him to help her to her feet as well. The connections of their bare palms sent a strange, new flutter skittering through her. She stared at him, swaying on her feet, feeling the effects of the whisky continue to burn through her.

"Will you allow me to continue to conduct my research?" she asked, feeling bold. And shaken. And all manner of things.

"Research?" He raised a questioning brow. "Do you mean will I continue to allow you to avail yourself of the privilege of viewing my club members in the pleasure chambers?"

She swallowed. *Yes*, that had been wrong of her. Her cheeks flamed with color. She had known it then and she knew it now, but she had enjoyed the shocking act of watching. "All of it, Mr. Kirkwood. I wish to continue my observations so that my story might be bolstered by both accuracy and attention to detail. If anyone is to become swept away in the world of *The Silent Baron*, I must be as realistic in my presentation as possible. The creative workings of my imagination alone will not suffice."

His fingers tightened on hers, and he stepped forward, into her body, crowding her. He was all darkness, all black, the embodiment of wickedness except for his golden hair and blue gaze. "Do tell what the *creative workings* of your imagination might have conjured, Lady Frederica. I admit, you have roused my curiosity, among other things."

Even her ears burned beneath the combination of his scrutiny and the subtle implications of his words. "Nothing as scandalous as the truth, Mr. Kirkwood."

"And did you enjoy watching yesterday, my lady?" he asked slyly. "Surely you must not have been disgusted, else you would not have returned today."

"My return here this evening was caused by my dedication, Mr. Kirkwood," she lied. "I wish for more information. I require the full picture of The Duke's Bastard."

And she did, she told herself. Even if once had been enough to provide her the bones for fleshing out the gaming hell in which her baron would lose his fortune, succumbing to the devils of vice. After all, there was no way she could capture the shocking, flagrant depravity she had witnessed here yesterday. No one would dare publish such an account.

"Ah, but I am not so inclined to allow such a thing." His thumb caressed her wrist. Just a simple movement—one slow, unending circle—and yet it made her knees nearly give out. "You see, Lady Frederica, this club is how I earn my supper. It is my reputation. My mistress. It is the livelihood of dozens of men and women. I will not have it destroyed by the whims of one spoiled, selfish duke's daughter who fancies herself an authoress."

He thought her spoiled and selfish? Why, he did not even know her. She tugged her wrist from his grasp, severing the connection and—she hoped—the ridiculous sensations careening unchecked through her traitorous body. He was toying with her, like a cat batting at a mouse he would eventually make his meal, and she did not like it.

"I am creating a fictional account, sir," she reminded him, keeping her tone frosty. "Your club will not be named. No one who reads *The Silent Baron*—should I be fortunate enough to find a publisher—would ever be the wiser. The repulsive acts you countenance within your walls shall remain your secret."

"Repulsive?" His eyes glinted. "I beg your pardon, my lady. Only yesterday, you did not appear repulsed."

Because she had not been, much to her everlasting shame. Nor was she now. Her father and mother would be horrified if they were to discover what she was doing in her father's absence. To know she had fallen prey to such wickedness. That even a lady who had been born and raised to a life of gentility, purity, and ease could become corrupted by vice.

Instantly, an idea for *The Silent Baron* entered her mind. The baron could fall in love with one of the courtesans in the gaming hell, intrigued by the disparity of their lives. It would be an ill-fated match, of course, with no future. Why had she not thought of it before?

She tipped up her chin, trying to hide the quiver of excitement running through her now. How she itched to flee home and put her pen to paper. But first, she needed to conclude her battle of wits. "Nevertheless, I was quite repulsed. How can you claim to know my inner thoughts and feelings? You do not know me, Mr. Kirkwood, and neither should I know you."

His sensual lips twitched. "More's the pity."

He was a bad man, Mr. Duncan Kirkwood.

A bad man who made her feel wicked things. Things she did not wish to feel. Her breath caught. She thought of his thumb on her skin, how his merest caress could still make her weak. What power did he wield?

She ought to go now. Run from him while her virtue and her dignity both remained intact. She could write *The Silent Baron* with the handful of details she had gleaned from her brief time in the gaming rooms the day before. It would be far safer. Far wiser to do so.

Frederica swallowed, banishing the feelings he spurred in her. She had far too many matters of import facing her. But then her mind prodded her that a lady of the evening was precisely the character she required to heighten the tension of the baron's fall from grace. She knew nothing about such females, having been raised to live her life as though the creatures did not exist.

If she was to write a harlot, she really ought to meet such a person. Speak to her. Understand her motivations. Her speech. Her aspirations. She could not leave. She had to convince Mr. Kirkwood to grant her more time at The Duke's Bastard.

She forced her countenance to soften, offering him a smile and taking care to remove every, last hint of ice from her voice when she spoke again. "Please Mr. Kirkwood, how can I persuade you of the necessity of my research here?"

CHAPTER 5

*D*uncan could think of at least five bloody excellent ways Lady Frederica could persuade him to allow her to remain within his club, conducting her *research*, as she phrased it. One of them involved her pretty mouth. One involved her hands. Another, her virginal cunny, and yet another her…

Damnation.

No need to torture himself.

This little game of theirs was at an end. Of necessity, it had to be.

"You cannot persuade me, my lady." He shook his head slowly, unable to keep his gaze from dipping once more to her loose coat, wishing he could see the true swell of her breasts. Just once. How tightly had she bound them? And why did the notion of her bound breasts make his cock rise hard and full in his breeches? Thinking of her in nothing but breeches, boots, and her bound breasts robbed him of the power of speech.

Those luscious midnight curls unleashed from their pins, trailing down her back. His hands cupping her arse. He would

SCARLETT SCOTT

direct her to unravel the bindings as he watched. And then, when her bubbies sprang forth, he would suck an erect nipple into his mouth. His fingers would make short work of the fall on her breeches. The breathy sounds of her need would fill the air as he moved to her other nipple, nipping this time with his teeth. He would part her folds, find her wet and hot...

Blast. Blast. Beelzebub. Hades.

A trail of epithets unleashed themselves in his mind. He had to stop this nonsense.

"Mr. Kirkwood, I beg of you," she pressed, those eyes, brilliant and glorious, wide upon his. "All I require is some additional research this evening, and then three evenings more at the most. A few hours of your time. You shall not even know I am here."

He would know she was there. If he was blindfolded, he would know she was in the vicinity. The scent of violets would forever make his prick go stiffer than a marble bust. *Holy God*, he was altogether certain the mere knowledge she was somewhere in London would be enough to make his cock hard.

He gritted his teeth. All the more reasons why he had to deny her. Her usefulness to him was at an end, and she was nothing to him now but a temptation and a distraction he could ill afford. He had worked too hard, for far too long, amassing his empire with one goal in sight.

It was all within his reach now. Glittering. Glimmering. Taunting.

Why, then, was he allowing the Duke of Westlake's chit to distract him?

"No," he bit out.

"No?" she repeated, her inky brows creeping up her creamy forehead. Her lips pursed.

He ignored how much he wanted to kiss them. He espe-

58

cially ignored means number one in which she could persuade him, by sliding his cock between them. "No."

She blinked, those thick lashes fluttering. "Forgive me, Mr. Kirkwood. I fail to see how my presence here could be such an imposition. You need not even speak to me. Simply grant me access to your club and I shall flit about with no one the wiser, observing and taking notes."

"There is the problem, Lady Frederica." He urged his cockstand to dissipate to no avail. How the hell could he deny her with the evidence of how much he wanted her scarcely restrained? Duncan cleared his throat. "I discovered your ruse within moments of first laying eyes upon you. Others will do the same. I cannot have the Duke of West-lake's daughter ruined within my establishment. No gentleman will dare to cross the threshold in the event of such a trespass."

She pursed her lips, and he could see her mind spinning. "But perhaps no one would need see me. You have viewing slots for your...chambers of ill repute. Surely you have the same sort of thing overlooking your tables."

She was a clever wench. He had to grant her that. Far wilier and sharper than he had imagined a sheltered duke's daughter could ever be. And damn him if it didn't make him want her all the more. He bloody well loved an intelligent woman, one who would argue politics, one who was well read, one who was unashamed of her mind, who wielded it like a weapon.

"I do have such viewing slots," he acknowledged. "But that has no bearing upon my decision. You must leave here this evening, never to return."

"Four more visits after this evening," she returned, unflinching.

"What manner of bargain is that?" He could not quite

keep the note of incredulity from his voice. "Mere minutes ago, you requested three."

Those bright eyes sparked into his. Even with the hideous strip of false mustache affixed to her upper lip, she was beautiful. "Your delay has increased my price."

The minx possessed gall. He had to acknowledge that as well. "You may remain for one hour this evening. That is all."

She took a step closer, her scent and her heat hitting him. "An hour today and four more visits thereafter."

His curiosity got the better of him then, and he cocked his head, considering her. "Tell me something, Lady Frederica. How is it you are able to escape from your father's home, dressed as your brother, no less, and venture to my club two evenings in a row?"

"My father is attending a matter of some import in the country on one of his estates," she ventured. "My mother is easily distracted, and my brother is young and ordinarily otherwise occupied."

"He is older than you are, my lady," he reminded her, for though he had never taken particular interest in the Marquess of Blanden, he had nevertheless memorized the details of his patrons and their families.

"Perhaps then he is merely easily distracted as well." A small smile curved her lips.

Again, he wished to pull the mustache from her skin. It seemed a travesty of the worst order that his view of her lovely mouth should be adulterated by the ludicrous thing. Whilst Lady Frederica in breeches appealed to his inner sense of depravity, the mustache presented a firm limit. It truly had to go.

He moved forward, his hand reaching out. Before he was even aware of his intentions, he had snagged the thing and pulled. It clung to her with tenacity, but a firm tug and it was gone, leaving a red line across her skin in its wake.

She clapped a hand over her mouth. "How dare you?"

The strangest thing happened then. There he stood in his office, opposite the key to his vengeance who had fallen—almost bodily—into his lap. She looked like an actress from a theatrical troupe that traveled the countryside, making a poor imitation of a gentleman with her half-unbound hair and her ill-fitting garb. It was all so ludicrous, so fantastical, that he could do nothing to suppress the laugh that rose in his chest, bursting forth, loud and unchecked.

He could not stop it. He laughed until his gut ached. Laughed until tears welled in his eyes and rolled down his cheeks. Laughed until he bent over, struggling to regain his breath. Laughed as he had not done ever before.

"Are you well, Mr. Kirkwood?" she asked above the din of his mirth, eying him as though he were a Bedlamite newly escaped and she was not certain if she ought to pity him or cajole him back to the prison he'd fled.

No, he was not well, in answer to her impertinent question. Else he would not be contemplating offering her a compromise. He should be ordering her to leave and forgetting she existed, not laughing at her haphazard attempts at deception. Not stuffing the scrap of a mustache inside his coat pocket. He already had one pair of her spectacles, so he supposed this latest acquisition could join the first well enough.

He caught his breath. "Perfectly well, my lady. It is merely the lightness of the moment. The sight of you…"

He allowed his words to trail off when he realized they said something rather different than what he had intended.

But she did not miss a word. Her brows snapped together. "The sight of me, Mr. Kirkwood? Are you laughing at me?"

Yes. No. Also, yes.

He was laughing at her. At himself. At the silliness of this predicament in which he now found himself. He was laughing because there had not been cause for much levity in his life, and he was grateful for this rare moment of indulgence.

But he did not wish to reveal any of that to the feisty, daring duke's daughter before him. Instead, he cocked his head, studying her. "I may be reconsidering your bargain, my lady. But first, you must answer another question. Precisely how have you managed to travel from your father's residence to my club each evening?"

The thought of her flitting about, so ridiculously costumed, a plump pigeon for any villain with a discerning eye to pluck, nettled him. He did not like it, not one whit.

She blinked at him, the spectacles magnifying her crisp emerald gaze. "I hired a hack, sir. It was reasonably easy. Far easier than I had imagined. Once again, it has proven an invaluable boon for my research."

A boon for her bloody research.

Did the foolish chit have no inkling of how much danger she was placing herself in with each of her rash actions? And it was not merely her reputation at stake but rather her innocence. Her body. How easily she could be broken. He had seen too many times the horrible consequences of a woman being taken against her will. His own mother had been one such victim, and he would never forget. It was one reason why he took such great care with the ladies he employed.

He stiffened, a protective surge overtaking him. "If I agree to allow you to return after this evening, my lady, it will be for one more occasion only. I will send a private carriage for you, and it will await you a discreet distance from your home. There will be no more hired hacks or wandering about the city unprotected."

Fire sparked to life in her vivid eyes. "I will accept nothing less than four visits, as I have already established. If you continue to debate the matter with me, I shall raise the number to five."

He barely held his laughter in check at her cheek. "Madam, I do believe you have no notion of the means by which a compromise is reached."

"Nonsense," she blustered. "Of course I do, else you would not be entertaining a compromise at all."

Damnation, the lady had a point.

He inclined his head, a new respect for her blossoming in his chest. She was not just lovely and brave, but intelligent and unafraid of pursuing what she wanted. Admirable qualities in anyone, whether male or female, but particularly so in a lady of her station. She could have entertained herself with balls, routs, soirees, and suitors. Instead, she was writing a bloody novel and infiltrating the ranks of the most notorious club in London, strutting about garbed as a gentleman, in the name of research.

His attraction to her was growing by the moment, and not just to the physical beauty of her body or the undeniable lure of her unattainable status—the forbidden had ever appealed to him—but to her. She interested him. He wanted to learn her the same way he had learned gambling: calculating the odds, learning which games of chance reaped the greatest reward, understanding just how much a risk to take without the chance of losing all.

How dangerous. Here was all the more reason to send the troublesome Lady Frederica on her way.

"Two visits and my carriage," he countered. "I will bar you from the door if you refuse to accept my means of conveyance."

Her eyes narrowed. "Three, and I shall continue the use of the hired hack. It does give one such a delightful sense of independence and freedom, the sort which I daresay I shall never again enjoy."

The sadness in her voice disturbed him. "Never again seems rather a hyperbole, my lady."

"To you, perhaps." Her chin lifted. "You are not the one whose father wishes to marry her off to any gentleman who will offer, regardless of how odious he may be."

His father had not wished anything to do with him. His father would not even acknowledge him or look him in the eyes. She was fortunate hers only wished to see her settled. His had never given a good goddamn about him.

"Have you no suitors?" he asked, curious. He could not fathom that a woman like her would not have every gentleman in London at her feet. She was as lovely as she was original. What man could look upon her without envisioning the bounty of her dark hair on his pillow?

"Not any I would wish to spend the rest of my life with," she said quietly. "I am approaching the age of spinsterhood. My father grows tired of waiting for me to make a match, and one of my suitors has been insistent. I am sure my future holds no interest to you. However, this may be my last opportunity to have such freedom of movement. The research I could conduct here at your club could last me for years. Or perhaps even a lifetime. That is why it is such a necessity."

Something about her words and the luminous sheen in her eyes caused a lump to settle in his throat. A strange sensation unfurled within him, one entirely foreign. He swallowed. Took a step away from her, rolled his shoulders, which seemed suddenly constricted by his perfectly cut coat.

"Three additional visits and the use of my carriage," he snapped, resenting her for the effect she had upon him. For the weakness she somehow created in him, a softening he had not suspected himself capable of possessing any longer. "That is my final offer, Lady Frederica. Accept it or leave it."

She was silent, her expression contemplative, for far

longer than he deemed necessary. But then at last she smiled, and damn her if that smile didn't take his breath.

"I shall accept, Mr. Kirkwood."

Why, in the name of all that was holy, did he find the pink mark on her upper lip so bloody adorable? And why did her triumphant tone make longing roll through him?

This was, quite possibly, the worst decision he had ever made in his life.

* * *

WHAT HAD SHE BEEN THINKING? Frederica could not help but wonder the next evening when the unmarked brougham awaiting her opened to reveal another occupant already inside.

A black-clad, impossibly debonair occupant with a smoldering blue gaze and lips she ought not to have imagined kissing the night before when she had been alone in her bed. Lips she could not help staring at now as a flush spread over her cheeks.

Frederica gaped, pressing one hand to her fluttering heart and using the other to tug down her hat in an effort to shade her face. "Mr. Kirkwood!"

In her shock, she forgot the necessity of lowering her voice lest anyone overhear her and question the feminine tone of the gentleman she pretended to be. *Blast.* She cast a furtive glance around her to make certain she had continued to go undetected. This was, without doubt, the riskiest decision she had ever made in her life.

Nothing seemed more dangerous than entering a confined space with Duncan Kirkwood.

"My lord." He quirked a brow, an edge of impatience creeping into his tone. "Are you going to get into the bloody brougham, or do you intend to stand on the street? You are already twenty minutes tardy."

She had not been able to arrive at the appointed time since her mother had returned early from her daily shopping expedition. Mother had even dined with her, being surprisingly solicitous rather than dashing away to add her spoils to her ever-growing collection. Her latest obsession was fans. At last count, she had one hundred and seventy-three of them. Most of them had never been used.

"I was unable to escape without notice," Frederica explained warily, not wishing to delve too deeply into her mother's eccentricities. "Forgive me, sir."

"Damnation, I am regretting my uncharacteristic munificence for at least the hundredth time today," he snapped, irritation as evident in his tone as it was in his bearing.

Oh, dear. She had a decision to make. She could either step up inside the carriage with the depraved owner of a gaming club—a man who did not blush or flinch at watching his patrons engaged in that amorous occupation which ought to be reserved for husband and wife alone—or she could turn and flee, forgetting she had ever made such a ruinous decision. She truly didn't have a choice, did she? *The Silent Baron* needed this research.

Moreover, whispered an insidious voice inside her, *when will you ever again get the chance to ride in an enclosed carriage, utterly alone with Mr. Duncan Kirkwood?*

She ignored the voice and her sense of self-preservation both, and mounted the steps. In two breaths, she was within, and there was nowhere to sit but alongside him. She swallowed as she settled herself as near to the window of the conveyance as possible. But he was so large, and his thigh, well-muscled and thick beneath his perfectly tailored breeches, nearly touched her.

His driver shut the door, leaving them in privacy.

"Nothing to say for yourself this evening, my lady?" Mr. Kirkwood asked.

His query jolted her gaze from her inappropriate examination of his thigh and the fit of his breeches to his face. She frowned at him, wishing his delicious scent did not permeate the air. Wishing he was not in such devastating proximity to her. Wishing she had more ability to resist his undeniable allure.

She cleared her throat. "Forgive me for my tardiness, sir. My mother delayed me by spending more time with me this evening than I anticipated. I was forced to wait until the appropriate moment to slip away from Westlake House unnoticed."

His mouth remained tightened. "I am of half a mind to deduct one of your three visits as punishment. My time is too valuable to be wasted."

What must it be like to be in complete control of his future? To be the master of his own fate? How glorious it must be to be Mr. Duncan Kirkwood, the man on all London's tongue, splashed across every gossip page, wealthier than most lords, feared and respected by his patrons and employees alike.

"I am sure your time is of great value, Mr. Kirkwood." She frowned at him. "I was not aware you would be awaiting me."

He raised a brow. "You imagined I would leave you unchaperoned? What manner of gentleman do you think me?"

She looked away from him, down at the idle hands in her lap, but then could not resist watching him once more. "You hardly qualify as a chaperone, Mr. Kirkwood. This arrangement is most scandalous. Why, your limb is nearly coming into contact with mine, and the entire carriage smells of amber, musk, and lemon. It is a very agreeable scent, I must admit, but could you not find something more subtle?"

His lips quirked once. Twice. "You find my scent agreeable, Lady Frederica?"

Oh, drat. Why had she mentioned it? Her mind was overtaxed. Burdened by her nightly deceptions and the risk of being caught, surely. "Overbearing is a more apt description, Mr. Kirkwood."

"Ah." His lips twitched again, this time developing into a full smirk. "I see."

"No," she huffed, "you do not. It was not intended as a compliment, but rather as a reproach. You ought not to be so vulgar, is what I meant to say. Everything about you, from your manner of dress, to your cologne, is intended to attract attention."

"Do I attract attention?" He stroked his wide jaw with a thumb. His gloves, too, were a deep, true midnight black. "Do I attract *your* attention, Lady Frederica?"

Of course he did, and the miscreant knew it.

The low timbre of his voice as he asked her the last question made a strange ache draw up inside her. "Why are you accompanying me, Mr. Kirkwood?" she queried instead, turning the subject to far safer matters. "You cannot have been serious when you claimed to act as my chaperone. Even a man who deals in sin for his bread knows what is proper and what is not."

"As does a duke's daughter, and yet it does not stop her from stealing away into the night, donning her brother's ill-fitting clothes, and worming her way into walls behind which I deal my sin." His tone had grown cool. *A reproach*, she thought.

She had displeased him somehow. Perhaps he did not appreciate the reminder of the path he had chosen in life. He was not wrong, however.

"Forgive my tongue, sir. I did not wish to offer you insult. I merely meant to speak plainly. You are correct, and I am acting in stark opposite to propriety's rigid strictures. My only defense is as a female, half the world's doors are closed to me. I cannot learn anything if I gad about as Lady Frederica Isling."

He leaned toward her, his stare piercing, seeing through to the heart of her, it seemed. Or attempting to, at the very least. "Fair enough, Lady Frederica. You and your tongue are all too easily forgiven. In exchange for my absolution, perhaps you might enlighten me. Precisely what is it you wish to learn?"

Her cheeks went hot. There was much she wanted to learn, most of which she could not tell him. Her gaze strayed back to her lap. A far safer, less tempting place for them to land. She cleared her throat. "The inner working of your club so I may understand why men are drawn to it and how they can go about losing everything they have in the name of one more game of chance."

He made a chiding sound, as though she were a child to be reprimanded. "Come now, my lady. I have already told you I'll not have my club's existence put in jeopardy to satisfy your missish sense of fairness. I will happily explain to you the rules to the games. But if you think to make trouble, I shall have the carriage turned around and you can return to your sheltered world and your closed doors.

What manner of trouble did he truly think she could affect? She had not even finished her book, let alone found a publisher willing to print it. Perhaps none ever would. Her gaze flitted back to him, finding him regarding her with an intensity and warmth that filled her with an odd combination of excitement and foreboding. Why had this powerful man capitulated to her demands?

"I do not wish to make any difficulties for you, Mr. Kirkwood," she told him softly, for it was true. She intended to be as unobtrusive as possible. "As I said, I merely wish to conduct my research."

"Hmm." He made another noncommittal sound, seemingly devouring her his eyes. "Where is your mustache this evening, my lady?"

She pursed her lips, reminded of his two small thefts from her. "The disreputable proprietor of the wickedest club in London stole it from me."

His lips quirked again. "Do tell."

"Indeed." She nodded, as if imparting a great font of wisdom. "I am currently en route to his club, with every intention of causing a great deal of uproar."

This time, his mouth rippled, two dimples in his cheeks making an appearance for just a flash, gone so quickly she may have imagined them altogether. "I cannot say I find fault with the mustache's absence, but I do not approve of this uproar you speak of. What shall it involve?"

She found herself grinning back at him, the knowledge she was capable of making his grim countenance soften with amusement—however brief—swelling her with pride. "I am afraid if I confide in you now, it shall spoil the surprise. You shall simply have to wait and see."

"Well played, Lady Frederica," he drawled, tipping his hat to her. "Well played, indeed."

CHAPTER 6

*T*he lady had a sense of humor.

Duncan would not have supposed it, looking upon her. For she seemed an odd little bundle of nervousness and propriety, of rebelliousness and caution. She was a dichotomy, Lady Frederica Isling. More intriguing than he could have supposed just yesterday.

For in addition to her daring and penchant for the absurd, along with her bewitching mouth, vibrant eyes, lush hair, and the loveliest arse in all Christendom, she was also intelligent. He discovered, as he allowed her the run of his private corridors and office, she was a true observer. She watched everyone. Studied everything, even the smallest nuances of someone's facial features.

"That fellow over there appears to be up to no good," she warned him now, her eye pressed to the viewing slot overlooking one of his faro tables. "His gaze is darting about, and I do believe he has been palming some of his cards up his coat sleeve. I have been watching him for nigh on to ten minutes, Mr. Kirkwood."

She spoke of Viscount Weston. Duncan did not even need

to press his eye to another viewing slot to be certain. He had been wary of Weston, a young dandy who had squandered some thirty thousand pounds in the last fortnight at The Duke's Bastard only to have his fortunes suddenly turned. Neither Duncan nor his men had yet been able to prove the whelp's treachery.

As he watched her viewing his patrons, dressed in her ridiculous coat and breeches, he could not help but think not of Weston and the cards up his sleeve but rather of the curves hidden beneath Lady Frederica's disguise. Her finely shaped bottom was all he could discern.

"Mr. Kirkwood?" she cast a glance back toward him.

Their gazes clashed, and an unwanted rush of desire washed over him. He was aware of her in a way he had never before experienced. *Bloody hell*, he needed to regain control of himself. Two days after first spotting her within his club, and he was already giving in to her ludicrous demands to conduct research and following her about like a puppy at its master's heels. Why had he felt the need to linger here in the dimly lit corridor with her, anyway?

It was locked for the evening, access to it restricted to just himself and Lady Frederica. There was no need to protect her or to watch over her. He ought to go about the business of running his club as usual. The Duke's Bastard was a machine, it was true, but it was a machine that required him to keep all the parts moving in unison. Lingering here with her was doing nothing but inviting folly.

His cock hardened when she licked her lips, her eyes settling upon his mouth.

All manner of folly, some of it more dangerous than others.

He wanted her, and he could not have her, and it was making him churlish. The need to lash out rose within him, a desperate urge to undercut the heaviness of the moment, the false sense of intimacy that had fallen betwixt them. She was quality. An innocent lady. Not for him.

"Leave the management of my club to me, if you please, Lady Frederica," he ordered with more harshness than necessary. "I have run The Duke's Bastard without the interference of an overindulged duke's daughter for years now, and miraculously, it continues to flourish.

Her thick lashes lowered, hiding the brilliance of her gaze from him, and he found himself hoping she would meet him with the reckless daring he so admired. But instead, her cheeks went pink. "Yes, of course."

Her meek response, along with the undercurrent of hurt in her tone, cut through him. He instantly regretted his impulse. For all that she was foolish and brave, she was also young and pure. He was jaded. Older. He had raised himself up from the meanest streets, from nothing, to where he was now. He ought to have known better than to allow her to return.

He gritted his teeth. "I do believe the carriage shall be ready for you within the half hour, my lady. Prepare yourself to return."

Her gaze jerked up from her study of the floor, wide and searching. He saw not a trace of manipulation in her expression, so different from most of the females of his acquaintance—the ladies who wanted a rough man's hands upon them in the bedchamber but would never acknowledge him by day.

"I have scarcely had any time at all to research," she protested softly. "Have I displeased you, Mr. Kirkwood?"

Lord God, if she only knew.

If she had an inkling of how much restraint he employed in this moment, how difficult it was to keep from pinning her to the wall and ravaging her sweet pink lips with his. From sinking his tongue inside to taste her, wrapping her legs around his waist so he could grind himself into the center of her as they kissed.

He swallowed. Conjured up images guaranteed to vanquish his fierce reaction to her, the discomfort in his breeches. He pictured his chef's face. A dead fish being cut open. Recalled, in desperation, the fists of one of his mother's paramours, smashing into his body when he'd been a wee lad.

At last, the overwhelming grip of lust began to dissipate.

"You have not displeased me," he said gruffly then. "But you have distracted me. I am a busy man, Lady Frederica. This club will not run itself, and I have much work awaiting me. I have been more than accommodating."

"Yes, you have." Her voice was quiet, redolent with an emotion he couldn't define, something soft and intimate. As if it were reserved for him alone. "I thank you for that."

Her gratitude made him roll his shoulders, clench his fists. He did not know what to do with it, how to accept it. Duncan Kirkwood was not a man of kindness or generosity. He had spent his youth clawing to survive, and as a man of means, he remained loyal and true to one goal, his need for revenge.

"Think nothing of it." He gave a flippant shrug. "I merely did not wish to have word of your murder or ravishment taint my club."

It wasn't true. He had wanted to see her. From the moment she had begun blustering, spinning her fantastical tale of an ill mother and a Melancholius Ague, he'd been fascinated by her. How bitterly ironic that the one woman he was drawn to as no other was also the perfect means for him to secure the vengeance he desired.

Another emotion crossed her expressive features, and this one he could discern well enough. Hurt. But how could it be that he, the bastard son of a duke and a Covent Garden whore, had the power to wound a true duke's daughter? Why would she care what utterances he spewed?

But then, her brilliant gaze searched his, probing, and he could not escape the notion she saw him. Saw straight bloody through him.

"I think you may have taken a liking to me, Mr. Kirkwood." A small smile curved her luscious lips, and he was once more grateful he had filched her ridiculous mustache. A mouth like hers did not deserve to be hidden. "That is why I am here. That is why you not only sent a brougham for me but also accompanied it. That is why you are wishing me to leave in such a rush as well. I make you uncomfortable."

Beelzebub's breeches.

Heat rose to his cheeks. He, Duncan Kirkwood—who made grown men weep, who did not possess the capacity for sympathy, whose philosophy of life was to make the first cut with his blade lest he be cut, who had presided over orgies and commissioned chairs upon which his patrons could cavort, who dressed in midnight black because it matched his soul—yes, *he* was blushing before her like a maiden in a schoolroom.

"What an imagination you have, my lady," he said coolly, irritated anew by his unwanted reaction to her, by the feelings she stirred within him. "Little wonder you have decided to try your pretty hand at scribbling."

He intended for his condescension to nettle her. To send her on her merry way, never to return to his club or his life, never to cause him further distraction. *Damnation*, he already had what he wanted, what he needed from her. Prolonging the torture was unnecessary.

But Lady Frederica again proved to him she was a woman with mettle and determination.

"What of the other chambers?" she asked suddenly.

He nearly swallowed his tongue. Surely, she did not

SCARLETT SCOTT

mean... *Christ,* but she did, the minx. He could read it in her countenance. She had a wicked, wild side to her he could not have fathomed.

"Other chambers?" he repeated in a hoarse voice, feigning confusion, though in truth he knew precisely what she referred to. *Damn it.* A raging, rampaging lust threatened to take the reins.

Her tongue darted over her lips, this time leaving a sheen he longed to lick. "The... depraved chambers. I wish to view those in addition to the gaming area."

Bloody hell. There was no way he could remain in this hall with her if she made use of the scarlet chamber's viewing window again. Watching her watch others, wondering if the acts she observed filled her with need...*damn it all,* corrupting her...thrilled him. It sent lightning through his veins, made his ballocks draw tight and his cock press harder against the fall of his breeches. The mere notion he could be the one to teach her. To undo the fall of her breeches as she watched and dip his fingers inside her sweet folds. What sounds would she make if he played with her clitoris? Would she be wet?

Somehow, he knew she would. She would soak his hand, drench his wrist. She would come like the wild tempest she was, loud and unapologetic, owning her pleasure.

The image in his mind had him grinding his jaw.

No. He could not surrender to his need. Duncan shook his head, sending the unworthy, dishonorable thoughts to the ether. "You have already seen them once, my lady, and even then, I ought never to have allowed such a travesty."

"Why did you allow it?" she asked softly, taking a step closer to him,

Undoing his resolve just a bit more.

He swallowed, fists flexing at his side. "I wanted to shock you. To send you from here with no wish to return."

Nearer still she ventured, unaware or uncaring of the danger she was in. "You did not shock me, as you can see. I must observe everything I can. Spare me from nothing. Show me all, Mr. Kirkwood. I need to learn. I must know if I am to accurately portray the baron and the netherworld he occupies."

"No," he denied her. Denied himself. No good could come of her lingering a moment more within his domain, the two of them alone, her delicious curiosity making his blood hum. "Remain where you are, my lady. I will go send for the carriage and have it brought discreetly to the back entrance so you may safely return home."

He forced himself to turn away, leaving her to watch him as he stalked to the door leading to his office. It was done. He had the willpower to leave her alone. Gaining his retribution upon the man who had sired him had nothing to do with him taking the innocence of a sheltered young lady. He would find someone else—anyone else—to slake the hunger she had kindled within him.

Trouble was, something told him no one else would quite do.

* * *

HE WAS GOING to make her leave his club after a mere hour.

Frederica stared at Mr. Kirkwood's broad, retreating back, trying not to notice the ripple of elegant strength beneath his perfectly cut coat as he stalked away. His shoulders were so large, larger than those of most gentlemen of her acquaintance. His entire air was a combination of primitive, dark, and debonair that left a quivery feeling in her stomach whenever he was near.

Or even when he was in the act of leaving her, as he was currently doing.

She had to stop him.

She needed more time.

"Mr. Kirkwood," she called out, her feet moving toward him. She could not chase in the shoes that dwarfed her feet—as it was, she'd needed to wedge several pairs of stockings inside the toe to render the things wearable—but she managed well enough.

He stopped just short of the door, stiffening, keeping his back to her. "Lady Frederica, it would not be wise of you to encourage me to linger in this hall."

The subtle implication of his words thrilled her. Sent heat blossoming in her, settling in the forbidden flesh she could not seem to ignore. The unspoken suggestion that she tempted him ought to frighten her, but she was reveling in her newfound freedom whilst it was still hers. When her father returned to town, she would not dare to be so bold in her escapes. And with his arrival would come a fresh wave of urging her to wed. Willingham would not wait long.

But it wasn't just her fleeting freedom making her heart pound and an ache pulse between her thighs. It was *him*. *This man.* He was not the sort of gentleman she would have ever been allowed to know. Mr. Kirkwood was scandalous. Dangerous. Even if his club was frequented by the peerage's loftiest lords, he was still the bastard son of a duke and a doxy. He worked to earn his living.

Polite society shuddered at such a plebian notion.

Frederica found it intriguing. Admirable. Attractive.

He was attractive. Frightfully so. He was forbidden, and it only made her long for more time in his enigmatic presence.

"Why should I not encourage you to remain here?" she asked, inwardly cursing herself for the breathless quality of her voice.

He already thought her a pampered, witless duke's daughter. She did not need to further his opinion. She was still speaking to his back. His head was bowed, almost as if he attempted to cling to his restraint.

She had seen the raw glint in his beautiful eyes. For a perfect moment, she had read his confusion. He, too, felt the connection between them—odd and unexpected yet so perfectly natural, as if it had been preordained. She knew it.

And he had not yet left. Or moved.

Temptation burned through her, along with an unaccountable boldness. Frederica scarcely recognized herself. The meek wallflower who was content to remain on the periphery of society was nowhere to be found. It was as if she had shed her old self in favor of her new identity. Here and now, she found herself in the midst of the most interesting bustle of people and vice and sin she had ever imagined. She found herself just a step away from the man she had only read about in scandal sheets.

One more step forward. She took it.

Frederica placed a palm on his back. She'd shucked her gloves, which had only hindered her ability to properly take notes, and the heat of him through his coat seemed to singe her skin.

"You did not answer me," she prodded, fancying her hand absorbed the steady, fast thuds of his heart.

He was rigid beneath her touch. Strong and male and lean. His scent washed over her, and the pulse in her core turned into a throb. She felt suddenly as she had when she had pressed her eye to the viewing slot and witnessed the most shocking acts imaginable. Hot. Achy. As if she needed something but did not know precisely what that something could be.

Only this time, it was magnified by one hundred.

"You should not touch me, my lady." His voice was rough and low, a decadent rake over her senses.

Naturally, his warning only made her bolder. She flattened her left palm to his shoulder as well, daring to slowly move her hands. The slope of his bones and sinew, the cords of his muscle, the solid strength of him—she learned it all, for the first time. She had only danced with gentlemen in ballrooms, driven with them in the park. So proper, a necessary degree of separation at all times. But this—Duncan Kirkwood—was real, and she could not deny how much she adored exploring his virility.

"Why should I not touch you, Mr. Kirkwood?" She continued her perusal of his back, unashamedly. It felt far too good. All of it.

She felt like a prisoner who had been locked away all her life, only to suddenly be handed the key. She wanted to fit the key to the lock, swing open the door, and run free. *Dear heavens.* Perhaps something was wrong with her. Perhaps she was inherently wicked. Whatever the case, she wanted her research to include *him.*

She could acknowledge it to herself if to no one else.

"Because you are an innocent," he growled then. "You are a lady of quality, and I am decidedly not a gentleman."

"What if I do not wish to be an innocent?" The question fled her unintentionally. Her tongue was always ahead of her mind, saying what she felt. Speaking out of turn.

Was it her imagination, or did he sway toward her?

"Lady Frederica, I can assure you that you are out of your depths," he gritted.

Was she? *Yes. Without question.* But that did not mean she longed for him any less. There was so much she wanted to know. So much she wanted to learn. Frederica was insatiable for knowledge. For research. To make her novels come to life.

Perhaps also to make herself come to life.

"Would you kiss me?" she asked, and she did not know

why. Kissing Duncan Kirkwood had not been her purpose in coming here this evening. Nor had her own ruination.

His silence seemed to fill the softly lit hall, echoing all around them, mocking her.

She had made a fool of herself.

Humiliation burning through her, she tore her hands from him and spun on her heel. It would be better if she allowed him to fetch the carriage and she remained where she was, too far away to further embarrass herself. Too far away for him to tempt her. She could only hope he would leave with haste.

She could not bear to return tomorrow. Not after begging for his kiss. A man like Duncan Kirkwood would have no use for a sheltered miss. What had she been thinking? Likely, everything she had read in him had been wrong. Drat her observational skills. They were flawed. Just as she was.

Tears stung her eyes.

How would she ever write a novel when she could not even understand herself?

She heard him mutter something behind her, and then the fall of footsteps.

Hands clamped on her waist, spinning her. She lost her balance and fell into him, into his hard chest. Perplexed, Frederica glanced up at him. "What are you do—"

But she could not finish her question, for his lips were upon hers. Firm and warm and so different from the one and only kiss she had ever received. This kiss was aflame.

She forgot her shame. Forgot her tears.

Forgot everything but Duncan Kirkwood's mouth on hers, his hands spanning her waist, his lean body burning into hers. His tongue coaxed her lips to part, and when she did, he shocked her utterly by thrusting it inside her mouth. Not roughly or rudely but slowly, a sleek foray as his kiss continued to play over her. It was voracious and yet gentle all at once, a breathtaking contradiction of slow seduction and sensual mastery.

Her hands went to his shoulders, holding herself steady against his devastating onslaught. At this proximity, one of his long legs thrust between hers thanks to her breeches, he made her dizzy. His scent filled her, and he overwhelmed her. He was everything she felt, thought, tasted.

She tasted *him*, she realized, giving his tongue a tentative nudge with hers. And he tasted of pleasure and passion, of the forbidden and...cocoa with a hint of anise. All this iniquity surrounding him, liquor on every sideboard, and Duncan Kirkwood tasted of chocolate. She felt powerful in that moment, as if he had divulged a secret to her alone.

Growing bolder, she tangled her tongue with his once more, and he rewarded her with a low sound in his throat, part growl, part hum, and all satisfaction. She never wanted this moment, this kiss, to end. Closing her eyes, she gave herself over completely to the sensations, to the passion vibrating in the air, in her, between them.

His lips moved over hers with reverence, soft and slow, steady and deep. She forgot who she was, who he was. Nothing else signified. He owned her with his passionate kisses. His hands began to move, sliding inside her coat, making her tremble as he traveled slowly upward, gliding over her waistcoat.

He did not stop until he reached her breasts. They burned and ached inside her painfully tight binding. His fingers splayed open, as if cupping the mounds he knew were hidden beneath her gentleman's attire, and through the layers, she felt that touch like a brand. His thumbs swirled, unerringly finding her nipples.

A fresh wave of sensation burst. Desperation laced through her—to tear away her coat, waistcoat, and shirt, to undo her bindings. She wanted those thumbs stroking her skin, easing away the sting, his fingers plucking at the tender buds until the only ache in them was caused by him.

Again and again, his thumbs moved while his mouth claimed hers. It was the most intimate touch she had ever received, and it changed everything. Something inside her shifted. Here was the key, in the lock, and she turned it. The lock opened.

She wanted to touch him everywhere, and so she did. Her hands found his neck first, strong and surprisingly soft to the touch above his cravat. And then her fingers sifted through his thick, sleek mane of golden hair. She framed his cheeks next, desperate to maintain their connection. Here, the tiny pricks of hundreds of his shaved whiskers abraded her skin in most delicious fashion.

His lips left hers burning, tingling, and forever altered, moving down her throat. Her fingers returned to his hair, so thick and lustrous. Somehow, his kiss upon her bare skin, directly above her madly pounding pulse, drove just as intense of a sensation through her as his kiss on her lips did. She hungered. Yearned. His mouth opened to suck her flesh above her neck cloth, his teeth delivering a bite that had her crying out, her fingers digging reflexively into his hair.

"So sweet," he murmured against her throat, his tongue flitting over her skin. "Forbidden fruit always tastes best." His thumbs raked over her bound nipples again, inciting an almost painful rush of pleasure.

Frederica was mindless. Breathless. She didn't wish to think about his words, what they meant. All she wanted was more of him. More of his mouth, his tongue, his touch. The heat that had been building within her made her arch her back, seeking, urging him to continue. She wanted him to open her waistcoat, unbutton her shirt, and lift it over her head. She wanted him to slice away her bindings. She wanted his hands on her bare skin without impediment.

She wanted…

A knock sounded. Quietly at first, and then more persistent. *Rap. Rap. Rap.*

Mr. Kirkwood stilled. For a beat, silence descended, and there was no sound save the muted din of the club and pleasure chambers beyond their private little viewing hall and the ragged sound of their breaths mingling until they became one. She fancied she could hear their hearts pounding in unison.

Rap-rap. Rap-rap. Rap-rap.

"Mr. Kirkwood?"

"Beelzebub's ballocks." Cursing, he tore away from her as if she were a live coal shot from the fire grate, and he had plucked her up from the floor with his bare fingers only to realize his folly and fling her as far and as fast from him as he could.

She swayed, wrapping her arms about herself as a sudden sense of loss hit her. Her lips felt swollen and tingly. Her body was alive as it had never been. Even the patch of skin on her throat he had sucked and nipped stung. Her mind seemed separate from her body. Mad thoughts rained through it.

Duncan Kirkwood kissed me. I kissed him back. He tastes like cocoa, and his hair is softer than a fine silk. His shoulders are every bit as hard as they appear. His hands on my breasts...

No.

She had to stay the wildness he had created within her. She watched as Mr. Kirkwood smoothed his coat and stalked toward the door, jerking it open without sparing her a backward glance. His words echoed in her mind, joining the tumult. *Forbidden fruit always tastes best.*

Was that what she presented to him? A challenge? The unobtainable? Perhaps he kissed every female of his acquaintance with such fiery dedication. After all, the man did employ harlots. He did have viewing slots dedicated for the pleasure of patrons who preferred to observe the depravities unfolding within his den of vice. He had created the perfect dwelling of sin at The Duke's Bastard—gambling, drinking, and worse. What sort of man was he?

Precisely who was the man she had just asked for a kiss? The man who had left her shaken and confused, questioning herself and everything she knew to be true? Right from wrong, honor versus ruin, freedom or safety, recklessness and care.

The interior of Mr. Kirkwood's office backlit the gentleman at the door, bathing his face in shadows. Frederica did her best to feign disinterest and act the part of a gentleman as she felt the fellow's gaze settle upon her for the briefest of moments before discreetly flicking away.

"Didn't realize you were otherwise engaged, sir," the man murmured. "My apologies."

Mr. Kirkwood flicked a glance at her over his shoulder, his brow furrowed, before turning back to his staff member. "His lordship is new to the viewing hall. I was merely providing him an introductory lesson in the art of pleasure."

Dear Lord, the manner in which the word *pleasure* rolled off his tongue, smoother than fresh cream, made her flush and wish for more such lessons at the same time. She ought to be appalled at herself, and part of her was.

But the other part of her—the part of her that longed for freedom and the pursuit of her own dreams—reveled in every second of what had occurred this evening. That part of her wanted more. And more. And then some more afterward.

"What the hell do you require, Hazlitt?" Mr. Kirkwood bit out, an edge of irritation blunting his tone.

He did not appreciate the disruption.

Good, then. Neither did she.

"Forgive me, sir. I would not ordinarily seek you out, but I am afraid there is a delicate matter underway. Lord Greaves has returned Monsieur Levoisier's dinner on no less than three occasions, claiming it is unworthy. Tonight, Monsieur lost his patience and he is, er, offering Lord Greaves his *opinion*. His distinct and unfettered *opinion*."

"I will attend the matter." Mr. Kirkwood sighed, passing a hand through the thick golden strands atop his head. He cast her a meaningful glance over his shoulder. "Remain where you are, enjoying the view, if you please, my lord. I shall return forthwith."

Naturally, since he did not wish her to accompany him, there was nothing she wanted to do more. How fascinating—the chef of a gentleman's club verbally assaulting one of the patrons. As discomfited as she still felt after Mr. Kirkwood had kissed her, her mind was ever spinning stories.

Here was an opportunity to witness a club's workings firsthand—its patrons, its staff, a conflict. Frederica could not ask for more. If she was not able to remain cloistered away in the hall, exchanging kisses with Mr. Kirkwood, she would happily accept the second-best fate in the name of her novel.

She cleared her throat. "I find I am famished, Mr. Kirkwood. I shall accompany you and have my supper whilst we are about it. Killing two birds with the proverbial stone, as it were?"

He glanced back at her, his expression startled for the briefest of instants before his mask of control once more settled into place. "Please, my lord. I insist you remain here until I return."

He insisted, did he?

All the more reason for her to ignore him. She flattened a hand to her midsection and rocked back on her heels as she had seen her father do on numerous occasions. "I fear I find myself ravenous, Mr. Kirkwood. I require sustenance before aught else. Do you care to lead the way?"

Mr. Kirkwood's gaze narrowed upon her. "Be that as it may, my lord, I am afraid I must suggest you remain here whilst I arrange a tray to be sent to you. That way, you can assuage any hunger you are currently suffering from."

Any hunger you are currently suffering from.

Had he intended the secret meaning to his words? Her gaze studied him, melding with his for a brief moment. It was a moment where their connection became so visceral and undeniable, she could not catch her breath.

But she had to. *Inhale. Exhale. Calm thyself.*

"No tray will be necessary." She sent him her sweetest smile, swinging her gaze to the befuddled manservant who awaited Mr. Kirkwood's response at the threshold separating the office from the den of iniquity. "I shall dine alongside everyone else."

"That would not be—"

"Mr. Kirkwood, I am afraid—"

"I wish to gamble," she announced, seizing upon the idea. With an audience, she was certain she could manage to convince Mr. Kirkwood to join her in any endeavor. "If you will not feed me, then perhaps you will lead me to the hazard table?"

"No." His answer was clipped. Dripping with an air of finality.

She raised a brow, both inwardly and outwardly. "I do beg your pardon. *No?*"

"No," he confirmed darkly before seeming to recall their audience. "That is to say, perhaps I shall escort you there if I've the time. Remain here and I will return."

How clever he must think himself. But she would not be denied this opportunity.

She pursed her lips and shook her head. "My use for this hall is decidedly at an end."

He pinned her with a glare. "Is that so, *my lord?*"

"Yes, it is," she challenged right back. "*Mr. Kirkwood.*"

"Sir?" the servant intervened; his expression as anxious as his tone. "I am afraid Monsieur may create a stir if he is allowed to continue unchecked."

Another foul epithet emerged from Mr. Kirkwood. He bowed his head. Looked from his manservant to Frederica, and then back. "Very well. Lead the way, Hazlitt. My lord, do as you wish until I can rejoin you."

Do as you wish.

"Yes." She beamed at him, a new sense of excitement bubbling up within her. "I shall."

He muttered something beneath his breath as they retreated from the hall, and she swore it sounded like *that is what I fear.*

Naturally, she ignored it. She would make the most of her time within the walls of his club. After all, her writing was her first and only love. There was not room for scornful owners of gentleman's clubs. No room at all.

CHAPTER 7

*T*he minx was going to borrow trouble, and he knew it. His mind should have been concerned with the possibility his chef was on the cusp of alienating an earl with deep pockets and a penchant for gambling poorly. Ordinarily, he would be calculating how much he earned from Lord Greaves' gambling losses and endless hunger for quim in a year and measuring it against Monsieur Levoisier's wages per annum, calculating how much of an attraction the proclaimed French was for his patronage, estimating the cost of procuring another, equally refined chef to keep his patrons well fed and sated. Balancing cost and reward, weighing the outcomes.

His mind adored facts. Ledgers gave him an odd sense of peace—numbers were familiar and comforting, and watching them add and grow without subtracting had long ago become a favored pastime. To a lad who had grown up picking pockets for coin and spending many a night with an empty belly, those growing figures represented the unattainable, stability. Happiness.

Raised voices reached him as he approached the dining

room, and he winced, reminding himself he had matters of far greater import requiring his attention. Lady Frederica Isling could remain where he had damn well told her to remain, or he would bar her from further entrance to his club. Indeed, he ought to bar her altogether after her foolish request and his equally witless acceptance of the gauntlet she'd thrown.

Why had he kissed her? When could he do it again?

Beelzebub's banyan.

"The soup bloody well requires salt." The agitated proclamation of Lord Greaves echoed through the dining hall as Duncan crossed the threshold.

Monsieur's face was flushed, his lip curled. The man was as volatile as he was gifted, but Duncan employed him for his culinary brilliance and not for his Gallic temper. He strode forward, Hazlitt at his heels, intent upon dousing this rather unwanted, ill-timed fire.

He had to thrust all thoughts of one midnight-haired lady from his mind.

"The soup is *parfait*, my lord," Levoisier spat. "Adding salt is *inconcevable*. The great masters, do you think they added more paint to their canvas, ruining it with too much pigment? *Non.* They knew perfection. *Alors*, you must admit too much of *une bonne chose* destroys that which is *déjà*—"

"Monsieur Levoisier," Duncan greeted in a calm interruption. He knew from experience that the more the chef reverted to his native tongue, the angrier he had become. The worse his outrage. The more astringent his venom. "I have a special request for you that must be addressed, if you please."

The chef blinked owlishly, distracted from his rage. "Monsieur Kirkwood." He bowed. "Good evening, sir."

Duncan bowed in turn to Lord Greaves, whose jaw was on edge. The earl was a young fop with the sort of classical features that made ladies swoon. He knew so because several of his lady consorts—bored society wives, all—had remarked upon his rakish allure. To Duncan, the fellow was a purse with hair that needed trimming and an ego that needed clubbing.

But the businessman in him would never attend to said clubbing. "My lord, please accept my sincere apologies for any deficiency in your soup course. If you think it requires salt, I am certain Monsieur Levoisier shall be more than happy to remedy the oversight."

The chef made a choking sound.

"The soup is bland," said the earl in a dismissive, cutting tone. His nostrils flared.

"Indeed, my lord," Duncan soothed. "Monsieur shall add salt as you recommend and return a fresh bowl to you forthwith."

"It is not mere soup," argued the chef, his ears going scarlet. "It is bisque of crayfish *à l'ancienne*. It needs no salt to the *discerning* palate."

Duncan gritted his teeth. "A correction will be made, my lord."

The earl raised a supercilious brow. "Excellent, Mr. Kirkwood. I knew I could rely upon your sound sense of reason in this matter."

The chef began to speak.

"A special request," Duncan reminded Levoisier. "From an *esteemed* guest to the establishment."

The Frenchman's eyes went round, and Duncan knew he supposed he was referring to Prinny, and while the Prince Regent had honored The Duke's Bastard with his royal presence on numerous occasions, this was decidedly not one of them. Duncan felt not a speck of compunction at deliberately misleading the chef, however.

The cost of the fellow's pride was not worth the loss to

Duncan's coffers should the Earl of Greaves choose to eschew his club after a rift with an overzealous French chef. He turned to address his man. "Hazlitt, you will see to the correction of his lordship's soup course, I trust?"

"Of course, Mr. Kirkwood." Hazlitt swept forward, retrieving the earl's bowl of soup and placing it upon a salver.

Hazlitt was more than capable of soothing ruffled feathers. As Duncan's right hand man, the unwanted task often fell to him, and he always handled it with aplomb. Like Duncan, Hazlitt had been born into the stews. He had come from nothing, and had fashioned himself into something. He was loyal, trustworthy, and capable.

With another bow to the earl and a pointed look at his chef that brooked no opposition, Duncan excused himself and his employee. When they exited the dining hall, Duncan turned to the Frenchman.

"I require a supper in my private office," he announced, even though he knew it was folly. "For two. Your finest effort would be appreciated."

Lavoisier nodded. "For you and your esteemed guest, sir?"

Esteemed guest.

He supposed one could call her that.

Or *problem.*

Minx.

Mayhem.

His downfall.

Yes, any of those would do.

But best to settle upon the former rather than any of the latter for the moment. He inclined his head. "Indeed, Monsieur. Add a pinch of salt to the earl's bowl and then send your finest to me within the hour. I shall be waiting."

* * *

"What do you prefer, my lord?"

Frederica blinked at the lovely, flaxen-haired woman before her and did her best to subdue her inherent jerk when her companion's small, dainty hand landed upon Frederica's thigh. "Ahem." She pretended to clear her throat, her mind whirling, searching for diversion tactics. "I do enjoy reading. What do you prefer, Miss? …"

Her companion giggled, natural color appearing in her round cheeks, heightening the pigment she had already applied there with her own hand. "You may call me Tabitha, if it pleases you, my lord. I was not speaking of something as decidedly boring as reading. I rather had *something else* in mind."

She frowned at Tabitha, wishing she was not so willowy of form and fair of hair. So lovely. This woman worked for Mr. Kirkwood. In his club. She did…unsavory, unspeakable things. A twinge of something she refused to call envy cut through her.

Frederica belatedly realized Tabitha was looking at her expectantly, running a tongue along one lower lip that seemed unnaturally red. She frowned. Was the woman hungry? Perhaps she had been inquiring after the sort of fare Frederica desired to eat.

She blinked, remembering to keep her voice suitably gruff. "I do like young rabbits, though I suppose that isn't the thing."

Tabitha's lips parted. "*Young* rabbits, my lord? How tender must they be?"

Foolish question from a tiresome woman. Frederica was growing weary of her company as it distracted her from her opportunity for unfettered observation. Why would she not simply go away?

She frowned. "Does anyone truly like meat that is old, tough, and dry?"

Surely that subtle chastisement would deter the woman from additional questions.

But Tabitha leaned closer, her scent tickling Frederica's nose, her golden curls, partially unbound and brushing against Frederica's shoulder. "What else do you like, my lord? Perhaps I can accommodate you. I may not be young, but I am not yet old."

Did she intend to cook Frederica a meal? This made no sense. Frederica had only just witnessed Mr. Kirkwood's man urging him to soothe the chef's irritation. Tabitha did not resemble a cook at all. "Oysters are tolerable as well if in patties à la Française."

"How wicked of you, my lord." Tabitha tittered, draping herself on the arm of Frederica's chair.

Good heavens, what was wicked about such a commonplace dish? Why did the creature insist upon crowding her so? She cast a glance about the sumptuous chamber, searching for a glimpse of a tall, blond gentleman before she realized what she was about.

Her frown deepened. "Wicked?"

Did Tabitha lack intelligence? Frederica felt unaccountably itchy in her brother's pilfered shirt and coat. For a moment, she longed for the comfort of her chamber, her books, her quill and ink and papers, the writing desk she loved. But then she forced herself to recall this was one of her final opportunities to investigate Mr. Kirkwood's club.

After this evening, she had only two visits remaining. She gritted her teeth, ignoring the disappointment surging through her at the realization.

"Very wicked." Tabitha's warm breath and warmer lips grazed Frederica's ear, startling her.

She swallowed. This was rather untenable. The other woman's hand landed on her thigh, stroking over her borrowed breeches. Stiffening, she thrust the hand away in haste, ignoring her companion's disapproval. *Blast.* Despite her best intentions, she'd managed to find herself in a *situation.*

She had wandered from Mr. Kirkwood's office in the wake of his abrupt departure, partially to irritate him and partially to answer her own curiosity. After all, she had research to conduct. He had closeted her away inside his office and hidden corridor, and she had yet to further experience the bustling atmosphere of the club. She required more time on the floor, mingling, overhearing snippets of conversation, taking in the sights, sounds, and smells.

Her innocuous observations of the gentlemen gathered to indulge their vices had been going precisely according to plan. No one had even paid her any heed. Until she had been pulled aside by Tabitha, who seemed intent upon the mauling of Frederica's person. Was this what gentlemen preferred, to be boldly pawed at by tittering females garbed in dampened dresses with their bosoms on garish display? Little wonder Frederica was still unmarried.

Her brows snapped together and she fixed Tabitha with a fierce, disapproving frown. "I do think I find myself famished, Tabitha."

But her words seemed to have the opposite effect of her intent, for Tabitha's errant hand returned, nearly grazing the apex of Frederica's thighs in search of Lord knew not what. Frederica bolted from the chair, in her haste, knocking into Tabitha, who nearly tumbled to the floor. Alarmed and sensing she was well out of her depths—fearing discovery or worse, more overtures from the persistent female—Frederica spun on her heel, prepared to bolt.

And promptly slammed into a male chest.

Hands steadied her. The familiar scent of musk and its accompanying notes enveloped her. She looked up into the eyes of Mr. Duncan Kirkwood. Her hands settled on his biceps, and not without noting how firm and strong they were. How they flexed and tightened beneath her touch. That brilliant gaze of his glittered with a combination of promise, menace, and something else…

Remembrance.

She could not help but look at his finely molded lips then, recalling how they had felt against hers—firm, hot, coaxing, and knowing, gentle yet devouring-all at once. Her ears went hot at the reminder of his bold kisses, her response.

"My Lord Blanden," he said at last, the decadent rumble of his voice striking a ripple of sinful want inside her that refused to settle.

She bit her lip hard enough to distract herself. It did nothing to alleviate the furious riot of sensation inside her. Duncan Kirkwood had taken her in his arms. He had kissed her. His tongue had been inside her mouth, his hands on her breasts. How could she ever look upon him again without wanting more of the same? Without *needing* it the same way she needed to breathe?

"This is a different manner of hare than I supposed."

The tart female voice broke Frederica from the spell of Mr. Kirkwood's eyes and lips and the haunting ghost of his kisses. She released her hold on him, taking a discreet step backward.

Mr. Kirkwood quirked a brow, settling his gaze upon the other woman. "Have you something to say, Tabitha?"

Tabitha pursed her lips. "This is the way of it then?"

Mr. Kirkwood's mouth tightened, his jaw clenching. "Perhaps you would care to make conversation with Lord Eversley. He appears in need of enlivening companionship, Tabitha."

Frederica had the distinct impression she was on the outskirts of a conversation about something other than what it appeared on the surface. She did not like it. Not one bit.

"Mr. Kirkwood," she said, finding her tongue without his blazing eyes devouring her. "Tabitha was kind enough to offer me sustenance. I was just about to partake."

A feline smile curved Tabitha's lips. "Yes, his lordship was. Perhaps you would care to join us, Mr. Kirkwood? The three of us could *dine* together. A feast, if you will."

"That will not be necessary, Tabitha," he said smoothly, a beautiful smile curving his lips and rendering him even more handsome than he ordinarily was. "His lordship and I shall *dine* together. *Alone.*"

Tabitha's mouth fell open for a brief moment before she collected herself and curtseyed. "I daresay it explains a great deal. Of course, my lord, Mr. Kirkwood. If you will excuse me?"

Frederica frowned as the golden goddess walked away, swaying her hips. What a strange creature. She could not shake the impression Tabitha harbored a *tendre* for Mr. Kirkwood, and she was ashamed to admit the notion sent a pang of jealousy straight through her.

Mr. Kirkwood's deep, delicious voice interrupted her musings then.

"Shall we, my lord? I for one am ravenous."

Her attention snapped back to him in a trice. Why, oh why, did the word 'ravenous' on his sinful lips incite such a trill of pleasure down her spine? And what, oh what, had she gotten herself into this time?

AN HOUR LATER, Duncan watched Lady Frederica Isling take her first bite of *Monsieur*'s famed Charlotte of apples with apricot marmalade, and he knew with a certainty that set his teeth on edge; he was the one who had borrowed trouble. Here she sat opposite him in the small table in his office where he ordinarily preferred to dine alone, beyond the eyes of his patrons, often whilst reading.

Trouble.

He had kissed her. Against the judgment that had never failed him in his life. Against his admittedly malleable sense of honor. Certainly, against his carefully wrought plans, which required her to return unscathed to her papa; the duke. All the better to allow Duncan's threats to permeate the august man's shroud of arrogance.

And he had not just enjoyed it, but he had reveled in it. The softness of her lips beneath his, the way she had responded to him, and the beauty of her surrender had all undone him. He'd gone mindless with the need to claim her. To kiss her with such ruthless abandon that his mark would forever be upon her memory and her mouth both.

She made a lusty sound of unabashed pleasure, and he gritted his teeth with greater force, trying to ignore the dart of her pink tongue over her full lower lip. Trying not to recall the sweet, tentative tide of that tongue against his.

Beelzebub's bottom, he had to think of something else. Anything else. To distract himself before he spoilt the perfect opportunity for revenge that had been all but delivered to him on a silver salver.

"I now understand why so many gentlemen flock to your club, Mr. Kirkwood," she said when she had swallowed the bite of moist, buttery perfection he knew Lavoisier's Charlotte to be. "The culinary mastery of your chef, despite his penchant for berating your patrons, is unparalleled."

He seized upon her words as the distraction he required, frowning at her. "My chef does not berate my patrons, madam. Do not put that in your book, else I shall become an object of supreme ridicule."

Her eyes glittered, a saucy smirk flirting with the corners of the mouth he could not help but want to kiss again. "I cannot fathom you being the object of anyone's ridicule, Mr. Kirkwood."

A strange thing happened to him. Warmth—*nay, a bloody inferno*—blossomed in his chest, in his gut, in his cheeks. He prickled with it. Blazed with it. He, who had for so long been lusted after and chased by females for the power he wielded or the pleasure he could bring them, experienced a novel sensation. He was flattered. He wanted to preen beneath her intelligent gaze. He had impressed a duke's daughter, and not just any duke's daughter, but one who was lively, witty, intelligent, and beautiful.

Trouble, a voice inside nettled him. *She is trouble.*

He ought to send her on her way. Two more such evenings were all he had agreed to, and if he had half the wits he'd been born into the rookeries with, he would have sent her home the moment he had learned her identity.

Instead, he found himself falling beneath her spell. In this moment with the din of his club beyond them and no one to interrupt, in the place he loved best, he felt at home. Having her in his zealously guarded space should have made him eager to be rid of her. Instead, his mind was swiftly inventing more reasons to keep her precisely where she was, eating Lavoisier's damned Charlotte with more pleasure than the most seasoned courtesan showed her lover.

"I have been the object of not just ridicule but scorn, hatred, disgust, and worse more times than I have fingers and toes, my lady," he told her solemnly, and it was the truth.

Though he may currently preside over the most sought-after club in London, he had been born the bastard son of a Covent Garden whore. He had been beaten. Tossed into prison. Spit upon. He had been derided and scorned and mocked. He had schooled himself on everything he knew. He was not ashamed of his past, but it made him wary. It made him aware how very fleeting everything in life was. Every candle sputtered out at some point.

"I am sorry, Mr. Kirkwood," Lady Frederica said with genuine feeling. "No one should have to endure such awful treatment."

He studied her, searching for pity and finding only empathy. His shoulders relaxed. He rolled them once. Twice. "It is the way of this world, Lady Frederica. Some men are born to great privilege, and others to great suffering. I was the latter, but I have fashioned myself into the former. Your Charlotte grows cold."

In truth, he wanted to watch her enjoy it. He had never supposed the sight of a woman reveling in a sweet would be erotic. Especially not an innocent like Lady Frederica. He had always harbored a fondness for the forbidden, but she was different. She was not just forbidden but wrong. A grievous lapse in judgment for which he could never forgive himself.

One he wanted more with each moment he spent in her presence.

Ever a fool, it seemed.

"Who dared to scorn you?" she asked instead of taking another bite of the delicacy before her.

A frown furrowed her brows, and despite her gentleman's attire, he could picture her as an avenging goddess, bearing down upon the ghosts of his past. *What the devil?* When had he become so fanciful?

"I am the bastard son of a duke, my lady, and my mother was a Covent Garden whore before her death," he forced himself to state the undeniable facts with a coolness he did not feel. He had loved his mother. She alone, in turn, had loved him.

Her loss had devastated him, and that, too, he laid at the door of the Duke of Amberly. Yet another sin among a myriad of them. "*Everyone* dared to scorn me, for I was nothing and no one. I was an urchin, a pickpocket, a thief. I stole for my supper. My mother lifted her skirts for the right amount of coin. The man who sired me will not speak to me or look upon me to this day, not even when I begged him as a motherless lad with an empty belly. Trust me, my lady, when I say I committed sins that would make you scorn me as well."

She did not appear shocked or disgusted as he had imagined she may. Instead, her frown deepened, her lustrous eyes intent upon him. "You love your mother."

Of all the observations she could have made, this one struck him like a physical blow as no other could. His mother's memory was the one part of him that remained untarnished and true. He swallowed hard, recalling her end, how she had died as she'd lived, with a man's hands around her throat. Duncan had found her, silent and still and cold, so cold to the touch, her eyes open wide. He had been just a lad then, not yet nine years of age, and he had been desperate for her to blink. To prove a sign of life.

Blink, Mama.

Please, Mama.

Blink.

Long after that horrible day, he could still hear the echoes of his childish screams, could still feel the panic swelling in his chest, making his heart heavy. Rendering it difficult to breathe. No child should have to see his mother's corpse. But he had. And he would not forget.

He would gain his vengeance upon the Duke of Amberly. Retribution was all he had left.

"I...loved her," he admitted thickly, uncertain why he would unburden himself to this troublesome interloper. "She was a good woman. Flawed and imperfect but nonetheless good. She deserved better than the life she was given."

Better than the life she had been left to suffer, begging for coin from men who would abuse her so she could fill Duncan's belly with bread. Meanwhile, the man who'd sired him had possessed enough gold to buy and sell half of London, and yet he had not offered Duncan's mother a single ha'penny. Instead, the bastard had wasted his fortune at the tables, so greedy he had been convinced another flipped card, another wager, another roll of the dice would make him richer still.

His avarice had led him to penury where he belonged.

Until the Duke of Westlake had bought Amberly's debts.

But that was where Westlake's daughter, seated so trustingly opposite Duncan in her foolish attempt at masquerading as a gentleman, came into the scene, fortuitously enough. It all rather had the makings of a Shakespearean tragedy, even he had to admit. For she did not realize she was a plump hen dining in the company of a fox.

And she was looking upon him now with... *Christ*, what had he been thinking, kissing her as he had? She was looking at him now as if he were someone dear to her. As if she cared.

Impossible.

Ladies of quality did not care for men like him. They used him. They allowed him to pleasure their bodies because it suited their need for the forbidden, much in the same way his use of them sated his desire for that which would forever remain beyond his reach.

"I am sorry, Mr. Kirkwood," she said softly. "It was not my intention to cause you distress."

How easily she could read him. He, who had bluffed his way through a thousand card games. What was it about this maddening woman that undid him? He was not a soft man, not given to sentiment or emotion. Indeed, he had fashioned himself into the man he was today a long time ago, a man incapable of feeling. A man who wore black, who forged his own way, who knew no weakness. "No need to apologize, my lady. Distress is for those capable of feeling emotion. Fortunately, I am not so cursed."

"Or so you would have yourself believe."

Her soft castigation nettled him. He stood. The moment was over. Their interlude was at an end. He had not felt so disturbed in a long time, and he did not like the way she shifted everything inside him, like an earthquake and then a hundred tiny tremors, reminding him his life could be upended at any moment. That he was not the one in control.

"Have you finished with your dessert, madam?" he asked coolly, careful to keep his expression and his tone equally neutral. He did not wish to show her how deeply she affected him.

What was it about Lady Frederica Isling that so undid him? She was his means for revenge, the final brushstroke in his masterpiece of vengeance, and yet he could not stop making one foolish decision after the next. He had given in to her demands to conduct research at his club, had even gone out of his way to ascertain her safety and wellbeing, and then he had thoroughly ruined it by compromising her. How could he make demands of Westlake, knowing how thoroughly he had kissed and touched the man's innocent daughter? Knowing he had introduced her to pleasures of the flesh, to sins the likes of which her carefully cultivated mind would never have even dreamt, let alone known.

"You are eager to be rid of me now," she observed in that uncanny manner she possessed, not rising from her seat.

He had never seen anything like it. "You must be delivered safely home before you are discovered to be missing from your chamber," he said calmly, as if he was driven by common sense alone and not by his mad need to remove himself from her bewitching presence.

"I have made you uncomfortable." She stood at last.

How odd it suddenly seemed to see her fully dressed in her gentleman's clothes when he knew she was as female as could be. For some inexplicable reason, he longed to see her in a dress. To see her as herself, stripped of all her disguises. To see Lady Frederica Isling. *Lord God*, he had no doubt she would be an incomparable if he ever chanced to see her in a gown. Her beauty was undeniable. Even through her silly adornments, he could still see *her*.

"On the contrary," he lied, because she had once again spoken the truth. Damnation, the woman could dissect him. What was it about her, a mere slip of a girl, an innocent, a virgin, the daughter of a duke? "I am merely busy, tasked with a myriad of duties this evening related to the running of my club. You may consider yourself fortunate I have allowed your intrusion this evening at all, Lady Frederica."

But she is also a lady who possesses more daring and bravado than anyone you know. The voice intruded upon his thoughts when he least expected it. And damnation, the voice was correct.

Her shoulders stiffened, her chin lifting. Here was her pride, coming into action. "Of course, Mr. Kirkwood. Thank you for your... generosity this evening. I could not have managed to conduct so much research without your assistance."

He should tell her she could not return on the morrow. He already had what he wanted. There was no need to prolong this madness. No need at all.

Except that which burned inside him, a flame kindled into a raging fire.

"Until tomorrow," he told her, because he could not bear to say farewell.

CHAPTER 8

*A*lthough Frederica expected Mr. Kirkwood to be waiting for her in the carriage the next evening at the appointed time, she had been thoroughly dismayed to find it empty. The short ride to his club had seemed interminable, her mind whirling with explanations for his absence. None satisfied her.

His defection after the heated kisses they had shared yesterday, after his revelations over dinner—when the mask he wore slipped to reveal the man beneath—left her particularly cold. She had returned home the previous evening, and she had written until her candles sputtered out and her fingers were ink stained.

To her surprise, the story had taken an unforeseen turn, and she realized the baron must be the villain. It seemed undeniable to her now, and she could not understand why she had envisioned it any differently. *The Silent Baron* was not the tale of a gentleman led astray, but of a flawed man struggling to find redemption.

As she made her way into his club, she reasoned their paths would necessarily cross here. Who else would hover

over her like a mother hen at the nest? But she was likewise disappointed when she arrived at The Duke's Bastard and his man of business instead of Mr. Kirkwood himself, met her with a bow and a frown.

"Lord Blanden," he greeted solemnly.

The man bore no expression, and yet he exuded an undeniable aura of disapproval. She could not help but wonder if he had suspected anything was amiss the day before when he had interrupted her interlude with Mr. Kirkwood. Heat scalded her cheeks and made her ears prickle. *Interlude* was such a tame, inappropriate word for what had occurred between herself and the gaming hell owner.

A man who mere days before had been a stranger. A man who now seemed hopelessly familiar. A man who was nowhere to be found. Who had brushed her off to the care of his staff members as if she were nothing more than a bothersome burden who must be shuffled from one person to another.

"Mr. Hazlitt," she acknowledged stiffly, trying to hide her displeasure over Mr. Kirkwood's glaring absence. Had she probed too deeply? Pushed him too far? He seemed a private man, a smoldering mystery wrapped in black.

She told herself she should be relieved. After all, he was also a wicked man, to be sure. His club was a haven for sin. He hosted and encouraged all manner of depravities, the likes of which she had never known existed. He ruined men to fill his own coffers.

Spending any more time in the man's presence would be ruinous. She had already proven herself quite the hoyden, begging for his kiss. Her face went hotter, misery multiplying until it threatened to drown her.

"Mr. Kirkwood has directed me to bring you to his office," Hazlitt said, intruding upon her thoughts. "Unfortunately, he is otherwise occupied at the moment. You may await him there, however. Will you follow me, *my lord?*"

Was it her wild imagination at work, or did Mr. Hazlitt just emphasize his form of address, as if to suggest he knew it was false? She swallowed the lump of disenchantment in her throat and nodded once. "Lead the way, Mr. Hazlitt."

Through the antechamber they traveled, Mr. Hazlitt's steps measured and brisk. Although her legs were long, her escort's were longer, and she struggled to keep pace as he led her through the series of well-disguised halls that led to Mr. Kirkwood's office. They entered in silence, and Frederica could not shake the sensation she was intruding. How strange it was to stand in a chamber that was so much Mr. Kirkwood—it even smelled of him, for heaven's sake, and yet for him to not be in it.

"Will you require supper?" Mr. Hazlitt asked coolly.

She eyed him over the rim of her spectacles, rendering him crisp and forbidding rather than blurred and frowning. "Do you dislike me, Mr. Hazlitt?"

His lip curled. "I dislike trouble."

He knew she was not a gentleman, then. The momentary thaw in his rigid expression was just the revelation she required.

She raised a brow, for the wallflower she was had been replaced with a different person entirely. In her disguise, she was free to do and say and act as she wished. If only it wasn't fleeting, her precious liberty, slipping away far too quickly. "Trouble, sir? You would dare to refer to a peer of the realm as trouble?"

The disdain on his countenance only heightened. "You ain't a peer of the realm, my lord. You're a cockish wench if I ever saw one, and I've seen many in my day. You may have Mr. Kirkwood under your spell, but I'm not going to allow you to lead him or this club into bad bread."

Bad bread?

She was not certain she understood Mr. Hazlitt's rude manner of speech, and she wished in that moment to record it lest she forget. Such speech could lend an air of realism to her characters.

Oh, dear. There she went again, worrying about *The Silent Baron.* Poor Mr. Hazlitt seemed to be anticipating a response. How easy it was to get caught up within her mind and story, rather akin to being trapped in a plethora of ivy vines.

What had he called her? *Cockish wench?* Dreadful. Her cheeks went hotter than ever.

She pursed her lips. "I do not like you either, sir, so perhaps we can dispense with formality and you may simply leave me in peace. Where is Mr. Kirkwood, and when might I expect his return?"

His gaze narrowed. "You're a cunning baggage, aren't you? I'll not be telling you where he's gone or why. You can wait here as you're told, or I will have you removed. The choice is yours, *my lord.*"

Ah, yes. There it was again. The bitterness lacing his voice as he exaggerated her address. "I am perfectly happy to remain here, awaiting Mr. Kirkwood. *Alone.* If you will excuse me, sir, I would appreciate some quiet."

She had already spied ink, sheaves of foolscap, and a pen awaiting her at Mr. Kirkwood's desk. If she must wait, she would make use of her time and Mr. Kirkwood's supplies. There was something about using his personal writing implements that seemed somehow intimate. Fitting.

"At the slightest hint of trouble from you, I'll have you tossed on your arse," Mr. Hazlitt warned, a hard edge to his voice.

"Noted, sir." She flashed him a smile she little felt. "Good evening to you."

"Nay, good evening to you. Tabitha may well occupy Mr.

Kirkwood's entire night." With a mocking bow and a dark-eyed glare, he added, "I predict you shall be wishing for that supper."

Tabitha.

Her mind traveled instantly to the beautiful, bold woman she had met the previous day. Tabitha with the lovely face, goddess-like form, and wandering hands. *She* was what had kept Mr. Kirkwood from this appointed meeting with Frederica? An unwelcome stab of jealousy pierced her at the thought. Only yesterday, he had been dismissive and cool. It made no sense, and yet it also made dreadful sense all at once. Men like Mr. Duncan Kirkwood were not gently bred. They were wild and unpredictable, uncivilized in their pursuit of pleasure.

With great effort, she kept her expression as serene as possible, showing nothing of her tumultuous thoughts. "Rest assured, Mr. Hazlitt, if I grow hungry, I shall call for you. You are dismissed, sir."

Hazlitt made an exaggerated bow and left the chamber, the door closing with more force than necessary at his back. Frederica winced, every bit of fight in her suddenly drained. She plucked her spectacles from her nose and tossed them against the wall, not caring if they smashed. Her hat was the next victim, torn from her head. Followed by a handful of leather-bound volumes atop his desk.

She rather hoped she cracked a spine or two.

Still fuming with pent-up irritation, she had no wish to feel, she devoted herself for a time to reviewing the titles of the books in his office. Poetry volumes, all of them save one, which was entitled *Views of the Seats of Noblemen and Gentleman.* Perhaps he studied the locations, architecture, and priceless artwork on display in the country homes of his patrons, all the better to know whom to fleece.

The unworthy thought reminded her of just how much a

stranger Mr. Kirkwood was to her. Today marked the fourth since he had appeared in her life, and already she was throwing tantrums, kissing him in hidden halls, and spying on lords engaged in shocking acts of depravity. There was also the matter of costuming herself as a gentleman and sneaking about London.

But *the kiss*. The kiss had altered everything.

A shiver trilled through her. What had become of her? Where was the sensible wallflower who was keener to devote herself to books and her secret passion for writing than anything and anyone else?

She has awakened from a long sleep.

Frederica approached his carved chair, noting the depiction of what was undeniably Hades on one half and Persephone on the other. Life and death, darkness and light, come together. She traced a lone finger over the intricate carvings, absorbing this small manner in which she could make sense of Duncan Kirkwood.

The man who had kissed her as if she were his life's breath.

The same man who had abandoned her the next day.

A fierce urge to write overcame her then. Words crept into her mind. Scenes and emotions unfurled. She had come here to be near her characters, their world, to bask in it and understand it in some small measure. Here was her chance.

Despite her misgivings and the tumult at work within her, she settled in Mr. Kirkwood's chair. Her fingers, still stained with midnight ink, itched to write more. She dipped his pen into the inkwell, trying to ignore the scent of him that seemed to permeate everything, especially her resolve.

Her quill scratched over the paper. The owner of the gaming hell appeared before the baron, and he rather resembled Mr. Kirkwood, much to her consternation. But she quickly became swept away by the characters and the plot.

There was a mystery afoot as well, one she had not previously conceived.

She wrote furiously, caught up in the scene, in the emotions, in the intrigue of it all. Losing herself in her writing could be so easy some days, and others, she arrived at passable sentences with great difficulty.

With a sigh, she dropped the pen back into the well and took a moment to read what she had written. To her surprise and delight, it was quite good. The thoughts were well formed, the plot growing in intrigue and strength. Even the dialogue had flowed exceptionally well, despite her irritation at Mr. Kirkwood's abrupt abandonment of her.

She had one more evening.

Perhaps she would not see him again before returning to the despicable monotony of her life as Lady Frederica Isling. The acknowledgment and the accompanying pang it sent through her fell into the recesses of her mind for a moment when her eyes unintentionally landed upon a packet of correspondence. The missive on top of the stack bore her father's name.

What business could Mr. Kirkwood have with her father? Her fingers hovered over it, the wicked urge to snatch it up and break the seal dashed abruptly when the door to his office swung open.

There he was, clad in black as always, his brow knitted into a frown that did nothing to diminish his beautiful features as he stalked into the chamber and carelessly flicked the door shut once more at his back. She stood, sending some of her frantically written manuscript pages flying to the plush carpet like sad little birds too soon fallen from the nest.

"Oh, bother," she muttered, hastening to scoop them up lest he offer to help and attempt to read her words. Lest he see himself in the debonair, rakish gaming hell owner.

"Lady Frederica."

Her name drawled in his deep rich voice made her skin pebble into gooseflesh and an answering surge of yearning blossom in her core. She did not look up at him, ignoring his greeting as she attempted to concentrate upon the recovery of all her pages. *Blast it*, why had she not thought to number the pages of her scene? Now they would be a hopeless jumble until she spent time collecting them back into their proper order.

Gleaming black shoes, in the height of fashion, approached her, stopping alongside a sheaf of paper that was beyond her reach. She surged forward, crawling on hands and knees, but he was too quick, and his long fingers descended, closing on the sheet.

"No," she cried out, scrambling to her feet and making an unladylike lunge toward him in an effort to recover her stolen manuscript page. "That is private material, Mr. Kirkwood."

It was certainly not ready for anyone else's eyes, having only been written. Moreover, with her rotten fortune, she was sure the page he held captive would also be the one bearing his description. She could hear her words, almost aloud.

He was a handsome man with a devilish air and a careless demeanor that hid a sharp, cunning mind. He bore an intelligence that belied his crude beginnings, a persuasive manner that could not fail to enamor all in his charmed presence...

Her ears went hot once more as he held the paper aloft and out of her reach, his frown deepening as his eyes settled upon the page. "What is this, my lady? You have been making free use of my ink and paper? This foolscap is quite dear, I will have you know."

"I shall recompense you." She made another ineffectual swipe through the air, rising on her toes to no avail.

He was taller, his arms longer, his reach well beyond hers in more ways than merely one. "In what manner?"

Her cheeks burned, too, her gaze flitting to his. Was he ungentlemanly enough to refer to the stolen kisses of yesterday? The kisses that were scorched into her memory forever? Did he dare suggest she pay for the pages she had used by kissing him again?

"If it is kisses you wish, perhaps you ought to request them from another," she bit out, horrified she could not recall the undignified outburst once it had been released. Why, she sounded horridly jealous. Which, of course she was not.

"Kisses." He lowered the paper, hiding it behind his back as he pinned her with his intense gaze. "An intriguing means of remuneration. I confess, it was not what I had in mind. But why should anyone other than you pay for the paper you have ruined without my leave?"

She pursed her lips, considering her response. "The paper is not ruined. I was passing the time by writing *The Silent Baron.*"

He quirked a brow, not appearing any further inclined to relinquish the page to her. "Ah. I might have known. Tell me, why the devil is the unfortunate fellow silent?"

"He loses the ability to speak," she grudgingly offered, hating revealing her plot aloud so simply, for it did not sound nearly as majestic as her mind rendered it. "His country seat burns down, and he rushes inside to save the woman he loves. He fails, though he escapes with his own life. After, the baron is never the same."

"How grim, Lady Frederica." His countenance remained unsmiling, his gaze assessing as ever. The missing page of her manuscript was still being held for ransom behind his back.

"Life is grim," she countered, for it was the bitter truth. Though she had been born to a world of privilege, it was not the world she would have chosen for herself. She had never truly felt as if she belonged. Societal constraints and expectations made her itch. The thought of marrying Lord Willingham made her ill. "The baron must do penance for his sins in one fashion or another, and the injuries he receives in the flames steal his capacity for speech."

"And what would a cosseted duke's daughter know of the grimness of life?" he asked, a mocking undercurrent to his delicious voice she did not like.

How she resented him for that question, for the assumption that wealth and rank necessarily brought happiness along with them. "Being forced into matrimony is rather grim, would you not agree, Mr. Kirkwood?"

"Forced?" His eyes seemed to burn into hers, so unnaturally light and bright.

She could not look away. "Forced, Mr. Kirkwood. Just as I said."

He curled his upper lip in obvious disgust. "To the unwanted suitor you previously mentioned?"

He had remembered. True, the revelation had not been made many days prior, but it struck her that her reference to her would-be betrothed had remained imprinted upon his memory.

She grimaced. "Yes."

"This suitor," he began, saying the word as if it tasted sour on his tongue, "has he ill-treated you?"

Though his tone was calm, she detected an undercurrent of barely leashed savagery. She thought of Lord Willingham's deft maneuvering on their drive so he could find a part of the park with enough privacy that he could force his suit. His hands had gripped her with a painful violence, his forced kiss as unwanted as his touch and courtship both.

For a brief, wild moment, she wondered what Mr. Kirkwood would say if she revealed the identity of her suitor.

Lord Willingham had certainly never spoken of Mr. Kirk-wood, and nor had the gaming hell owner ever mentioned his lineage, though the name of his club said it eloquently enough. She still could not reconcile the two men sharing blood.

"He has kissed me when I did not wish it," she admitted softly.

Something indefinable flashed in his eyes. "Does your father not care for your opinion in the matter?"

She thought of her father's ultimatum before he had left for the country. "He wishes to see me settled as soon as possible. I am afraid his choice for me is not my own, and having grown impatient, I must say no. He does not particularly care."

"And who is *your* choice, my lady?" he asked, his voice as strained as his expression.

What an odd dialogue to be having with the wicked Mr. Duncan Kirkwood. If she did not know better, she would almost swear the man cared for her. But, of course, she knew better. She knew he only cared for his own gain, his own pleasure.

She considered his question for a beat. "Someone who is caring, who is kind. Someone who will not frown upon my writing. A man who will champion me rather than attempt to silence and stifle me. A man who is bold and adventurous of spirit."

For some ludicrous reason, the man she pictured inside her mind resembled Mr. Kirkwood in much the same manner the character in *The Silent Baron* did. *Oh, dear. This would never do.*

"Does this paragon have a name?" He stiffened, his entire body going rigid, a hardness that had not been previously present underscoring his words. "You need but tell me, and I can vouch for his integrity or lack thereof."

Frederica shook her head swiftly. "He does not bear a name. There is no one."

A slow, beautiful smile lifted his lips. "Good."

She did not understand. "You are pleased a worthwhile husband does not exist?"

He shook his head, stepping forward, crowding her with his large, warm body. She retreated a step, uncertain of his intentions, every part of her screaming to remain where she was and raise her face to beg for more of his kisses. But then she recalled why he had been absent for so much of the evening. She remembered a beautiful, golden-haired woman named Tabitha, who had been the cause of his defection.

"I am pleased you do not have a suitor you are enamored of, Lady Frederica."

His revelation was not what she had expected. It stripped her down, cut to the marrow. The question that had been eating her alive could be contained and ignored no longer. She set it free. "Where were you this evening, Mr. Kirkwood?"

His lips flattened, nostrils flaring, but the intensity of his gaze could have scorched her, set her aflame. "I was settling one of my ladies. She and a patron had an unfortunate clash. If you are looking for shame or an apology, you may continue your search elsewhere, my lady. I run a den of vice. The Duke's Bastard is not a church, though men may come here to worship at the altar."

"At the altar of sin," she finished for him, her blood growing cold. *One of my ladies.* This reminder, like his absence, struck her in a way nothing else could. How easy it could be to forget their disparate circumstances. But she must not confuse her interest in him, his club, and the life he led for anything more.

"Sin indeed." He stalked forward, sending her backward once more.

One step, two, three, four, until there was nowhere left to flee. The sharp edge of his wooden desk bit into her tender flesh. Her hands found the polished surface.

He planted his hands on the desk alongside hers, bringing the missing page within her reach at last as he pinned it to the surface. But all thoughts of repossessing it fled when he lowered his head until their gazes clashed at the same level. Heat and danger smoldered from him. He had never been more glorious.

"It is the reason for every patron's attendance at my club, Lady Frederica. Sin. Depravity. Wickedness. Unless you have failed to realize it, you are so far from your sheltered world of balls and soirees and evening musicales. No one here gives a damn about propriety or dancing the minuet or sipping orgeat. The men here have assembled for one reason and one reason alone. It is how I have earned my bread all these years."

The bitter sting of jealously was eating her alive from the inside out. "Did you kiss her as you kissed me?"

He stared at her, darkness rolling off him in waves. It was almost a tangible thing between them, the part of him he held at bay. "Who?"

"Tabitha," she whispered, hating the name, hating the woman, her angelic face and her dampened skirts and her hands that seemed intent upon stroking a man's... *Good sweet God*, she fervently hoped the woman had not...that Mr. Kirkwood had not... He did not seem to be the sort of man who sampled the wares of those beneath him, but it was true that many such men existed. "Did you kiss her?"

Please say you did not.

Please.

Please.

What a shocking demand to make of him. Did she have no shame? And why did she care so much whether or not he had dallied with the beautiful Tabitha? Why did the wait for his response seem to take a century? Why should the notion of Duncan Kirkwood kissing another woman make her feel ill?

His gaze glittered with emotion. "Nothing I did this evening is any of your concern, my lady. You are temporary. Fleeting. Like a candle's flame. After tomorrow, you will be gone, never to return, and you shall have to find another unfortunate soul to torture."

His words made her feel as if the floor had opened up beneath her.

But she persisted. His body, strong and lean and hard against hers, injected her with a rare fearlessness. "Did you *kiss* her?"

"No," he bit out. And then in the next instant, his hands were cupping her face, insistent and yet gentle, so large and capable of inflicting hurt but nevertheless so tender. "You are the only woman I want to kiss."

His words should not have thrilled her, and yet they did. Something warm and delicious shot straight to her core, reverberating in waves throughout her entire being. He had not kissed Tabitha, but he wanted to kiss *her*. Frederica Isling, wallflower and oddity. Female who felt more at home in gentleman's garb, sneaking her way into clubs, spending most of her time on penning stories until her fingers were stained with ink and her vision went bleary.

Duncan Kirkwood had seen her—the true Lady Frederica Isling—in a way no other man had before him. In a way, she knew instinctively, no other man would after. She fell into his fathomless gaze. Lost herself in the intensity of the moment and the thrill of his regard boring into her.

The only words that made sense rose within her, begging to be spoken aloud. Foolish words. Words she may later regret. But she was beyond the point of caring. She set the pages she'd collected aside, somewhere strewn atop Mr. Kirkwood's desk. And then she linked her arms around his neck, turning her face up toward his, her eyes dipping to his lips, so full and sensual, so kissable.

Hers.

That mouth was hers.

For tonight, even if it was now and then never again. She did not care. She would gladly pay any price for this one chance to sin with him.

"Then kiss me, Mr. Kirkwood."

* * *

WITH PLEASURE.

He could not be certain if he spoke the words or if he thought them. All he *was* certain of was that he was going to seize her offering. Duncan tarried not a moment more. The instant the invitation had been issued from her gorgeous lips; he had gone mindless.

Every intention he'd had to keep a respectable distance between them vanished, replaced by his mouth on hers. Kissing her was a horrid idea. Altogether wrong. He endangered his opportunity for vengeance with each reckless moment of abandon, and yet he could not help but to want more.

Her lips parted for his questing tongue. She sighed into his mouth. Lady Frederica Isling tasted sweet and dangerous all at once, a thousand times more delicious than the forbidden fruit that was responsible for man being banished from the Garden of Eden. The Bible verses came to him now as he kissed her with all the driving need inside him. Voraciously. Ferociously.

For dust you are and to dust you will return.

He would gladly be the dust for this woman. She was a

confusing clash of innocence and an inclination to sin, of womanly curves and male attire, of nonsensical stories and soul-jarring clarity. She was temptation incarnate; it was undeniable.

His hands were on her, moving from the desk to slide beneath her coat. His palms found her arse, and it was high and full, soft yet firm. He squeezed gently, catching her lower lip between his teeth and giving her a gentle bite. She made a startled exhalation that ended on a breathy sound of need he felt in his ballocks.

He forgot she was an innocent. The daughter of a duke. The means by which he could achieve the one goal driving him since his youth. He lifted her, setting her atop his desk, not giving a proper damn what papers she sat upon. They were either covered in her flowery script or marked by his rigid scrawl, and he did not care if they blotted out every word in the English language with their lovemaking as long as he could keep her here and ravish her to his liking.

And ravish her, he would. As far as he could go whilst leaving her innocence intact. She never should have told him to kiss her. Never should have bloody well invaded his territory from the first, pretending to be her brother, dressing as a man, inventing preposterous stories that only made him want her more. Because now he could not stop.

He inhaled violets and dragged his lips down her throat. The cravat had to go. Duncan kept one hand on her waist, her heat and curves tantalizing him even through the twin layers of her waistcoat and shirt. With his left hand, he plucked open the knot on her neck cloth—not even a passable Mathematical—and tossed it to the floor, leaving the smooth skin of her throat open for his exploration.

"Oh," she whispered, her hands landing upon his shoulders, her fingers digging into his flesh when he licked the place where her pulse gave her away. "You should not have untied that knot. I need to reuse the dratted thing."

"You ought not to return here," he felt compelled to warn against her skin, even as he licked her again. She tasted different here, flowery with a slight tinge of salt. The best damn thing he had ever tasted, including any miracle Lavoisier had ever managed to whip together. "Can you not see, Lady Frederica? Coming here the first time was a mistake. Returning? Sheer folly."

She gasped when the hand on her waist traveled slowly along her curves until he found the buttons of her waistcoat and undid each one. But she said nothing. Offered nary a hint of protest. Her fingers dug into his muscles, spurring him onward, it seemed. Heat rushed through him, the desire rising as fast and furious as a flood, sweeping away all else. Nothing remained—no caution, no conscience, no honor— nothing but the way she responded to him. Nothing but her delicious femininity awaiting his discovery.

But he wanted to pace himself. Wanted to go slowly for both their sakes. The pleasure between them could not be rushed. He kissed her ear, finding the soft lobe and taking it between his teeth before bringing his lips to the finely formed shell above it. "You stole my paper and ink, my lady, and you heaved my books to the floor."

Yes, he had noticed the small evidence of her destruction. When he had first entered his office, he had been torn between irritation at her thorough purloining of his private office— sitting in his bloody chair, using his pen and ink and paper, tossing about his books—and immense satisfaction at the real- ization she was jealous of the time he had spent with Tabitha.

"Your man of business told me I was to make use of your office," she protested on a throaty sigh when he ran his tongue along the dip behind her ear.

He nipped. Licked. Kissed. *Beelzebub and hellfire*, she was a feast and he could not stop partaking. "Did he also tell you to throw my books to the floor?"

She stilled, swallowed in a ripple he felt against his open mouth as he worked back down her throat. "No."

"Were you jealous, my lady?" Beneath her waistcoat, nothing but the fine layer of her lawn shirt between their bare skins, he swept his hand over her in a caress that ended over her bound breasts. His thumb pressed until he felt the compressed bud of her nipple. Using his blunt nail, he raked over it once, twice, thrice. Until she arched against him, responsive as ever. "Tell me, is that why you desecrated my office?"

"Why should I be jealous, Mr. Kirkwood? I am merely conducting research," she murmured, fingers digging into his shoulders a bit harder. "How…interesting it is to see the side of life denied to me as a gently bred female."

He did not like her answer. Did not like that she still had the presence of mind to goad him and match him wit for wit. Something had changed between them from the moment he'd swept open the door to find her seated in his chair, at his desk. A primitive sense of possession had blossomed, and with it, a desperate need.

For her.

Only her.

Four days. That was how long he had known her. That was how long it had taken for her to put her mark upon him. It was ludicrous and laughable, and yet there it was. Duncan Kirkwood, a man who had belonged nowhere and to no one, was so enthralled by one eccentric duke's daughter that he could not concentrate on his club or even his retribution.

"Interesting," he repeated her bothersome choice of word against her skin, accompanying it with another slow scrape of his nail over her bound nipple.

Her moan rewarded him.

"Yes," the minx dared repeat, taunting him. "My research has proven most enlightening, Mr. Kirkwood."

Most enlightening? He would rob her power of speech. Render her breathless and helpless. He kissed a necklace around the base of her throat, stopping at the dip where her pulse galloped even more than it had just moments before. His hand found the fall of her breeches. The fastenings. He plucked one button free of its moorings. Then another.

"Mr. Kirkwood," she said softly. Shakily. "What do you think you are doing?"

He smiled against her silken skin. Button three was removed. Then four. The fall dropped. His fingers slipped into the opening, happy to discover her flesh, warm and silken and so damned glorious he could not resist dipping his fingers between her folds to truly feel her for the first time. Wetness kissed his skin, and he found her pearl unerringly. It was even more responsive than the rest of her. Her hips jerked, and she cried out.

"I am helping you with your research, my lady," he said, answering her question at last. He stroked her with increasing firmness, noting her wide, glazed eyes and shallow breaths. If this was how it was between them the first time, what would it be like the second? The third?

No.

He could not think in those terms. As adrift as he was in his own lust, even he could acknowledge tonight would be the only night he could allow himself to misbehave with Lady Frederica Isling. Her reputation was important. As was her innocence. He required both to remain intact in order for his plan to succeed. Did he not?

Perhaps not whispered an insidious voice inside him.

"This…Mr. Kirkwood…I…*oh.*" She made a delirious

sound of pleasure, her head tipping back as if it were too heavy for her neck.

Precisely, and he had not even had his tongue upon her yet. He kissed her again, inhaling her sweet scent, like a sugared flower, before dropping to his knees on the carpet. He had not locked his office door, and the cautious part of his nature reminded him he ought not to take such a chance. If they were discovered, any witnesses would instantly imagine he was servicing another man. It was the sort of rumor from which he doubted he could ever recover, though dalliances of that sort were common enough among the *ton*.

And yet, with Lady Frederica, he did not care. He could not summon the will to leave her. All he wanted was just one taste, he promised himself. He would give her pleasure, restore her costume to rights, and send her on her way assured she would never again wear a gentleman's breeches without thinking of him.

But first, he wanted his name on her lips when she came.

"Duncan, my lady," he told her, caressing the generous curves of her hips. She had clamped her legs shut during his descent, and she watched him shyly now, cheeks flaming.

No sight had ever been lovelier than Lady Frederica Isling disheveled and unbuttoned atop his desk, her mouth swollen from his kisses, her gaze glistening, pupils black and huge.

"Mr. Kirkwood." Her protest was small and husky and redolent with uncertainty.

He could see in her eyes she wanted whatever he would give her, but she did not know what that something was or how to achieve it. What it would mean for her. When was the last time he had been this near to innocence? When had he ever been so untouched, so pure?

Never. Was it why he wanted her so badly? Did some primitive part of him think to regain what he had lost by claiming it from her? He wanted her. Wanted to consume her. To lick and taste and suck. And yes, to fuck, though he would restrain himself from the last. He was Hades, and his Persephone was seated before him.

For tonight, he could drag her brilliance into his dark world. She would leave, but she would never be the same.

"Duncan," he coaxed again, gliding his palms down her thighs. Her heat scorched him. He stopped when he reached her knees, and he gently urged them apart. "Open for me, sweet."

Her lips parted, her lashes fluttering on her cheeks. For a beat, he thought she would deny him, that he had pushed his intrepid virgin too far. Until she responded, her knees gliding apart with the cajoling pressure of his hands.

One word escaped her. A whisper of sound. "Duncan."

The sweetest sound he had ever heard. It was like a promise on her lips. He dipped his head to trail a line of kisses up her inner thigh. The fall of her breeches slipped down, revealing her to him. He guided her legs wider, mesmerized by the exquisite sight, like a blossom opened just for him. Pink and pretty.

He lightly scored his nails back up her thighs as he leaned forward. The earthy musk of her arousal consumed him, and he could not wait a moment more. He ran his tongue along her slick seam. A hum of approval tore from him. She was sweeter than a candy. Up and down he licked, slow and lingering, allowing her to adjust to the newness of the sensations. To the delicious intimacy of him pleasuring her with his mouth.

He parted her folds with his tongue, finding her pearl, flicking over it with steady, quick pulses. She jerked, hips rising up to meet him, and he obliged, burying his face deeper, breathing only her, tasting only her, hearing her rapid breaths, the soft cries of pleasure she made no effort to contain. When he suckled the needy bundle of flesh, she writhed against him, her fingers delving into his hair.

Damnation, he had scarcely begun, and she was about to spend.

She was so responsive, and he was harder than he had ever been, his cock desperate to sink inside her tight, wet cunny. But he could not. All he could do was lay his tongue to her, bring her to the precipice.

A low, keening sound burst from her. She quaked as her pinnacle gripped her, fingers tightening in his hair, a small flood of wetness slipping from her channel. He lapped it up, savoring it on his tongue as if it were the finest nectar. He stayed with her until she rode out the final spurts of pleasure, using his tongue and teeth to heighten and prolong it.

At last, he pressed a final kiss to her sex before he gently fastened the fall of her breeches. He slid the buttons into their moorings and rose to his feet. She wore a dazed expression, cheeks flushed, eyes closed, almost as if she did not dare to look at him after what had transpired between them.

He smoothed a stray tendril of midnight hair from her forehead and pressed a kiss to the smooth flesh, ignoring the pang in his heart he had never felt before. Tamping down the tender surge of protectiveness. Lady Frederica was not and would never be his, but he had been the first man to help her experience passion, and he would always relish that knowledge.

"Your research for this evening is at an end, my lady." He kissed her forehead again, then her furrowed brow before straightening and forcing a stern expression to his face. "It is time for you to go."

CHAPTER 9

"*G*ood heavens! Frederica Rose Isling!"

"Do hush, Leonora," Frederica chided her friend lowly, blushing furiously, and casting a glance around to make certain the outburst had gone unnoticed. "I have no wish to be the target for scurrilous gossip."

Thankfully, in the crush of the Aldersley rout, two wall-flowers in their usual place on the periphery of the entertainment did not garner much interest. The orchestra was insufferably loud this evening, the ballroom was unseasonably warm, and the lemonades were weak and watery.

Not much to recommend the affair in Frederica's mind.

But the temperature of the chamber and the quality of the beverages were not her greatest concern. Her friend's shocked countenance was. Or rather, the reason for Leonora's shocked countenance was.

Had she truly believed, even for a moment, that confiding in her beloved friend—who had always been more practical and proper than she—would be a wise idea?

"I simply cannot believe you returned to that den of vipers," Leonora hissed, her tone lower, less strident. Still accusatory, however. "I warned you against it, and you promised you would not, Freddy."

Frederica pursed her lips, searching for the proper response before deciding upon honesty. "I lied."

Leonora's eyes went wide, her incredulity incapable of being restrained. Her lovely face was ever expressive, and anyone who gazed upon her in this moment would recognize her undisguised outrage. "How dare you lie to me? We are sisters, are we not?"

Their unlikely friendship had begun two years before when the Season's reigning belle, Lady Maria Athcourt, had begun spreading tales of "Limping Leonora." Frederica had deliberately spilled her punch all over Lady Maria. They had been inseparable ever since. In Leonora, Frederica had found a calmer, pragmatic foil to her eccentric nature. They complemented each other, and together they were a formidable team, always looking out for the other.

But that loyalty did not necessarily mean they always agreed.

"Of course we are sisters," she reassured her friend. "But you are also a sister who tends to disapprove of my inclination toward...adventure."

Leonora's brows shot upward. "Adventure or ruin, Freddy? For ruin is precisely what you are inviting by returning to a cesspit of vice with that horrid man." She shuddered. "They say he is a hulking beast who ill uses all the ladies of the evening he employs. That he is without a hint of kindness or compunction. Do you know how many men he has left destitute?"

Frederica ran her tongue over her suddenly dry lips, her gaze darting about once more. She did not like to think of Duncan's profession or the nature of his business, for if she did, then she could not like him. And if she could not like him, she could not welcome his kisses. Nor could she allow him to sink to his knees and…do what he had done to her.

She hadn't a name for it yet, but whatever *it* was, the sensation had been so intense and pleasurable, that for a moment, she had been convinced she had been catapulted into the stars. The mere memory of his tongue playing deftly over her flesh was enough to make her ache even now, in a chamber filled with others.

"He is not a hulking beast, nor does he abuse his power in regard to the female members of his staff," she countered. "I cannot deny he runs a den of vice but despite that, he is a good man."

And he was. She felt certain of it. Felt it all the way to the marrow of her bones.

Her friend gaped at her. "You dare to defend him? He is a monster, Freddy. What has he done to you?"

Heat burned her cheeks. She diverted her gaze to the couples twirling about the ballroom beneath the glinting candlelight. The evening should have been a welcome diversion. A happy excuse to reunite with her friend. Instead, it was an impediment that kept her from being where she truly wanted to be. Her brother, who ordinarily eschewed balls of all sorts, had suddenly decided they all simply must attend this one. Mother had been happy to comply, presented with the opportunity to display her newest fan.

"What has he done?" Leonora repeated, suspicion coloring her tone. "Good heavens, Freddy. Tell me he has not…that you have not…did he *hurt* you?"

"Decidedly not," she said coolly, growing rather irked with her friend for her reaction. One would think Duncan was a scoundrel of the first order. A soulless, evil, morally deficient man with an incessant appetite for destruction and greed. "Quite the opposite, in fact."

Oh dear. She should not have added the last.

And she knew it the moment her friend pounced. "Freddy! Have you been *ruined*?"

Leonora posed the last question in a shocked whisper, but Frederica nevertheless made another furtive inspection of their surroundings. The answer to her friend's question was simple, though she had not thought of it in those terms until this moment.

Yes, she had been ruined. The liberties she had allowed Duncan Kirkwood to take with her body—shocking, wonderful, wicked—meant she would be damaged goods in the eyes of society should anyone discover the truth. But her secret was safe, and no one would ever know.

"Leonora," she protested softly. "Let us speak of something else."

Her friend's mouth opened in a perfect circle of surprise, her eyes going wide. "You have been! Frederica! What can you have been thinking? Something must be done. He must pay for his actions."

Frederica's cheeks went hot. "I did not confirm anything untoward occurred."

"He must marry you." Leonora ignored her half denial, fanning herself wildly in her agitation. Blond curls that had been artfully arranged to frame her face flapped about. "What if you are *enceinte*?"

Her friend posed her last question as if she were proclaiming the sentence of death.

"I cannot be," she said with certainty, for that much at least was true. "Nor will he marry me."

Though she could not deny the sudden flare of warmth such a notion produced in her. It lit a spark, grew a tiny flame.

"How do you know? Such delicate matters take time to be revealed. Oh! I knew I should never have kept silent about your plan." Leonora waved her fan even harder, creating a breeze that was strong enough to whip over Frederica's arms as well.

"My brother has…literature," she explained. "I discovered it amongst his old coats and breeches when I was searching for my disguise."

Shocking literature. Literature she had pilfered along with the outgrown waistcoats, breeches, and shirts. Naturally, she had secreted it in her chamber, and she had read it from cover to cover. Twice. The book was quite clear that a man had a seed which emerged from his member, and without such an event, a woman could not bear a child.

"*Frederica*." Leonora—sweet, tender, kindhearted, always above reproach—looked aghast at Frederica's revelations.

Well, and there was the trouble, was it not? Leonora would make a fine wife to any gentleman. She was proper and perfect, a veritable saint among mere mortals, and yet her limp caused her to be overlooked. Frederica knew how much her friend longed for a husband and children of her own. Whilst Frederica, on the other hand, had been courted more times than she could count until she decided to become a wallflower. Frederica wanted adventure, freedom, the chance to pursue her dream of seeing her words in print.

She also wanted Duncan Kirkwood.

"He has debauched you," Leonora charged quietly.

Had he? Frederica pursed her lips. Yes, she supposed so. In the last five days, she had lived more, seen more, and understood more of life than she had in all her two-and-twenty years combined.

She regretted nothing.

The realization made her stomach go fluttery, as if inhabited by butterflies. She reached out a staying hand, capturing Leonora's agitated fan. "You must stop bandying about such incendiary words, my dear. I am merely conducting research for *The Silent Baron*. You know better than anyone how important this is to me. Pray do not grow cross. If I do not have you, I do not have anyone."

Leonora was her only true friend. She had her father and her brother Benedict, both hopelessly inept at conducting meaningful conversation with the fairer sex. Her father's idea of speaking with her involved a rapid succession of questions, an inquiry into the use of her pin money, and a reminder that she was expected to make a great match. *Soon.* Her brother's conversation was abbreviated, often punctuated by distraction. They were six years apart in age—their mother had lost three babes and buried one stillborn child in the time between their births—and given her penchant for ignoring anything that did not give her immediate gratification, Mother was not any more comforting a figure.

Leonora fixed her with a pointed look and a frown. "I am not cross, Freddy, so much as I am outraged on your behalf. You are the Duke of Westlake's daughter, for heaven's sake. That man is the illegitimate brother of your future husband, and he has earned his fortune by capitalizing upon the misfortune of others."

Frederica preferred not to place the Earl of Willingham and the phrase "future husband" anywhere in the same vicinity. She could not suppress her shudder at the thought, but she feared sooner rather than later, it would become her reality.

Yes, there was a part of her that well knew what she was doing was wrong. That it was not fair to Duncan to allow him liberties whilst knowing she was almost promised to his half brother. Just as it was not fair for her to flagrantly ignore propriety and allow another man such intimacies when she knew she was bound for the altar with Willingham.

"He has made his fortune in the means that were afforded to him," she defended Duncan then, realizing as she said the words just how true they were. "Just as any gentleman in his place would. He has built something truly incredible, Leonora. You would be horrified if you saw it, I know, but it is breathtaking. It is garish and beautiful, horrible and thrilling all at once. I cannot quite describe it. The air of the place is so alive, thrumming with the forbidden."

Leonora stared at her, mouth agape, her fan stilling in its frenzied motion. "It is worse than I feared, then."

"The club is not as bad as you may think." Frederica frowned, growing rather irritated with her friend for all her naysaying. Did she not understand Frederica wanted to dream? She had lived more excitement in the last few days than she had experienced in the entirety of her days on earth.

"I do not speak of the club," her friend said lowly, through gritted teeth. Her gaze flitted over Frederica's shoulder for a moment. "I speak of *you*, Freddy. You have feelings for him."

"Of course I do not," she denied hastily, shocked Leonora would even suggest such a ludicrous possibility. She had known him for mere days. That was not time enough to…a sudden ache in her breast told her she was wrong. She should know better than anyone the heart did not care about time, distance, funds, titles, or any of the other trappings of society.

"Hush now, here comes Lord Willingham." Leonora murmured, lifting her eyebrows meaningfully.

Bother. "Have I time enough to feign a need to attend the lady's withdrawing room?"

One could always dream.

Leonora gave a small shake of her head.

Frederica stiffened just as the earl appeared before them, offering a bow.

"My Lady Frederica, Lady Leonora," he greeted in that signature manner he possessed, as if he were paying them the utmost compliment by his mere presence.

His purple coat and emerald breeches were an affront to

the senses, in keeping with his usual attire. His thinning brown hair was untamed, the ends reaching skyward as if pleading for the intervention of a higher power. His cravat nearly touched his chin. It had been precisely six days since she had last laid eyes upon this preening rooster of a man, and his appearance before her now was far too soon.

She curtseyed. "My lord."

"Would you care to take a turn about the room, my lady? We shall fetch some lemonade if you prefer." He turned to Leonora, condescending. "Pity you cannot accompany us, my lady. Shall we bring a glass back for you as well?"

"That would be lovely, thank you," said her friend, not showing a hint of insult at Willingham's thinly veiled reference to her limp.

Frederica narrowly resisted the urge to stomp on his instep in retribution. Instead, she allowed the earl to guide her on a meandering journey around the outskirts of the festivities.

"That was most unkind," she snapped when they were beyond Leonora's earshot.

He leaned toward her, and the scent of his cologne— cloying and spicy—tickled her nose. "Forgive me, but I have been in a dreadful state these last few days, missing you, my dear. I was most disappointed when you were not at home after I called to take you for a drive two days ago."

With her father absent, and her mother a flimsy guardian easily distracted by the beacons of Bond and Oxford Streets, Frederica had taken advantage of the opportunity to refuse Willingham's overtures. She feared a ride with him would only mean more unwanted kisses from which there was no escape, and so she avoided him instead.

"I do believe the turtle soup I ate at the Farthingale supper was spoilt," she lied blithely. "I fear I was far too ill for a jaunt."

"Of course, my dear lady," he said, but there was an ill-disguised note of disgust in his tone. "I am indebted to Blanden for bringing you to this ball at my request."

Blast her brother. That explained his sudden desire to be in attendance this evening. *Et tu, Brute?*

"Yes," she drawled, taking great effort to keep her irritation from her expression and voice, "it was lovely of him to intervene."

Frederica's gaze roamed over the earl's face, searching for signs of resemblance to Duncan, and found none save the dimple marking the tip of his chin. How could one brother turn her body to flame whilst the other made her stomach curdle? Duncan was taller, broader, stronger. His was a lean, powerful grace cloaked in elegance and dipped in darkness. Lord Willingham was, by comparison, a court jester.

"I am hoping, my lady, to speak to your father when he returns from Oxfordshire," Lord Willingham said then, stopping to retrieve a watery lemonade for Frederica, one for himself, and another for Leonora.

He wanted to speak with her father. As soon as he returned.

Why, that would be in just two days.

Two days until her freedom ended. How could it be? She tried to envision a life in which she was married to the earl. In which she was Lady Willingham. In which he could press his cool, flat lips to hers and do to her as he wished. Her gaze dipped to his mouth, which was unsmiling and glinting with saliva. Why were they always so wet?

Frederica took a lengthy sip of the lemonade, finding it far too tart. Nothing but bitterness, much like the emotions blossoming inside her. She felt as if she was going to be ill. Her stomach clenched, bile rising in her throat.

"My lady? Would it please you?" he pressed.

No, it would not please her. She thought of his hands on

her, how tight his grip had been, the purple half-moons left behind by his fingers. His words. *You will learn to enjoy it, my dear. I will make certain of it.* More threat than promise, she feared.

She swallowed another sip of lemonade, wishing it was Duncan's fiery whisky. Wishing she was there, at the Duke's Bastard, trading wits and kisses. Wishing, for once in her life, she could be free.

But she was Lady Frederica Isling, daughter to the Duke of Westlake, soon to be married to the Earl of Willingham, and she could never be free. She forced a smile to her lips, stared into his flat brown eyes, wishing they were blue. "Nothing would please me more."

* * *

SHE HAD NOT COME.

Duncan sat in his chair, gulping a whisky, rage burning through him like the fires of hell. But the whisky did not numb him. Nor did it do a damned thing to mitigate the fury scorching him alive. Around him, his club bustled, business as usual. The dice dropped. Cards shuffled. Laughter, clinking glasses, and the hum of voices barely seeped into his awareness. All he could think was that she was not there.

It was to have been their final evening. The last time he would ever see her. He had attempted to resign himself to that unwanted reality ever since he had watched her delicious arse flounce out of his office the night before. *Without success.* And now, she was the only one in his thoughts. Plaguing him. Calling to him. Taunting him.

His name on her lips had been pure poetry. He could still hear it now, the throatiness of her voice. *Duncan.* And Christ if it didn't make him hard, right then and there in the midst of all his patrons on a bustling evening, with not a woman in sight except for the one haunting his mind.

Bloody, blazing Beelzebub.

The carriage he sent for her at the arranged time had returned empty. His driver offered no explanation. *His lordship* had failed to appear, reported Marmot to Hazlitt. The conveyance had lingered for three-quarters-of-an-hour. Finally, needing to take a piss, Marmot had returned to the club.

Can't take a piss on the street in Mayfair, wot?

Hazlitt had guffawed as he related the last, expecting Duncan to laugh as well. On another day, in another time and place, had the empty carriage not been missing one Lady Frederica Isling—the woman he had brought to a deliriously lovely spend the night before—he may have been amused. As it was, he could still taste her on his tongue, could still smell the sweet, musky perfume of her slick flesh.

To say Duncan was in a foul mood would be an understatement. He was furious. Outraged. In the blackest humor of his life.

He could not remain in his office, for sitting at his desk reminded him of the sight of her upon it, legs spread, sex pink and glorious and ready for his tongue. He could not stalk the hidden hall with viewing slots, for her ghost was there as well. It was where he had first kissed her.

Even in the main gaming hall, she was there. It was where he had laid eyes upon her. And though it had been mere days before, she had already become an inextricable part of his world.

He was not sure how it happened. Christ knew he had not wanted to allow her to affect him, had not wanted to soften toward her. He, who had prided himself upon having no softness in his life. She was the means for his revenge, the retribution he had been seeking for twenty years as hatred and bitterness had eaten away at him.

Why?

The question, unbidden, surged. He could not tamp it down, no matter how hard he tried. Why did it have to be her? Why was the one woman who set him aflame also the one he needed to gain what he wanted, his worthless sire begging him on hand and knee?

He drained the remnants of his glass, about to signal for another, when his gaze lit upon a familiar figure. An arse, to be specific. Curved and full and high, ill obscured by the coat tails. Luscious calves beneath white stockings, trim ankles. No spectacles perched on her delicate nose because she had left her second pair in his office the day before, and those, too, he had scavenged alongside a forgotten manuscript page like a vulture, two more objects in a growing collection he would use against her. His prick went even more rigid, springing against the fall of his breeches. His body knew before his mind—it was elemental. Inevitable. Unavoidable.

There. She. Was.

And she had come without the benefit of the safety his enclosed carriage and driver would have provided her. He shot to his feet, his empty glass and need for another whisky abandoned. His body and his mind collided. *Mine* said something deep inside him. *Mine.* Each footfall that brought him closer to her rang with finality. *Mine. Mine. Mine.*

Until she was close enough to touch. He wanted his arm sliding around her waist, her soft curves nestling into his hardness. Wanted to draw her against him, stake his claim, but at the last moment, he recalled she was dressed as a man.

Instead, he drew alongside her and lowered his lips to her ear, in such proximity his lower lip brushed over the delicate whorl. "Are you looking for someone, *my lord?*"

She stilled. Swallowed. "Yes, in fact, I am. The owner of

this establishment." She sent him a flirtatious glance that landed in his cock and ricocheted throughout his body. "Do you know him?"

He ground his jaw, lust for her rising so strongly within him he could scarcely maintain his focus. "Aye. Promise me something first?"

Her expression turned wary. "What promise would you have from me?"

"If you ever take it into your foolish head to traipse about London alone again, come to me first. You need but to send a servant. I will make certain my staff is aware Lord Blanden and Lady Frederica both have the use of any carriage they wish, on any day, at any time." The notion of her gadding about in hired hacks made his skin break out in a cold sweat. Even if he would never see her again after this night, he would have the solace of knowing she was safe.

Her brows rose. "That is a generous offer indeed. One I cannot accept."

Duncan was not in the mood for opposition. "You can and you shall. Promise me, or forfeit your final day of research, and I will send you home at once."

Her lips compressed, and she was silent for a beat before giving a jerky nod. "Very well. I promise."

Thank Christ.

A tiny measure of the disquiet inside him abated. "Excellent. Now come with me, if you please."

That particular battle won, he stalked away from her, knowing she would follow. Trusting it the same way he trusted each new breath would rise and fall, filling his lungs, giving him life. The same way she did. He could not deny it. All the darkness in him had vanished the moment his eyes had lit upon her form. She was there after all, and though he fully intended to reprimand her for not arriving safely using his appointed carriage, he could not deny the delight—the sense of rightness—bubbling forth within him.

Through the din of drunken revelers they went. He did not stop until he burst inside his office, throwing the door wide and stalking inside. When he spun on his heel, she was there as he knew she would be, her countenance hesitant. Her eyes searching his. She closed the door behind her.

Wise lady.

He stalked toward her, unable to resist. *Bloody hell*, but he was in a frenzy. He did not stop until she was within reach, though he did not touch her. "Where were you?"

Duncan did not intend for his question to reverberate like a demand, but it did, snapping and humming in the air around them. He waited for her answer. For her excuse, certain nothing would be sufficient.

"My brother escorted me to a ball," she said solemnly. "At the behest of the man who wishes to make me his wife, it would seem. I had no choice but to attend."

The need to commit violence rose inside him, stark and strong and undeniable. His hands clenched into fists at his side. The reminder that she was not his, and that she would one day soon become another man's, killed him. It hit him in a vulnerable part of himself he had not even been aware existed. He closed his eyes, counting inwardly to ten, willing his anger and resentment to abate.

To twenty when it did not.

Then to thirty after that.

Fifty.

One hundred.

Fuck.

"Did he touch you?" he growled.

It was not what he intended to say. Not what he meant to ask. Indeed, even if the bastard had touched her, it was none of Duncan's business. He could do nothing, say nothing about it. Of course she would wed another man, and it was well beyond his control.

What would she do?

Marry Duncan Kirkwood, the bastard son of a duke, gaming hell owner, man who had never given a bloody damn about the rules by which she had lived her life? Laughable, for he did not wish to marry anyone.

Did he?

The notion did not disturb him nearly as much as it ought. Indeed, it had rather a different effect entirely when he joined marriage and Lady Frederica in the same sentence. When he thought of making her his. Forever. Was it the idea of possession that thrilled him, or was it binding himself to Lady Frederica?

"No," she said softly. "He did not touch me. Not as before. There was not opportunity, and I made certain he did not take one. We danced. He fetched me lemonade."

Her words did nothing to ameliorate the warring emotions inside him. He did not want any other man to touch her. Ever. And she had indicated the suitor had forced unwanted attentions upon her previously. That thought set his teeth on edge.

He wanted her to be his.

Alone.

It was a hell of a development. One he did not know precisely what he could do with just yet. One he could not act upon. Not now, and likely not ever. For to do so would be nothing less than sheer folly. Would it not? Of course it would. She was the means by which he could at long last watch the bastard who had sired him pay for all his sins.

Every, last one. Especially the sins against Duncan's mother. He would exact extra penance for those when the time came.

The breath he had not realized he had been holding

141

hissed from him. "This is your last evening here at my club." He said it because he needed to hear it. Needed to acknowledge it. Perhaps in so doing, he could convince himself never seeing her again was best for him. Best for the both of them.

"Yes, it will be the last," she agreed quietly. "My father returns tomorrow, and I expect my betrothal will be announced soon. I must thank you for your kindness in allowing my trespass here at your establishment."

Her affirmation somehow set him on edge even more than he already had been. He did not want it to be the last, *damn it all to hell.* Nor did he like the detached manner in which she spoke, as if they had never kissed. As if he had never tasted her.

"Kindness," he repeated, his lip curling, thinking of what he must do, how he would betray her to gain what he wanted. "I am not a kind man, Lady Frederica. I would think you wise enough to recognize greed when you see it."

Show her the floor, urged a voice inside him. *Allow her to roam for the evening and complete her research. She is the key to everything you have ever wanted. See her father upon his return and gain your revenge at last.*

He knew he ought to heed the voice, but what if she was the key to everything he had ever wanted in more ways than just one? What if he could have his vengeance and her both? The question was too dangerous to entertain, too fraught with implications he did not dare to examine.

She stared at him with her fathomless gaze, *seeing* him in a way no other before her ever had. "I do not think you are greedy at all, Duncan. Nor do I think you unkind."

She would change her mind if she knew he was using her to gain what he wanted. If she knew she was his pawn. If she ever learned the truth, she would hate him. Her every memory of his touch and his kiss—the passion he had awakened within her—would burn and fade into ash.

But he did not want to think of that now, because she was wrong about him. He was greedy when it came to her. She had called him Duncan, and she was staring at him as if she longed for him every bit as much as he did her. It was an ache in his loins, a fire in his veins, like the waters of a river flowing, leading him inevitably forward.

"If I was kind, I would not do this." He closed the distance between them, framed her lovely, pale face in his hands, and lowered his mouth to hers.

She opened for him with a sweet sigh, her lips moving against his in a wild, untutored hunger that only made him want her more. His mind could only comprehend small, violent bursts as a rush of pure need washed over him. Violets. Warmth. The tart bite of the lemonade she had consumed earlier. His tongue against hers. He caught her lower lip between his teeth, wishing he could consume her.

The kiss deepened. They were moving backward as one, his hands still on her hot, smooth skin, their mouths never parting. Toward his desk. Tongues dueling. Breaths intermingling. Desperation lit like a flame. Shame burned him. This was wrong. He was wrong for her, and he knew it. Kissing her was wrong. Wanting her was wrong.

But he couldn't stop because she was the sun, the moon, and all the glittering stars in the blanket of the night sky at once. Fierce, brilliant, glorious. No other woman before her could compare, and he knew instinctively no woman after her would either.

Her fingers were in his hair. Her delectable arse met with the edge of his desk, and it was the night before all over again. Unlike last night's frenzied lovemaking, however, tonight he wanted to savor. If it was indeed his last night with her, he would not act with haste.

He kissed her. And kissed her. Their lips melded perfectly. Kissed until his lips bruised hers. Licked into her mouth like he was delving inside her perfect, untouched cunny with his cock.

Everything in him screamed to take her, then and there. To sink home inside her, and allow their bodies to make the decision for them. But he could not. He tore his mouth from hers, knowing he would end it here this evening. Knowing he must, for both their sakes.

He stared down at her, breathing harshly, absurdly pleased by the contrast of her masculine hat, bound hair, and gentleman's dress to her full, kiss-swollen lips, dazed eyes, and feminine beauty. "Tell me I am benevolent and without avarice now, my lady."

She stared at him, silence deepening between them, as she slid her gloved hands from his hair, caressing his face, cupping his jaw. "You are a good man, Duncan Kirkwood. This I know."

Her faith in him made his chest swell. But she was wrong. He shook his head. "I am not."

She would learn soon enough who he truly was. A man without compunction. A man who cared for no one else. A man whose goodness had died the day he had seen his mother's lifeless corpse on the floor when he was but a lad. A man who had seen and endured far too much of the world to ever be worthy of her wide-eyed worship.

"We shall disagree, then," she said softly.

Damnation. Here she was, his Persephone. And he wanted to keep her, in his dark underworld, at his side. Forever. Something inside him broke open. Jagged shards rained. He was awash in her. In the way she saw him. In the man he saw reflected in her eyes.

But it was not meant to be.

"We shall disagree," he repeated, pressing one last, lingering kiss to her lips before releasing her and disentangling himself from her touch. "This is your last visit here. Tell

144

me, my lady, what aspect of the club would you like to research for your novel?"

Her gaze followed him as he put some distance between them, glittering. "I want to see the scarlet chamber."

Beelzebub's ballocks.

CHAPTER 10

*I*n silence, Duncan led her to the chamber where such shocking depravities had occurred the first night she had visited his club. It was not in use for the moment, meaning she could wander through its sumptuous appointments, taking notes as she wished whilst Duncan looked on.

Bereft of its lewd occupants, the space seemed somehow less wicked. Indeed, it was almost as proper as any drawing room, with the exception of the dark crimson wall coverings, immense bed, and shocking pictures depicting nude men and women cavorting. One caught her attention for its ribald subject matter, a woman on her knees before a man, his member in her mouth.

Gasping, she glanced back to find Duncan watching her. His brilliant gaze upon her felt like a caress. In his eyes, she saw the same need that had not stopped burning inside her from the moment he had first set his lips to hers. Each moment she spent in his presence, each kiss, each touch, stoked the fire until it could not be banked.

She was an inferno.

Just yesterday, he had laid his tongue upon her. He had licked her most intimate flesh, had brought her to throbbing release with nothing more than his mouth. The picture and the memory of him pleasuring her made a steady ache throb to life between her thighs. Would it be the same for him if she took him in her mouth?

She wanted to ask, but she dared not give voice to the forbidden words. Cheeks stinging, she turned away from him at last, walking about the chamber and taking notes she knew she would never use later. The research she was currently conducting was not for *The Silent Baron*, for she could never relate such scandalous details and hope for publication.

No, indeed. This research was for her.

She noted an assortment of riding crops and whips laid out on a table, varying in length and thickness. Puzzled, she turned back to Duncan once more, only to find he had followed her and stood near enough for her to close the distance between them with a single step. His jaw was rigid, his large body radiating tension.

"What is the purpose of these?" she asked.

He shook his head in slow denial, his gaze continuing to burn hotly into hers. "Such detail should not be included in your novel, my lady. It would be beyond the pale."

It was a fine time for him to draw a line between the depravities he would teach her about and those he would not, and she was having none of it. "Tell me."

"Some prefer pain with their pleasure." Though his tone was soft and low—gentle, almost—it possessed an undercurrent of darkness.

Pain with their pleasure. Shock flared as understanding dawned. The men and women who made use of the pleasure chambers at The Duke's Bastard reveled in all manner of debaucheries, and apparently taking riding crops and whips to each other was yet one more.

She swallowed against a surge of something inside her, part revulsion, part curiosity. "Do you?"

He did not respond immediately, holding her in the potent thrall of his stare. "I enjoy giving pleasure," he said at last. "Like gambling, it is something I excel at."

Yes, he did, and she could attest to that. His words were neither a denial nor an admission, however, and they sent a shiver through her. She wondered how many other women he had pleasured. Did he kiss them all the way he kissed her, as if he was ravenous for her taste on his lips? The heat inside her suddenly cooled. She turned away, putting some distance between them once more.

"I see, Mr. Kirkwood," she managed to say, gratified when her tone did not waver or reveal even a hint of her distress.

How foolish of her to think, even for a moment, that what they shared was special. For her to think he may have some tender feelings for her just because her heart seemed to swell two times its normal size whenever she thought of him. An icy tendril of despair crept up inside her as she thought of the longing she felt for him.

It was their last evening together.

The final hours in each other's presence.

If only that hard truth did not make her want to weep.

She continued her exploration of the chamber, but the thrill of discovering that which should forever remain a secret from her had abated. In its place was a morose combination of jealousy and futility.

"My lady."

His voice was near. Too near. She spun about, clenching her pencil and notebook. "Mr. Kirkwood?" She raised a questioning brow, aware of the awkward formality that had fallen between them.

She wished she had never asked to come to this chamber, for now that she was within, she felt as if she had opened Pandora's box. *I will never see him again*, she thought, *and I have ruined our final kisses*. If only she had fled on that memory, something to which she could cling.

"I have never made use of this chamber, my lady," he told her quietly.

Her heavy heart lightened instantly at the revelation. But she was embarrassed he had sensed her question. She had no claim on him. She had not yet known him for a full sennight, and this was to be the end of their association. "It is not my concern whether or not you have, sir."

"I tell you freely." Still watching her intently, he brushed her chin with his fingers. Just a glancing touch, and yet she felt it everywhere. "This chamber is for the entertainment of my patrons."

Relief slid through her. The thought of him with Tabitha or some other beautiful goddess in this chamber had been enough to make her ill. "Have I seen the worst or is there more?"

"There is more." His jaw clenched. "Though I feel confident you have already seen more than enough. What is the meaning of this research, my lady? I do not believe you can use it in *The Silent Baron*."

She allowed her eyes to linger upon the finely hewn features of his face, the blade of a nose, full lips, the dimple in his chin. He was so beautiful, like a god among mortals, dressed all in black and come to rule the land of the living with his call to sin. She would gladly heed his call if she were free to. In that moment, she cursed the fate that would have her married to Duncan Kirkwood's brother instead of him.

"Curiosity," she answered honestly. "When my freedom has been taken from me, and when I must become a proper wife, I want something to remember. Some small promise of

149

daring and passion and yes, even sin. I find myself fascinated by your world, Mr. Kirkwood."

And fascinated by you, she added inwardly, for it would be far too much of a confession. Her pride would not allow it.

"You astound me." He plucked her hat from her head suddenly, finding the pins in her hair and setting them free one by one. "And confound me."

She knew she should stay him. Each thud of a hairpin on the rug was akin to a bell that, once rung, could not be undone. Her thick dark hair began to fall in heavy waves to her shoulders. His hands moved in reverent strokes, smoothing it around her face.

No one had ever touched her with such delicate care before. Her lady's maid was deft in her ministrations but jerky, with a tendency to pull at the roots of Frederica's hair as she ran the comb through it. It seemed at once odd and breathtaking to be touched with such tenderness, and by the infamous Duncan Kirkwood.

"You are ruining my disguise," she protested without heat, for she could not summon even a drop of outrage. She wanted his touch. Welcomed it. Longed for it.

"Your hair is too glorious to be bound and hidden beneath that monstrosity of a hat." More pins fell to the floor until none were left, and still, he stared as if memorizing the sight of her, his hands stroking slowly over her locks. "Damnation, you are the loveliest woman I have ever seen."

His flattery made her cheeks go hot and started a queer fluttering in her belly. "Flattery," she dismissed softly.

"Nay." He stilled, staring down at her with the gravest expression she had ever seen him sport. "Truth."

She fell into his brilliant gaze, headlong. Wishing this was not goodbye. Wishing she could see him one more time. Did it truly have to be? "May I come again tomorrow?"

"I am afraid not." His expression turned rueful, but his

denial smarted nonetheless. "I am holding a masque tomorrow, and I shall be distracted by my duties as host. The guests will be unsuitable company for you, and these affairs tend to get rather…ribald."

"Oh," was all she could manage to say, hurt bubbling up at the reminder he was not her suitor, and prolonging their interactions would only prove fruitless and reckless should she continue on this path.

When she would have extricated herself from him, he held firm, forcing her to remain. His eyes glittered. "I will not be the man who ruins you, Lady Frederica. We are dancing perilously close to your fall from grace, and I will not be the one who forces you over the edge."

His hands were warm and large on either side of her head, caressing her hair in soft, soothing strokes that did nothing to take away the sting of his rejection. He was being honorable, the last thing anyone would have expected of the infamous Duncan Kirkwood. She wanted to throw herself into his arms and fuse their mouths. Wanted him to take her innocence so she would not have to surrender it to the Earl of Willingham.

His half-brother.

A man who was nothing like him.

"What if I wish to be ruined?" she asked boldly. Desperately.

He closed his eyes for a moment, and then lowered his mouth to hers for a slow, soft kiss that was over before it had even begun. And then he released her, taking a step back. "You do not want to be ruined, Lady Frederica."

But she did. Only by him. Only if he wished to. Here was her answer, however unwanted, he did not wish it. She stood before him, hair falling to her waist, clad in her brother's thieved clothes, and the pain inside her chest was so fierce and unexpected, she nearly doubled over. He was telling her goodbye. She was a burden he did not wish to bear, and how could she blame him?

"I must go," she said, blinking back the tears threatening to fall and humiliate her.

He startled her then by taking her hand and bringing it to his lips for a kiss. "My carriage will deliver you safely home."

His voice was flat. Final.

She nodded, feeling as emotionally drained as he sounded. "Goodbye, Duncan."

He released her and bowed with an elegant formality that would have been at home in any ballroom or drawing room. "Goodbye, my lady. I'll not forget you."

CHAPTER 11

*T*he Earl of Willingham had sent her a bouquet of lustrous white lilies.

They did not bear a scent, being solely for viewing pleasure, and when Frederica gazed upon them, she was struck not by their beauty but by their transience. Groomed for cutting, the hothouse flowers had been tended to and raised in their isolated world, fit only for a display. Trapped in a vase before they wilted, their petals falling.

She saw herself in those lilies, and she wanted to have them removed.

She wanted them cast away before they had the opportunity to wilt and die. She wanted to escape before the same happened to her. One day soon, she would be culled, sold, and kept, much like the lilies. The thought of being the earl's inanimate object of beauty, his to display or ill use, made her shiver with revulsion as she looked upon the flowers.

Predictably, her mother thought they were glorious, for she adored anything new. "Such a beautiful token of his lordship's affections," she had clucked upon their arrival. "How fortunate you are, Frederica, to be the recipient of an earl's attentions so many years after your comeout."

Frederica narrowly resisted the urge to crush one of the blossoms in her fist, or to send the entire affair flying to the floor with one vicious swipe of her arm.

She pressed her lips together, staring at the immense white blossoms, which somehow seemed garish despite their lack of color. "It seems such a shame they do not bear a scent. What is the result of merely being beautiful to look upon for a handful of days before fading?"

"The result is being admired, for however long a span of time that may be," her mother said. "You do not look as if you have been getting enough rest, dearest. Your eyes appear tired. I shall get you a pot of cream whilst I am shopping later. It will not do for Lord Willingham to think his bride *mature*."

In Frederica's mind, it would not do for Lord Willingham to think of her as his bride. *Ever.* She shivered, wishing the lilies would disappear. Wishing she could return to The Duke's Bastard the night before and take the reins into her own hands.

She did not bother to feign a smile. "That would not do at all."

"Three pots," her mother decided, smiling. "One can never have too many. Perhaps a new fan as well? When Lord Willingham asks your father for your hand tomorrow, we will go immediately to Madame Ormonde for your trousseau. Oh! It shall be wonderful."

Wonderfully awful.

Sickness coiled in Frederica's stomach. Though he had informed her himself he wished to speak to her father, she had somehow been hoping he would delay. "How do you know the earl will ask for my hand tomorrow?"

Her mother traced the delicate shape of one petal admiringly. She was a lovely woman, though lines marred her visage. With white streaks shooting through her raven tresses, she often tucked them beneath a turban, and today's choice was deep red, ornamented with pearls. "Lord Willingham was good enough to indicate his intentions to Benedict in order that His Grace may make haste back to town."

One day remaining.

Tomorrow she would be betrothed to Lord Willingham when all she could think about was his illegitimate half brother. How cruel was fate? Icy tendrils closed over her heart. "What if I do not wish to wed the earl, Mother?"

Her mother turned her attention back to her. "Dear heavens, Frederica do not be silly. You will make a fine countess."

"But I do not wish to be a countess," she persisted, pressing the matter as she had never before dared. The last few days had left her feeling liberated. "I want to write novels."

Her mother shook her head, an expression of ill-concealed disgust pinching her features. "Nonsense. You are the daughter of a duke, and you shall be a countess. In time, you will forget your childish yearning for ink-stained fingers."

Her mother's careless dismissal of Frederica's writing never failed to hurt her, regardless of how many times it was issued. "It is not a childish yearning, Mother."

"Ladies do not waste their talents in needless endeavors," said her mother with a sniff.

"Such as shopping?" she could not resist asking.

"Shopping is a lady's art," her mother snapped in an uncharacteristic show of ire. "I despair of ever making a proper lady of you, Frederica. When you become Lady Willingham and assume all the duties associated with that noble title, you will understand just how trivial and foolish your old yearnings were. Nothing shall make you happier than being a wife and mother. It is your greatest obligation in life."

Frederica knew she ought to refrain from pursuing the matter further, as arguments with the Duchess of Westlake were akin to spinning in a circle too many times. It made one terribly dizzy. "Are you happy, Mother? Is that why you spend most of your days buying fans and creams and gewgaws?"

Her mother's gaze was inscrutable. Her shoulders stiffened, the feather on her turban bobbing comically. "Of course I am happy."

"Perhaps I want to seek my own happiness," she said softly. "If Father would only grant me my dowry—"

"His Grace will not countenance such folly," her mother interrupted coldly. "You will marry, or you will become a companion to Lady Ogden."

Of course. She was more than familiar with the threats issued by her father and upheld by her mother. Frederica was to marry the odious Lord Willingham or languish in the country with no prospects and no hope of ever completing *The Silent Baron* or seeing it published. How unfair life was for a female. Had she been a male, she could have made something of herself like Duncan Kirkwood had. At the least, she would have been taken seriously. She would have had a choice in her future.

Just then, their butler, Elmwood, appeared to announce the arrival of the Earl of Willingham. Dread unfurled within Frederica as her mother instructed Elmwood they were at home and would be happy to receive his lordship.

The earl appeared, dressed in a claret waistcoat and buff breeches that was not as garish as his ordinary mode of dress. His cravat made up for it, a jarring cerulean tied in the Mathematical style. He bowed as Frederica found herself once again comparing the earl to Duncan. Mr. Kirkwood as she must think of him now, for she had used the last of her visits to his strange, exhilarating world.

Where one man blazed with vitality and sensual charm, owning any chamber with his presence, the other merely filled the room with his pomposity. Lord Willingham thought himself a catch, and he made no secret of it. Frederica knew precisely why he had settled upon her—Willingham's father was rumored to have beggared his estates by gambling away nearly everything he had. The earl wanted Frederica's dowry, and she did not fool herself for a moment into believing he had more innocent motivation.

He was exchanging pleasantries with Mother, and Frederica scarcely paid them any heed until it was too late. He turned to her, offering his arm. "Thank you, Your Grace," he said smoothly to her mother. "A turn about the gardens will be ideal on this fine day. Come along, won't you, my lady?"

Willingham did not even wait for her response before leading her reluctantly to the small walled garden in the rear of the townhouse. The day was unseasonably warm, but Frederica could not stifle either her shiver or her misery as she walked alongside the earl in silence, her slippers crunching in the gravel along with his boots. She supposed he would go riding today, and for a moment, the most ridiculous urge to see Mr. Kirkwood atop a horse struck her.

She squelched it, knowing she did herself no favors in continuing to think of him. The man at her side was her future. They stopped before the hedges in the center of the garden, which had been trimmed into a perfect square. At its center was an assortment of long grasses, Sweet William, peony, and white Mignonette.

"You are radiant this morning, my lady," he said with a remarkable lack of passion.

"Thank you," she said, staring at the bold flowers and proud blades of grass swaying in the gentle breeze. Here were flowers she could appreciate, planted in the soil, roots dug into dirt, standing resilient day after day beneath the sun and moon. They would not be removed by the hands of a diligent servant in two days' time, never to be thought of again.

"I will speak to your father tomorrow, Lady Frederica. It will be my honor to make you my countess." Willingham's voice was low in a pleasant enough sense, though it possessed none of the velvet suggestion laden in Duncan's.

She turned to him at last, looking up into his rigid countenance. He was so proper, so foppish, so at odds with everything she wanted but could not have. "My lord, I have a confession to make. I am in the midst of writing a novel."

"A novel, my lady?" His brows rose in question, disbelief evident in his tone and expression both. "Surely you jest."

"I do not." She did not flinch, continuing to meet his gaze. "I wish to see it published. As my husband, will you object to such an endeavor?"

"My dear Lady Frederica." He laughed as though she had made a sally. "As the Countess of Willingham, you will find more than enough duties to occupy you. The woman's place is as mother and wife. You shall be so fulfilled; I expect you will forget all about such childish fancies."

Her future loomed before her, inviting as a grave. The earl would take her dowry and her body, owning her. She would provide him an heir, and he would strip her of everything she valued. It was entirely possible he would forbid her to write, and how would she gainsay him? What rights would she have as his chattel?

None.

She did not want to be the cut lilies, scentless and pure, untouched by the wildness of nature, never ruffled in a wind or soaked in the violence of a lashing rainstorm. She wanted to be the flowers thriving in the dirt.

She could not marry Willingham.

"I expect your countess would," she told him. And the smile curving her lips had nothing to do with the earl and everything to do with the plan that had begun to blossom in her mind. "It is such a lovely day, my lord, but I do think we ought to return to my mother lest she suspect us of challenging propriety. I would so hate for my pristine reputation to bear a mark so soon to our nuptials."

"Have patience, Lady Frederica," he ordered, his tone clipped, his hands on her upper arms sudden and unexpected as they gripped her, biting into her tender flesh. "Before you flee, I would have what I have come for."

Frederica did not have time to defend herself from the inevitable onslaught of his mouth, rough and wet. His tongue speared between her lips, aggressively darting into her mouth. He tasted bitter and unpleasant. His hands on her arms tightened painfully until she was sure the morrow would bring more bruising, and he made a low sound in his throat, as if he was enjoying this forced, unskilled meeting of lips. She held her breath and remained still, hoping he would stop.

But oddly, her indifference only served as encouragement. He kissed her harder, one of his hands going to her waist and then sliding higher, cupping her breast, his fingers biting into her flesh and sending a jolt of pain through her. Unlike Duncan's skilled, masterful caresses, Willingham's painful fervor made her cold. His tongue plowed deeper into her mouth. She reacted instinctively, biting it.

He released her at last, staring down at her with a new gleam in his eyes that sent a tremor through her. "I look forward to making you my wife, Lady Frederica. You will learn me, my dear. I will take great pleasure teaching you."

She vowed it would never happen. As he escorted her back to her mother, she began to formulate a plan. It would either end in her ruin or her salvation. But in either case, she would never be the Countess of Willingham, and she would never have to suffer his kiss or his punishing touch again.

* * *

HE HAD DONE the honorable thing.

Duncan stood on the periphery of the crush, watching men and women whirl and twirl. Throaty laughter rose above the din of the orchestra, which had just begun a sinful waltz. On any other evening, he would have been struck by the pageantry of it all, the notion that a lowly street urchin and duke's bastard could create all that was before him from nothing. On any other evening, he would have felt like a king surveying his courtiers.

This evening, he raised a glass of champagne to his lips and drained it as he watched with a disinterested eye. Masked lords and ladies of the night surrounded him, bosoms on display, ripe and full and creamy, dampened skirts. Contraband whisky and the finest French champagne were being liberally served. The night would end with satisfaction for many.

But for Duncan, it would end as it had begun, with a hollow ache in his chest and the daunting fear he had made the greatest mistake of his life in allowing Lady Frederica to leave him. He had watched her from above, being handed into his carriage. Had pressed his palm to the cool pane of glass as the conveyance lumbered forward, disappearing into the London night. Had wished the smoothness of the glass was instead her hair, silken and luxurious, her face, soft and beautiful, her cunny, lush and wet.

He had not made a mistake, he reminded himself, hoping if he repeated it enough in his mind, he would believe it. Lady Frederica still maintained her virtue. She would go to her husband with an unburdened mind and a maidenhead intact.

He gritted his teeth, catching a servant bearing champagne and trading his empty glass for a full one and draining half its contents in one gulp. He needed to numb himself. To become mindless and uncaring. It was the only means by which he could fumble through the night.

"Duncan."

The throaty voice at his side, uttering his name in a sultry tone, was as unwanted as the thoughts rampaging through him. He turned to find Lady Clifford. She was dark-haired and beautiful, a jewel-encrusted mask of ivory doing nothing to hinder the effect of her loveliness. Creamy complexion, rosebud lips, wide blue eyes, and a bosom a man could happily lose himself in.

Once, she had stirred him.

Now, he looked upon her and felt nothing. "My lady," he acknowledged, his tone as stiff as his entire body felt.

She pursed her lips. "Do you dare to treat me as someone unfamiliar to you?"

He sent her a mocking smile. "Never. I am all too familiar with you, I daresay."

Her nostrils flared, the only sign of her displeasure. She inhaled, the effort making her breasts rise higher above her tight bodice and indecent décolletage. "I have missed your cutting wit."

Ah, but he was not flirting. He no longer had the capacity to be entertained by women of her sort. Something had changed inside him, and he could not help but to be disgusted with himself for ever allowing Lady Clifford to use him. He thought now of the things he had done to her, at her request, and he felt ill.

"I have not missed you at all," he told her coldly, offering her a mocking bow. "If you will excuse me?"

He did not wait for her response before striding away. Thankfully, his gaze lit upon his friend Cris, the Duke of Whitley, with a flame-haired siren on his arm. Cris had been through hell, fighting against Boney in Spain, and he had returned to a mountain of responsibilities. It would seem his friend had found a distraction to make him happy, at least for the evening.

As he approached the masked pair, the strains of Cris's conversation reached him.

"...wholeheartedly do not regret my decision." His friend spotted him then and flashed Duncan a rare, welcoming smile. "There you are, old fellow."

Cris's lovely companion turned to face him, and even beneath her mask, Duncan could clearly discern she possessed a staggering beauty. He hoped to hell this was the governess Cris had been mooning over, and that his friend had finally won her affections.

"Miss Turnbow, Mr. Duncan Kirkwood, owner of this fine establishment," Whitley introduced them.

Duncan bowed, and Miss Turnbow offered a well-practiced curtsy. He took her gloved hand in his and raised it to his lips, deciding to needle his friend. "A pleasure, Miss Turnbow, to make your acquaintance. Would you care to dance?"

Cris stepped forward, scowling. "I am afraid you are too late. I have already claimed this dance with Miss Turnbow."

He muttered something else that sounded like, *And every bloody other one.*

Duncan grinned. *Ah, yes,* this would be the governess, and it would seem his friend was rather besotted. *Good.* "Perhaps the next dance, then."

Cris's gray gaze glittered with irritation behind his mask, his jaw clenching. "Haven't you an unsuspecting patron in need of fleecing somewhere?"

His grin deepened, his improved mood untouched by Cris's ire. He had never seen his friend so possessive of a woman before, and he could not quite temper his enjoyment.

"As a wise man recently said to me, if only everyone else thought you as droll as you find yourself, friend," he said, repeating the words Cris had said to him not long ago. But all levity dissipated when his gaze traveled, as if by instinct, to a masked woman dressed in a diaphanous pink gown, dark hair styled artfully atop her head. His body reacted with a savagery he could not contain. *Mine*, it hummed. It simply could not be her. But then she turned and smiled at a masked gentleman, and recognition hit him like a fist to the gut. "What the devil is *she* doing here?"

"She?" Cris asked, sounding concerned. "Is something amiss, Duncan?"

Duncan's gaze remained fixed upon her, watching as she laughed. He was going to rip the man standing far too near to her limb from limb. Whoever the hell he was, his breaths on earth were numbered. "Nothing I cannot manage, Cris," he forced himself to say, offering a bow. "Enjoy the evening, lovebirds."

Without waiting for a response, he moved toward her, drawn as ever. Part of him wanted to kiss her senseless. Part of him wanted to throttle her. How had she managed to come to the club again tonight, and looking as she did, like a Venus risen from the sea?

It was the first time he had seen her dressed as a woman, and she was so beautiful he ached. If he had been drawn to her in her ill-fitting male costume, he was bloody well slavering over her now, even as he stalked closer, agitation and irritation mounting.

The instant she noticed him; her eyes went wide behind her mask. He did not stop until he reached her side, inserting himself between her and the unlucky gentleman who was going to meet an untimely end if he did not step away from Duncan's woman.

His woman?

Beelzebub's ballocks, he had to do something about this foolish infatuation, this untenable weakness she caused in him, the fever she lit in his blood. His jaw tensed. He bowed to her, ignoring the interloper he had maneuvered to the side. She was all he saw, her eyes glittering, her full pink lips glistening, her long, graceful arms, throat bedecked with winking gems, her bosom...holy hell, her bosom at last. Perfect handfuls straining against her bodice.

"Madam." Into that lone word, he infused every emotion roiling through him. Outrage, frustration, jealousy, and desperate need.

"I beg your pardon, Kirkwood," sputtered the fellow behind him. "I was about to have my waltz with Angel."

He spun on his heel and pinned the masked gentleman—the Earl of Darby, unless he missed his guess—with a meaningful glare. "I am afraid you are poaching, my lord. This ladybird is mine."

Duncan hoped like hell the earl read his imminent murder in his expression. It would seem he did, for he lingered but a moment before conceding. With a bow, he melted into the crowd. Snarling, Duncan turned back to her.

Damnation, she was gorgeous. "*Angel?*"

Her creamy skin flushed red. "What would you have me tell him? My true name?"

"No, my lady." He stepped nearer, so close her skirts billowed about his legs, almost ensnaring him in as cloying a grip as Lady Frederica herself did. He lowered his face to hers, wishing he could snatch away her mask so he might see her in her full, womanly glory. "I would have had you stay at home where you belong. How the hell did you find your way here?"

The thought of her attempting to hire a hack made him want to smash his fist through a damned wall.

Her generous lashes lowered over her vibrant eyes, shielding her from him for a moment. "You promised me the use of your carriage whenever I wished it, did you not?"

Beelzebub's breeches. She had outmaneuvered him. Had routed him with the cunning persistence of a military genius. "Not to come to this masque, damn you. This is not a proper ball where your infatuated swain will fetch you a ratafia as you're being watched by the careful eyes of a dozen dowagers. This is a glorified Cyprian ball. The gentlemen in attendance are either in search of a mistress or have arrived with one. The women in here are the feasts laid before a herd of starving wild boars."

The analogy made him grit his teeth, but it was true. To think someone could have touched her. Kissed her. Led her to one of the pleasure chambers. *By God*, what would she have done?

She stared at him, licking her lips slowly.

He tracked the movement of her tongue, feeling every bit the starved boar he had likened the other men in the chamber to. Where she was concerned, he wanted nothing more than to claim, possess, taste, touch.

Lick. Bite. Suck.

His cock went inconveniently hard, and he had no one to blame but himself and the lecherous bent of his thoughts. Damnation, his body was on fire for her. Everything in him crying out to haul her in his arms, throw her over his shoulder, and take her away from this debauched crowd.

"Arthur seemed rather kind," she said softly. "Not at all like a wild boar. I do believe he may have made a thinly disguised reference to my bosom, however, now that I think upon it…"

A growl tore from his throat. He was going to bloody well

hunt *Arthur* down and end him. Tonight. Duncan took Frederica's hand in his, lacing their fingers together in a grip that was not as gentle as he intended. But he was a man consumed by lust and jealousy and the violent need to protect her, to remove her from this den of iniquity before it tainted her. Before she was ruined.

Ah, yes. There you are, Duncan, you fucking fool. Save her reputation so she can be married off to the milksop who forces kisses upon her and brings her watery lemonades.

He ignored the voice inside him and hauled her through the crush, intent upon getting her alone so he could send her on her way. She did not wear gloves, and why would she to an affair such as this, where many of the female attendees were practically naked beneath their dampened skirts? But damn it if the contact of her skin upon his did not feed the hunger for her that had already rendered him ravenous.

"Mr. Kirkwood," she protested.

But any other words she may have said were drowned out in the din of revelers and the orchestra as it struck up another waltz. He did not care to hear them anyway. Inside, he was in tumult. She had defied him. Had returned. And for what purpose had she put her reputation and her innocence in such jeopardy?

Through the sea of faces, painted lips, bared bosoms, and black masks, he led her. Finally, he found the almost unnoticeable door in the western corner of the chamber that would lead him to the intricate series of inner halls that were the veins of his establishment. He opened it and pulled her through, closing the door at their backs. Tonight, the hall was dimly lit in keeping with the nature of the evening.

He could not see her in as great a detail as he wished, but it would have to do because he did not think he could make it another step. He whirled her so her back pressed against the wall. He followed her, pressing his body mercilessly to hers, knowing she could feel every hard, hot part of him pressing against her. His cock was rigid, and he did not spare her modesty. There was no room for anything less than the visceral betwixt them now.

"Why have you come?" he demanded, dipping his head until their foreheads met in a parody of the kiss his body screamed to claim.

She expelled a breath, and it was warm, champagne-scented. "I do not know."

He recognized the tone of her voice. Understood that Lady Frederica Isling was not a female who ever took a step without rationalizing it and planning where it would lead her.

"Liar," he charged softly.

His hands, of their own volition, had come to cup her face. Her skin was so soft, like the petals of a fresh rosebud. He wanted to stroke her, strip her bare. Taste and touch her everywhere. She was like a revelation. A miracle. A sacred text only he could read.

"Duncan." His name slipped from her lips in a sigh.

Or an invitation.

It required every modicum of restraint to keep from slamming his lips to hers. "Frederica. Tell me the truth, damn it. You were meant to never return. Your reputation was intact. You conducted your research. What more could you want? Why are you here tonight, in defiance of me and everything that is right and proper?"

"I wanted to see you," she said on a rush. Her eyes closed. "I need you, Duncan."

Damn it to hell. Her admission robbed the air from his lungs. One moment, he stood still and silent, gazing down upon her as his world changed, and the next he was assaulted by an almost violent surge of want. Pure desire. Animalistic need. He wanted to lift her skirts, rut with her here and now, against the wall, mark her as his forever. Plant his cock and his seed deep inside her.

The realization shook him. He could not afford to want this woman, to take her for his own. Doing so would dismantle everything he had worked so hard to gain. He could not abandon his course. Not now. Not ever. Did not his mother deserve some retribution? Should not Amberley be made to pay for the manner in which he had abused, used, and abandoned a gentle soul with his own flesh and blood growing inside her belly?

He muttered a curse. Never before had he been so torn. So conflicted. "Why?" he demanded of her because he could not seem to keep the question within himself as he knew he ought. "Why did you want to see me again, my lady? Does the forbidden thrill you? Do you wish for a taste of passion before consigning yourself to the life your father would choose for you?"

Her eyes glittered up at him in the semidarkness. *Tears.* The realization made everything inside him turn to dust. He had never been a particularly superstitious man, but it seemed to him in that moment that a part of him died while another part of him was born.

"Perhaps I wanted to know what it is truly like before the right is taken from me forever," she said, her voice hushed.

Damn her. She was making this difficult. Too difficult.

He made short work of her mask, flicking it from her lovely face without a hint of contrition. Spectacles, mustache, mask—he had stripped her of every barrier she used to keep her true self from him. She was on display now, just as he had imagined her since the first night he had caught her in his club, only a hundred times more lovely than his mind had conjured.

She was radiant. Persephone, goddess of spring and life, of fresh buds and turned dark earth and planted seeds and shoots of renewal. She was beautiful beyond description. She called to him as no one before her had. As he instinctively knew no one else after her ever could.

"What *it* is truly like," he repeated, his voice gruff, laden with the promise of all he wished to do to her. To show her if he would but allow himself. "Tell me, Frederica. What do you speak of?"

He closed his eyes and inhaled sharply, warning himself against temptation, but the scent of violets filled him. As did her breath, the frantic thump of her heart, the heat of her, radiating into him.

Her hands, which had previously been settled upon his shoulders, moved higher, locking around the back of his neck. "Making love."

She said the two words so quietly he thought he must have misheard her. "Making?"

"Love," she whispered. "I want to be yours, Duncan. Even if it is only for one night."

Raw, unadulterated need pounded through him, fiercer and hotter and stronger than ever before. He couldn't stop himself from pressing his lips to hers then, kissing her, open-mouthed and furious. He kissed her with all the longing burning within him. With all the anger, all the confusion, all the frustration. He wanted her so much, and yet she could never truly be his, not just because of his quest for vengeance but because she was Lady Frederica Isling, daughter to the Duke of Westlake, and he was Duncan Kirkwood, bastard son of a Covent Garden lightskirt.

Because there was no world in which they could ever be one.

And if that bitter acknowledgment made him kiss her harder, and if it made his tongue slide into her mouth with a deeper insistence, and if she mewled in her throat and clung to him as if he was all she had ever wanted, who was he to deny it? His hands slid to her breasts, cupping them for the first time through her bodice. They were high and full, her nipples erect, hard little gems cutting into his palms. He tore his mouth from hers and planted it on her throat, inhaling deeply of her scent, warm woman and floral musk.

Bloody hell, he was lost. Lost in her. He planted kisses everywhere. Opened his mouth to taste her succulent skin, used his teeth upon her flesh. His hands roamed. Claimed. Every curve and swell, each new temptation comprised of sweet-scented, warm, womanly flesh.

He was aflame, the sizzling heat of desire licking through his veins. There was something about Lady Frederica Isling that made him want to claim her. To strip her bare, pin her to his bed, sink home inside her. To unleash his seed in her womb, an act which he had never before committed with another woman. An act he had never wished to commit, being the product of a loveless bedding himself.

"Oh, Duncan," she whispered, her voice at once a soft balm and a promise of more.

Bleeding hell, how could he resist her?

And then another voice inside him whispered *what if?* What if he ruined her? What if he took her to his bed? At the least, it would keep her from an unwanted match with her forceful suitor, would it not? Moreover, there had always existed within him the niggling knowledge that leaving her innocence largely intact could mean her father would deny him the payment he wished in exchange for his silence. He had not wanted to damage her reputation or cause her harm, but how could it be so if the lady herself wished it?

A light began to burn within his darkness. Beseeching. Tempting. *My God, I can have her. For one glorious night, I can make her mine.*

He took her mouth once more, his hands tightening on her waist. She tasted of champagne, intoxicating and tart. His tongue slipped past her lips, and she sucked it. His cock twitched in approval. An innocent lady she may be, but Lady Frederica possessed the passion of a woman.

He tore his lips from hers, pressing their foreheads together so they remained nose to nose, bodies flush, their breaths mingling. Before he could do it, he needed to be certain she was aware of the consequences. She was reckless and passionate, inquisitive and bold, and these were characteristics that could often land one in a spot of trouble. "You do not know what you are asking, my lady."

"I know well enough." Her bright gaze burned into him, unflinching. "I do not want the life that has been chosen for me. Tonight may be my last opportunity to be truly free, and if it is, I choose you."

I choose you.

His heart thundered, her words reverberating with each life's pulse. The undeniable pull he had felt for her—right from the moment he had first seen her arse at his hazard table—increased, mingling with the fierce, primitive need to make her his. He needed to be inside her.

She made him greedy. Made him weak. In that moment, their skins touching, bodies pressed together, two hundred revelers on the opposite side of the plaster, he knew he had made his choice as well. An air of finality mingled with rightness.

Another thought jolted through him like lightning. Frederica's brother, the real Lord Blanden, was in attendance this evening. How easy it would be to arrange for Blanden to accidentally discover Duncan and Lady Frederica in a compromising position? What better means of proving, beyond a doubt, he had compromised her?

He would never have taken her innocence, but if she offered it to him, would it not be the irrefutable, indisputable argument he needed to force Westlake's hand? More so than threat and innuendo, the knowledge his daughter had been ruined would surely move Westlake to relinquish Amberley's vowels.

Could he be so ruthless? She had asked him to bed her, not to ruin her. Could he hurt her to gain what he wanted? He searched inside himself, and felt only the darkness blossoming and spreading, a nothingness where emotions should dwell. He could have everything he wanted, all at once. Frederica and his revenge. Both would be fleeting.

Duncan pressed a quick, hard kiss to her lips before withdrawing, taking her hand. "Come with me."

And both would be worth the black marks upon his soul. Of that, he had no doubt.

CHAPTER 12

Their fingers laced together, Duncan led her through the labyrinth of secret halls and up a flight of stairs to a chamber she had never seen before. He released her hand to light a lamp. A warm glow spilled over polished dark wood. On a separate floor from the main gaming and pleasure rooms, it was nevertheless luxuriously appointed. A large bed dominated the wall.

A burst of warmth unfurled in her belly, leaving her tingling and terrified.

The door had scarcely closed behind them before he turned, crowding her with his large body. He framed her face in his wide palms, his handsome countenance inscrutable as he looked down upon her. He searched her gaze, it seemed, for the answer to a question that had never been posed.

"It is not too late, Frederica," he said softly, and her name in his deep, dark voice sent a thrill through her. "One word from you, and I shall bundle you into my carriage."

Guilt struck her then, an emotion she had done her best to suppress with champagne upon her arrival at his forbidden masque. Who would have thought Duncan Kirkwood, purveyor of vice and sin, would have possessed such a tender heart? Before she had met him, Frederica would not have believed it. But he was so much more than his reputation. It did not surprise her he was not simply taking what she'd offered. He was giving her every opportunity to change her mind, should she wish it.

She would not. Lord Willingham's visit had made it clear to her what she must do. She regretted the necessity of involving Duncan, for deceiving him after all they had shared felt horridly wrong, but there was no other man she would have ruin her. And ruined, she must be. It was her only hope of escaping the grim future of life as Lady Willingham, recipient of forced kisses, brutal touches, condescension, and heaven knew what else.

She did not want to know, and that was why she was here, body pressed indecently to Duncan Kirkwood's, on her way to ruination. His scent, like his heat, invaded her senses. He was all she could think, see, breathe. She could be honest with herself; her decision to facilitate her ruination had not been selfless. It had been greedy, shameless, and wanton. She longed for Duncan, his mouth, his touch, his body.

For a brief, mad moment, she wondered if she ought to confess her plan to him, but fear he would not wish to aid her, spurred her on. She told herself she had no other option.

"My lady," he pressed, taking her hand in his once more and squeezing it. "Your final decision must be made."

Ah, but hers had already been made before she had even entered his establishment earlier that evening. Everything was in motion, leading her inexorably to the next chapter of her life.

Onward, she promised herself. When her father was presented with irrefutable proof of her fall from grace, she felt certain he would have no choice but to forego any hopes of a match with Lord Willingham. And then, perhaps Frederica could at last convince her father to grant her freedom.

She shook her head. "I shall not change my mind."

His jaw tightened as his gaze searched hers. "Good."

His lips took hers. Hot, hungry, insistent. Devouring. She opened for him, tasting him, savoring the silken heat of his tongue in her mouth. Willingham's hard, forced kiss had been as bleak as a winter day, cold and harsh. But Duncan was the voluptuous warmth of a summer day. In his arms, she forgot about her plans. Forgot about the need to be ruined. In his arms, she came to life.

He kissed her breathless, raising his head to gaze down at her. His eyes glistened with possessive fire; his expression fierce. "I have wanted you since the moment I first saw you, dressed as a man, scribbling notes on your ivory pad."

Her mind whirled at his revelation. Duncan's kisses and his heady masculine scent had wrapped her in a fog. Facts and reality intruded, like cold little pinpricks. She was misleading him. Using him for her own gain. But if she managed to conduct her plan properly, he would never be affected. Indeed, he would never even know.

"How did you know I was a female?" she asked softly amidst a fresh twinge of guilt. *Tell him*, said the voice inside her. But the rational part of her knew she must not. If he knew what she meant to do, he would not be here with her now, looking down upon her with such tenderness and need.

And now that she was here, so close to him, their bodies pressed together, his lips near enough to kiss, his hands coasting up and down her spine in a slow, steady caress, she could not stop. She was a carriage, hurtling forward, propelled by her own selfish need for him. Propelled by the promise of the forbidden, the chance to know what it was like to be Duncan Kirkwood's, even if just for one night.

Not even for a whole night.

Hours. It was all they had. Perhaps this was the last time she would ever see him, and that knowledge made an ache bloom inside her.

He kissed her slowly, deeply, taking his time. There was nothing hurried about this meeting of the mouths. When he withdrew, his thumbs gently tracing her cheekbones, he blessed her with one of his rare, beautiful smiles. "There are not enough false mustaches, ill-fitting coats, or hideous spectacles in Christendom to hide your beauty, Frederica."

Oh. He hurt her heart. She had never thought herself particularly beautiful, but she believed the vehemence in his voice, the frank appreciation in his gaze. Why had he not been born Lord Willingham? If only she could have been promised to Duncan instead. She would have married him gladly, if only because it meant she could kiss his beautiful mouth whenever she wished.

"You flatter me," she said, breathless.

He shook his head slowly, his smile fading. "I told you before. I do not flatter. I speak truth."

She stared at him, absorbing the haunting beauty of his features, committing them to memory. For as long as she lived, she would never forget the handful of wicked nights she had spent with Duncan Kirkwood. He had changed her forever.

She caressed his cheek tentatively, for she had never before touched a man thus. "Thank you, Duncan."

"For ruining you?" A self-deprecating smile quirked his lips. "Do not thank me for that, Frederica, for I am doing you no favors. Indeed, I am not a gentleman. I am a man who seizes what he wants, when he wants it, regardless of how long it takes."

There was something in his words, a harshness, a hardness, that had been previously absent. She could not be certain of the cause of it. "Not for ruining me, but for the time you have granted me. I will never forget you."

"Nor, I, you." His countenance, like his tone, was rigid and unyielding.

"What is this chamber?" she asked him then, for the question had been prodding at her. She could not help but wonder. It looked as if it was his, but she could not be certain. "Why did you not take me to one of your pleasure rooms?"

His gaze grew shuttered. "This chamber is mine. I use it occasionally, on evenings when I am too weary to return home at the conclusion of business."

She thought of Tabitha and all the other beautiful ladies working at The Duke's Bastard. Did he bring them here as well? Was this where he kept his women? Was she just another woman wooed by his charm and his handsome face, going to the same bed so many others had occupied before her?

Her feelings must have shown on her face, for his thumbs stilled on her skin, his expression changing, tightening. "I have never brought another woman to this chamber, Frederica. You are the first."

The knot of trepidation inside her eased, and in its place was longing and warmth and a desperate need. Her instincts took over, and she rose on her toes to seal her mouth with his, kissing him. He kissed her back with a fiery fervor, openmouthed and deep. There was promise in that kiss, mystery and heat and untold passion.

She wanted more.

The time for talking and worrying was over. Her body was singing with life and pleasure. Her tongue moved against his, sliding inside his mouth as he had done to her. She wanted more than she understood. She wanted everything.

To make her mark upon him. To make him hers, in the same way she would become his.

Their kisses were a battle. A delicious, seductive battle.

But she was ready for the war, and so, it seemed, was he. Without removing his lips from hers, he swept her into his arms. She was weightless as he carried her across the chamber, and the sensation was at once decadent and intoxicating. Her arms went around his neck as an unladylike squeak emerged from her, straight into his mouth. He swallowed down the sound of her surprise. Strode across the chamber while kissing her with such slow care she could not squelch the embarrassing mewl of need that rose from her throat. He was so powerful, so strong. And yet capable of such sweet gentleness. An enigma. A conundrum she longed to unlock.

He was the only man she had ever wanted, and he was the one man she could not have. Not beyond tonight. The knowledge made her kiss him deeper, made her sink her fingers into his thick, soft hair. Made her inhale his scent and trap it in her lungs like her own private spoils. Made her lose her inhibitions when he set her on her feet by the bed.

He was dressed in his black evening finery, staring down at her as if she was a revelation. And she did the only thing she could think of. She spun around, giving him her back so he could open the fastening of her gown. He kissed her nape, his fingers working with ease. His mouth trailed to the side of her neck, opening, sucking. She gasped at the raw pleasure of it.

And then her gown was slipping from her body. Large hands found her waist, clamping down, spinning her back to face him. He was so beautiful, the lamp illuminating the stark lines, angles, and planes of his face, the hard musculature of his body.

"You're the loveliest thing I've ever seen." His words were

low, almost guttural. His gaze swept over her, as tangible as a touch. "Take your petticoats and chemise off for me."

He wanted her to disrobe before him. To strip away every last scrap of fabric shielding her from him until nothing remained between them. She swallowed, hesitating, a sudden shyness hitting her. Thanks to the wicked tome she had read, she knew, at least in a broad sense, what her ruination would entail. Imagining it had been one thing, but finding the boldness to be completely nude before him was another matter.

"Now," he prodded firmly, sensing her hesitation. "I want to see you, darling. All of you. Won't you show me?"

He asked so nicely, with such sweet pleading. He made her feel powerful and desired. Brave and strong. A mortal becoming a goddess in her god's eyes. She swallowed, finding her courage, and did as he asked, whisking away petticoats and chemise. She stood before him in nothing more than stockings and shoes, her body on display in the chill of the night air.

But she was not cold. His eyes devoured her. A flush stole over her skin, and she became aware of new sensations. Her nipples tightened. Her breasts ached. Between her thighs, the flesh he had pleasured before throbbed.

"Holy God," he swore. "You are even more beautiful than I imagined, Frederica."

She shivered. It was strange, how she did not feel embarrassed or ashamed. Instead, she stood proud. How natural it felt to reveal herself to him. How strange to feel as if he was a part of her now, as if she were his in truth and not just for the night.

"I am not beautiful," she could not help but deny once more, though his appreciative gaze made her feel as if she was.

"Yes," he said starkly, "you are." His hands gripped her waist again, and this time it was skin on skin as he guided her backward until the edge of his bed prodded her thighs. "Sit, darling."

She obeyed because he was Duncan and she trusted him implicitly, seating herself primly on the edge of his bed. She stared up at him, acutely aware he was fully clothed while she was almost entirely nude. She felt wicked, wild, and free. It was wrong, forbidden, and the knowledge only made her want him more.

He dropped to his knees before her, his hands on her ankles, kneading softly. He kissed one, then the other. His hands swept up her calves, warm brands. Claiming.

She could not suppress the soft moan of appreciation that emerged from her. She was recalling his mouth on her flesh, his tongue. His teeth. She remembered all too well the pleasure he had brought her, and even now, her core throbbed. Perhaps something was wrong with her. She was lacking in morals, it was certain, for she could not dredge up a speck of remorse or shame.

He took off her shoes. His fingers found the arches of her feet, massaging as he kissed his way to her knees. Even though her fine stockings provided a barrier between his lips and her bare skin, she felt those kisses in the center of her body.

His hands swept higher, leaving her feet to glide over her ankles, up her calves, all the way to her thighs. He caressed her. Raked his nails gently over her skin. She jerked at the sensation, meeting his gaze.

"Open for me, darling," he ordered gently.

She did as he asked, her legs falling apart. He was between them in an instant, fully clothed and gorgeous in his black coat and trousers. His golden head dipped low like a suppliant. He pressed a kiss to her right knee, then her left. Then higher still, up her inner thigh. His hands and his mouth worked in concert, skimming her everywhere, licking, sucking, gently nibbling, all whilst he avoided the part of her he had so thoroughly pleasured before. And now that she knew the pleasure to be had from such an action, she wanted it again.

And again.

And again.

But she would settle for once more just now. One more touch of Duncan Kirkwood's wicked mouth upon her sensitive flesh. One more flick of his tongue, suck of his mouth.

He kissed higher still, and she jerked, arching against him.

"Do you like this?" he asked as his tongue flitted over her flesh.

Near enough to where she wanted him but not the same. "Please, Duncan," she whispered.

His hands, so large, so knowing, ran up her outer thighs. "Please what, darling? Please lick you? Please make you spend? Say it. Tell me everything. Every wicked little thing you would have me do. I want it all, your complete surrender. Tonight, you are mine alone, Frederica. Tonight, you belong to me."

Of course she was his. Always his. Only his, and she would do whatever he asked of her. Anything if it meant more of his touch upon her skin, more of his mouth on her, more of the torturous pleasure only he could deliver.

Up and down his hands traveled, over her thighs in slow and steady strokes, touching her so softly, so sweetly, as if he feared she was as delicate as the finest porcelain teacup. He kissed a path back to her knees. He had made her greedy, and she wanted more. But the words would not leave her tongue.

"I want words, darling." He kissed his way back to the juncture of her thighs, pursing his lips and blowing a tantalizing burst of humid air over her pulsing sex. "Give them to me."

"Ah," was all she could manage at first. "Your mouth. I want your mouth."

"Here?" He moved higher, teasing her, pressing a kiss to the jut of her hip.

"No." She moved, restless. "You know where."

"Ah, I believe I do." He smiled up at her, both dimples on show, and he was wicked and beautiful all at once. He kissed her other hip bone. "Here? I want to worship you, Frederica. Tell me where."

His words, delivered into her bare flesh with the tantalizing brush of his warm lips, made a slow, steady ache pulse in her core. She could not speak. Her hands were starving for him. She sifted her fingers through his thick, golden hair, absorbed the strength of his broad shoulders, flexed and beautiful beneath his coat.

"If you will not tell me," he growled, kissing a path up her side as he caressed her waist, "I shall have to kiss you everywhere." He cupped the fullness of her breasts. "Here." His mouth closed over the peak, sucking. He released the nipple. "Here." He moved to her other breast and kissed it as well. "Here, where you are the same pretty pink as your cunny." He sucked and lightly bit with his teeth.

She gasped. Her need for him was built like a fire stacked with dry kindling and then doused with oil. She wanted to be nearer to him. Pressed against him. Wrapped around him. She arched helplessly, undulating against him in an effort to assuage the ache.

Her hands were desperate for him now, traveling over his back, her face dipping into his glorious hair to inhale. Lemons and musk and ambergris and warm, delicious man. *Duncan.*

She could love him.

She could so easily give him her heart.

The realization hit her as he ran his tongue over her

nipple, holding her gaze as he sucked it with such strength she cried out, shooting forward on the bed. Her thighs splayed open, her aching sex pressed against his waistcoat. It was not enough. She wanted his flesh. She wanted to be as wicked as she could be with him.

But she must not allow herself to feel more. All they had was tonight. Now. These stolen moments together. Pleasure, passion, and sin. She did not dare fall in love. He was a wild stallion, meant to be admired from afar. Untamable. Unbreakable. Hers, fleetingly.

He continued his game, dragging his lips up her neck, finding the mad fluttering of her pulse. His mouth opened, and he sucked as if he wished to consume her, and she wished he would. She wanted him everywhere. Wanted his arms, his embrace. Wanted to become one with him, their bodies and skin and beating hearts indistinguishable.

"You even taste sweet here," he murmured, his tongue flitting over her tender skin. "Sweeter than any confection. Violets and sugar." He worked his way to her ear, licking the hollow behind it until wetness slid between her thighs, and she jerked once more against his solid body, seeking relief and finding none, only more aching stimulation. "Better than chocolate. You are delicious, Frederica."

She rubbed her cheek against his, eyes closed, drowning in decadent sensation, awash in him, on fire for him. How she wished she could stay here forever, in this chamber, at his side. With him. His kisses skimmed over her throat, along her jaw. And then his mouth was on her again, and she was lost.

* * *

INSATIABLE. That was what he was. Lost in her. *Ravenous.* He inhaled her delicate, floral scent, willed himself to slow down, to savor her the way she deserved. He took her mouth as he would take her body, with reverence and gratitude. Her tongue played against his, her fingers dragging over the wool of his jacket. There was desperation in her hands, need in her touch, in the soft sounds of surrender in her throat.

Those sweet hums of pleasure urged him on. He forgot about his teasing game to make her demand what she wanted from him and gave in to his own rising need. One hand cupped the ripe fullness of her breast, thumb strumming over her hard nipple, while the other parted her folds. Slick dew coated his fingers as he found the plump bud of her sex and stroked.

She jerked against him, and he swallowed her cries with his kisses, taking everything he could. But it was not enough. He wanted more. Wanted her on his tongue, to drink her, to lick her, to make her scream. His hunger for her was a potent, raging beast inside him that demanded to be fed.

He tore his mouth from hers, raining kisses back down her body to the curve of her breast. Then lower, until he was between her spread limbs, caressing the silken skin of her inner thighs.

"If you won't tell me where you want my mouth, darling, I'll have to choose myself," he warned.

She was open to him, and he took a moment to admire her before he lowered his head, his tongue parting her folds, licking up every trace of her he could get. She tasted so good. He could eat her and eat her and never have his fill.

He hummed his approval, his lips closing over her pearl. She thrust her cunny into his face shamelessly, her cries ringing through the chamber. He slid his hands around her arse cheeks, parting them, opening her even further. Slowly, he worked his way to her entrance, running his tongue gently over her in slow, steady swipes.

The urge to possess her, to stand, open the fall of his

breeches, and sink home, was strong and relentless. He had never bedded a virgin before. The notion of being her first, of introducing Frederica's body to pleasure, being the only man who had ever been inside her, made his cock hard as marble. He kissed her there, gently, tenderly.

And then he was feasting on her again, sucking her into his mouth, using his tongue and lips until he sensed how near she was to exploding. Her fingers were in his hair, gripping fistfuls and tugging, and he did not give a damn, for the surprising sting of it pleased him.

He continued plying his torture, working her needy flesh as she grew wetter. She was on the precipice now. Her breaths emerged in ragged pants, her low moans the headiest sounds he had ever heard. One more swipe of his tongue, and she cried out, her body tremoring beneath his hands and mouth as she sobbed her release.

But he was a sinner, and when it came to Lady Frederica Isling's pleasure, gluttony was his vice. This time, he did not stop, even after her shudders subsided. He continued sucking, exerting greater pressure, and then used his lower teeth to gently graze the sweet spot where he had noted she was most sensitive. When she moaned and writhed beneath him, he bit that plump, delicious bud, and he was almost instantly rewarded by the rush of her spend. He caught it with his tongue, swallowed it down, a part of her that was now part of him.

And then his body was moving of its own volition, standing. Shedding his jacket, tearing off his waistcoat, hauling his shirt over his head. She watched, eyes glazed, mouth slack, her breasts rising like offerings, those luscious nipples hard and eager for his mouth. Her legs were still spread, the swollen, wet lips of her cunny glistening like a beacon. She looked like an angel who had been ravished by the devil, and in a sense, that was precisely what she was.

He toed off his shoes, and in a rush, he stripped away his breeches and stockings until he stood before her in nothing but his smalls. In one swift tug, they were gone as well, and he was nude, her wide eyes going to his prick. He was large and thick, and he knew it. Her tongue swept over her lower lip as she stared. Duncan gripped himself, groaning at how ready he was, that the touch of his own hand could elicit such startling sensation, his ballocks drawing up and heat shooting straight to his spine.

"That is your member?" she asked in a hushed tone, her vivid eyes never straying.

Beneath her curious gaze, he grew larger still, straining against his hand, which could not resist another pass over his turgid flesh. The way she watched him—wide-eyed and riveted—made him want her even more.

"Aye," he said, running his thumb over the head. He stepped into the vee of her thighs then, positioning himself at her channel, her cream making the tip wet. It took every bit of his restraint to hold himself still, to keep from pressing forward as his body demanded. "This is the part of me that will go inside you. Here." For one brief, breath-claiming moment, he canted his hips, his cock sliding against her.

"Oh," she said, eyes still wide, gaze burning into his at last. "I know."

She knew? This gave him pause. He raised a brow, studying her, his wayward little innocent who had somehow found herself in the clutches of London's darkest beast, and who, instead of running, had begged him to take her innocence. She possessed so much depth. Just when he thought he had peeled back her last layer, he found yet another.

"How do you know, my wicked angel?" he could not resist asking. Perhaps her mother had warned her, in anticipation of her impending nuptials.

Thoughts of Frederica marrying some spoilt fop, of

another man touching her breasts, taking her nipples in his mouth, and claiming her cunny for his own, enraged Duncan. She was his, damn it. Except she was not. Not beyond this night, and he had to remember that. He closed his eyes for a moment, gripping his cock harder, trying to battle the warring factions of possessive rage and delirious lust careening through him.

"A book," she whispered, looking suddenly shy, a glorious flush tingeing her cheeks. It was so at odds with the brazen manner in which she was nude before him. So very Frederica —at once pure and yet capable of such divine depravity.

Of course it was a book. He ought not to have been surprised at her admission. Part of him was, and yet part of him understood curiosity and observation were her nature. She wanted to see, know, experience everything. Perhaps that same inquisitive spirit was behind her decision this night. Whatever it was, he did not dare question it, not when he was so near to everything he wanted.

With his free hand, he cupped her cheek. "Where did you find such corrupt literature, my lady?"

She turned her head, pressing a kiss to the center of his palm that arrowed straight to his cock, all the while holding his gaze. "It was my brother's, I believe. I found it in one of his trunks.

"And, of course, you read it all rather than leaving it to its mysteries." He smiled. That was his Frederica, fearless and undaunted by the forbidden. Her boldness had brought her to him, and regardless of what came to pass after this night, he would always admire her for it.

No other lady could compare.

"Twice," she said, confirming his thoughts.

"And? Are you disappointed with the flesh and blood version of the fiction you read?" He dragged himself up and down her seam, making both their hips twitch. It felt so damned delicious. She felt so damned delicious. Her wet heat silken, and he wanted to take her now. Wanted inside her. So. Very. Badly. He licked his lips and tasted her, musk and honey.

"*Oh*." The gentle exclamation left her once more, but this time with an aching resonance he did not miss. "I must say, as much as I appreciate the written word, there is something to be said for flesh and blood."

"Something?" His fingers delved into her folds now, finding her already sensitized pearl and stroking.

A lusty moan tore from her, the heat of her expelled breath brushing over his lips like a kiss. He toyed with her slowly. Softly, knowing from the way she writhed impatiently against him that she wanted more. Harder. She wanted to come again, his wanton goddess.

And he would allow her to. But not yet.

"A great deal," she amended.

He removed his fingers, slick with her wetness, and held them to her lips. "Suck, my lady."

There was something infinitely stirring about maintaining formality with her whilst they were naked and he had licked her cunny into devastating submission twice. When he was holding fingertips kissed with her dew to her perfect mouth and ordering her to taste herself.

Her lips parted, obeying, and he suppressed a groan at the sight of that perfect, lush rosebud mouth opening for his fingers. Her lips closed over his two fingers, her tongue lapping. Hades and hellfire, he had no words. No thoughts. The suction of her mouth on his fingers made his cock pulse as if he had just spent. And if he endured her innocent torment for another moment more, he feared he would do just that.

He withdrew his fingers, drew them to first one nipple, then the other, painting lazy, glistening circles around each.

And then he lowered his head to draw them into his mouth. He lingered on the last nipple, tugging with his teeth until she cried out.

He wanted to prolong their joining for as long as he could. Wanted to make this night last, for the memories of it would be all he had left of her come the morning. He shoved that miserable thought from his mind, unwilling to acknowledge or examine it, for all he wanted in this moment was her, and he could not imagine anything beyond it. Could not fathom ever wanting anyone the way he wanted her, or feeling this soul-deep desire with another.

Duncan released her nipple, met her gaze once more, falling into mossy brilliance. He knew she was as lost as he was. "I need you."

She nodded. "Yes." Caught his face in her small, elegant hands and drew him to her for a kiss.

He poured all of himself into that meeting of mouths. Lips. Tongue. She tasted of herself and of raw desire, of the forbidden, of need. Their tongues tangled. Moans rose between them. Hands were everywhere. His. Hers. Traveling, caressing, learning, memorizing, and tantalizing. Her skin was supple, warm and smooth, at once innocent and yet debauched. He could touch her forever. Kiss her forever.

But a voice inside him reminded him their time was limited.

He guided her to the center of the bed and joined her there, fitting naturally between her thighs. They kissed, alternating between long and slow and fast and hard. He tore his lips from hers, looking down at her, their ragged breaths mingling to become one, their eyes locked.

"Are you certain?" he asked, for he would not proceed without knowing she harbored not a single doubt. It did not matter how much he wanted her. He had no wish to be her regret.

"Yes, Duncan," she said with aching seriousness.

Her hands were on his shoulders once more, caressing with bold, tender strokes. She branded him. As long as he lived, he would never forget the sensation of Lady Frederica's body, willing and lush beneath his, her hungry hands roaming his flesh as though he were someone worthy of her.

Plainly, he was not.

But neither was he such a gentleman that he would attempt to dissuade her of the wisdom of her decision—or lack thereof.

"You want me?" he had to ask again, for some part of him could scarcely credit that Lady Frederica Isling—beautiful, innocent, bold—wanted him, misbegotten illegitimate son who lived a life of sin and decadence.

That the god of the underworld and the goddess of spring could so meet.

"You have woken me from a great sleep," she told him then, her voice vehement, stirring an answering understanding deep within him.

They were meant to be.

For tonight, he reminded himself.

Only for tonight.

But *oh*, what a glorious night it would be.

He kissed her, allowing his entire body to press against hers, from chest to ankle. The delicious fullness of her breasts, her hard nipples, the softness of her belly, the sweet mound of her cunny, the curves of her legs—they were fitted together everywhere. Perfectly.

Their kiss deepened. Tongues and moans intertwined. Hands roamed. Bodies arched and flexed, accommodating, begging, needing with a desperation that seemed impossible. She had invaded his life for a sennight, and yet, she was all he could think about, see, breathe. She consumed him, and he wanted, in turn, to possess her. He wanted her to never forget the night when a baseborn bastard had given her pleasure.

He would not last much longer. Not now, not with her tongue in his mouth and their bodies almost joined as one. He reached between them, stroking her flesh as he had learned she liked it. She rewarded him with a breathy sigh, a quick puff of air over her lips. His middle finger worked her nub from side to side, readying her.

She jerked against him.

"The time has come, my lady." He kissed her jaw, her ear, her throat. "I am going to enter you. I will take care not to hurt you, but I have never before had a virgin, and I do not know what to—"

Her arms wound around his neck and forced his lips back to hers, silencing him. He surrendered easily, readily, kissing her deeply, notching his cock to her entrance.

"Hush, Duncan. Just take me," she said against his lips.

It was all the encouragement he needed. His fingers did one last sweep of her slick flesh, gathering her dew to stroke over his cock. And then he was poised at the center of her. His mouth took hers, tongue delving deep. With an agonizing slowness, he settled the tip of his cock inside her. Testing. Waiting. He had never been more terrified of hurting another in all his life.

Her hips moved. Her muscles clenched, bring him deeper. Inch by inch, he entered her. Laboring over it, loving it, savoring every moment of her hot, slick channel swallowing his prick. *Yes,* sighed every part of him. His hips rolled, and he sank inside her a bit more. *Yes.* His kisses never wavered as he sank his tongue deep and thrust his cock inside her another infinitesimal increment. *Yes.* Kiss. *Yes.* Thrust. *Christ, yes.*

She was so tight, so small, engulfing him, claiming him. The squeeze of her internal muscles surprised him. So tough and yet so willing to give, much like the lady herself. One more thrust, and he felt the barrier give. Her maidenhead was gone.

Gasps stole through the silence of the chamber, his and hers intertwined.

He stilled, fearing he had caused her pain. Dropped a gentle kiss on her lips before raising his head, his gaze locked on hers. "Have I hurt you, darling?"

Tears glistened in her luminous eyes, unshed. She caressed his face with more care than anyone had ever shown him. "You could never hurt me, Duncan."

Her trust in him was misplaced, but it nevertheless made a hot, stinging burst of gratitude crack open in his chest. The sweetness of her touch undid him. Her surrender, her acceptance, the offering of her body and innocence, all into his care...it was immense. Bigger than he was. He kissed the corners of her eyes, setting the tears free with his lips, licking the salt of her so that this, too, he could forever keep.

He whispered her name as he moved his hips. Reaching between them, he found her bud, stroking. She responded with a mewl, a tip of her hips. Her muscles grasped him harder, drawing him in, her body welcoming him. Her mouth opened for him. Her tongue dueled with his. She moved beneath him in instinctive rhythm, taking him deeper. Deeper. Deeper.

And he went with her, moving slowly, claiming her with as much tenderness as he could manage. Until he was fully sheathed inside her, and she was so warm and slick and constricting. He moved, just a tentative glide out then in, and she cried out. He worked her pearl relentlessly.

Their mouths fused as their bodies joined. Words abandoned him, and so he spoke to her with his kisses, with the leashed savagery of his desire for her. With each stroke, he worshipped her. She stiffened beneath him, and he swallowed her cries as the next wave of release rushed over her. Her cunny tightened with such sudden force he nearly spent inside her. He had never wanted another woman the way he wanted Lady Frederica Isling.

He moved faster, made his shallow thrusts deeper, and with a low moan of his own, withdrew from her, clenching his cock in his hand as his release hit him. Thick white spurts landed in the bedclothes alongside her as he came so hard his head thundered.

Duncan fell to his back alongside her, heart pounding as his wits returned in gradual stages. *Sweet Christ*, he had just taken his first maidenhead, and not just any maidenhead but *hers*. Frederica's virgin blood was smeared on his cock like an accusation, marking him. A sickening realization dawned.

She had been wrong.

He could hurt her.

And, inevitably, he would.

CHAPTER 13

*S*he was ruined.

How odd, for she did not feel ruined. Indeed, save for the soreness between her thighs and the lingering warmth pervading her body as she attempted to restore her wardrobe to some semblance of order, precious little evidence of her fall from grace remained.

The secret, for now, belonged to her and Duncan alone.

As if her heart had conjured his touch, his arms wrapped about her waist from behind, hauling her back against his firm chest as if he longed to forever keep her there. Her heart ached as he pressed a reverent kiss to her nape, and then another to her ear.

"How do you feel, my lady?" he asked, his warm breath brushing the shell of her ear and sending a trill down her spine.

She allowed herself the luxury of covering his bare hands with hers, her head falling back to rest on his shoulder. In the aftermath of their lovemaking, he had exhibited such exquisite concern for her wellbeing. He had tended to her with a cloth and water, softly cleansing her aching flesh before once more settling his mouth upon her. His tongue had played over her overstimulated sex, and it had not been long before her body was taken once more by beautiful oblivion. She had shuddered beneath him and had fallen briefly asleep in the safe cocoon of his arms.

But all too soon, reality had intruded, and he had roused her with a chaste kiss. She dressed with a heavy heart, not for what she had done, but for the knowledge she would never again see Duncan Kirkwood. Never again know his touch, his lips, or the delicious weight of his body atop hers.

"I am well," she forced herself to answer him at last, attempting a smile she did not feel.

For how could she carry on with her life, knowing she could never again see him? How could she pretend saying goodbye to him forever would not split her heart in two?

He kissed her throat, pressing his nose to her skin and inhaling as if he, too, was beset by the same painful musings. As if he was memorizing her scent for when she would be gone, nothing more than a ghost who had flitted into and then out of his life for one charmed sennight.

"Regrets?" he asked, his lips grazing her as he spoke.

That we can only ever be together once.

But she did not dare speak the thought. Did not dare to say the words aloud. She swallowed against a sudden, unwanted rush of tears. "None."

Except giving you my heart.

For she understood as she stood there in the warm glow of his chamber, surrounded by him, his body a hard, protective wall at her back, her body still humming with his possession, his arms around her, his mouth on her skin, that she had fallen in love with him. She had fallen in love with Duncan Kirkwood, a man who was not just unsuitable for her in the eyes of society but one who should be shunned. He was a man she was never meant to know, and yet, having known him—truly *known* him—she could see the sad hypocrisy of the world she inhabited for the first time.

She had begun her time at The Duke's Bastard thinking to write a novel that would condemn men like Duncan Kirkwood, and she was ending it knowing there was no story she could write save the truth. The baron was not the hero at all but the villain. He was not the victim of a cruel gaming hell owner. He was a slave to his own greed. And, like Duncan's father had done to him, the baron would turn his back on his duty to those he should have protected. The baron would earn his silence.

And Frederica...she would never forget the man who had changed her forever.

Duncan kissed her neck, then her cheek. After the wild passion and unimaginable intimacies they had shared, something about his lips on her in such a chaste kiss felt like a confession from him. Or at least the only sort of confession a man like Duncan could willingly give. It occurred to her then how little she knew of him. Just small fragments, tiny pieces, jagged shards to explain the man he had become.

"Thank you, my lady," he said, his voice a low, beloved rumble. "You entrusted me with the greatest gift anyone has ever given me."

She closed her eyes against the fresh sting of tears. No matter what happened after they left this chamber, they would always have this stolen time together. They would always have the remembrance of the night when she had been Frederica and he had been Duncan, and together, they had been perfect.

"It is yours. I am...a part of me shall always be yours, Duncan," she returned when she was certain she could speak without a tremor in her voice to give her away.

"Do you promise?" There was something in his voice—a hardness, the gritty texture of desperation.

"Of course."

She would have said more, but for the sudden, abrupt rapping on the door. She jumped, jarred from the intensity of the moment to cruel reality. Somehow, she had allowed herself to become so overwhelmed by their idyll that she had not expected the outside world to intrude so soon. But she supposed she ought not to be so surprised, for his club was akin to a living, breathing beast. It needed constant tending.

He stiffened, his arms tightening around her, almost protectively.

"Kirkwood!"

The voice burst through their insulated world, disturbing the last, fleeting moments of their time together. But it wasn't the interruption itself that made Frederica's heart thump with painful intensity in her breast. Rather, it was recognition.

She knew that voice.

Her brother's voice.

"Kirkwood, you lowly miscreant, I demand you open this door at once."

Duncan's hold on her tightened. Behind her, his body too stiffened. "Damn it to hell," he muttered.

Though her entire purpose in attending the masque this evening and in slipping away to Duncan's private chamber with him, allowing him to take her to bed, had been nothing but intentional—a decision she had made the moment she had first laid eyes on those curst lilies from Willingham—shock still claimed her. She had not expected anyone to discover her actions. Indeed, she had relied upon the fact that she alone would hold all the answers when it came to the extent of her downfall. Her plan had been to confront her father with the suggestion she was ruined, to reveal to him the various occasions upon which she had infiltrated The Duke's Bastard.

She had been hoping he might see reason at that point. That he would agree she had been compromised beyond all reason, and that she must necessarily withdraw from the marriage mart. She would not be forced to marry the earl, and she would decide where her lift would next take her.

But she understood, as her brother began pummeling the door separating herself and Duncan from the outside world, that her creative mind had perhaps taken liberties. That there would be no graceful means by which she could either extricate or redeem herself from this mess.

Perhaps there was a small chance he did not know she was within…

"What have you done with her, you cravenly bastard? I will break down this door if I must." Her brother's angry snarl, almost unrecognizable for the angry vehemence of his tone, dismissed that false hope instantly.

Somehow, Benedict knew she was there. He was deliberately avoiding calling her by name in an effort to salvage what remained of her reputation.

Duncan kissed her cheek once more. "I am sorry, angel. So very sorry."

Then his arms slid away from her, his strength and solidity leaving. She was bereft. Alone. Impossibly cold. She turned to face him, hugging her middle, watching warily as he strode to the door. Why had he apologized?

* * *

WHY THE HELL had Hazlitt set the Marquess of Blanden upon him so soon?

Duncan reached the door to the sound of her brother's irate pounding and escalating threats. He had not yet been ready to say his farewell to her. To let her go. And now, he had no choice.

He must.

With the sinking weight of sick dread in his gut, he unlatched the door. Blanden stood in the hall, fist raised for another round of furious knocking. He hardened his expression, banishing all emotion, all thoughts, save one: his mother's broken body. He could do this for her. He *owed* her this.

"Ah," he drawled. "The real Blanden has arrived at last."

"There is no other," the marquess snapped, rudely attempting to shove Duncan out of the doorway.

He held firm. He was taller, broader, stronger, and a hell of a lot more determined than his lordship. "I do beg your pardon, my lord, for there has indeed been another Marquess of Blanden here at my club nearly every evening for the last sennight. Though he claimed to be you, I saw through his ruse instantly."

"Are you mad or soused, Kirkwood?" Blanden demanded, his tone sizzling with rancor. "I fail to follow your lunatic ravings."

"Neither, more's the pity." He sneered, looking over the marquess's shoulder to where Hazlitt stood sentry.

His man of business's countenance was grim and disapproving. Duncan gave him a nod, indicating he could leave his post. The marquess, in addition to being boring as a stick, was as weak as a stripling. Duncan would mercilessly crush him in any match of fisticuffs. Hazlitt gave him a meaningful look before bowing and silently departing.

"I demand entrance to this chamber at once," the marquess was ordering.

"Benedict, you must calm yourself." The quiet, husky voice—the voice that had not long ago wept his name with pleasure—interrupted the impasse. She drew alongside him, pressing a hand to his coat sleeve, her gaze on his part beseeching, part questioning.

Her eyes slayed him. She was so damned beautiful, a

black-haired angel he could not keep. He was not a man given to sentiment, but in that moment, something inside him, a fragile piece of himself he had not realized yet existed, broke into ten thousand tiny, splintered fragments.

He wanted to reassure her. To tell her all could be explained. But he could not lie. Could not bear to hurt her any more than he already would.

"Explain what you are doing here, my lady," growled Blanden, attempting once more to launch himself into the chamber.

Duncan deflected him with ease, his eyes only for Frederica. "Your faith in me was your downfall, my lady," he warned softly.

"Duncan." She gripped him harder, tears swimming in the brilliant depths of her gaze, as if she were drowning in the sea and he was the last bit of flotsam to which she could cling. "What is the meaning of this?"

He shook his head. He was not her flotsam. He was not her anything, except for the first man who had known her. Gritting his teeth against the knowledge he was her first but another would be her last, he tamped down the bile and forced himself to speak.

"I arranged for his lordship to be informed of your whereabouts. He has come, I would gather, to take you home where you belong." Coldly, Duncan turned back to the marquess. "Is that not accurate, Blanden?"

"What the devil is she doing here with you?" His lordship once more threw himself at Duncan with a violent savagery that took him by surprise. "If you have harmed my sister, I will challenge you to pistols at dawn."

"Ah." He forced his lips to stretch into a wolfish grin, one that was unrepentant. One that said more than his word possibly could. "I did not hurt her. Did I, m'lady?"

He turned back to Frederica, who looked stricken. The

expression on her face was akin to a booted foot to the gut. "Of course you did not hurt me. Not yet."

She was intelligent, his angel. It was one of the many traits he admired about her. Her boldness, her unassailable curiosity, her determination, her fearlessness. Her mind. He had read the manuscript page she had left behind in his office, a treasure he could not bear to forfeit. Her talent was undeniable.

She knew now what was about to unfold. He could read the devastated acceptance in her eyes. In her voice.

"Not yet," he agreed softly, regret slithering through him like a deadly serpent. He turned back to the marquess, whose complexion had gone mottled and red in his outrage. "You may enter now, my lord, but only if you promise to behave. I will not have upset or violence in my club."

Blanden's lip curled. "Your club will be a smoking waste-land of ash and greed by the time I am finished with you, Kirkwood."

"You will eat those words, Blanden," he promised with deadly menace, stepping away from the threshold and away from Frederica, too, as if she was not everything he craved, everything he wanted and needed. As if she was not necessary to him.

Blanden stormed into the chamber, slamming the door at his back, stalking toward Duncan. Duncan recognized himself in the marquess in that moment: bitter, angry, needing to draw blood.

"Benedict, please." Frederica rushed forward, grabbing her brother's arm and staying him when he would have been foolish enough to continue forward, intent upon delivering a blow, Duncan had no doubt. "I beg you, do not make this untenable situation any more difficult than it already is."

He hated himself for the hitch in her voice, almost unde-tectable. Caused by him.

"You will accomplish nothing with fists, Blanden." He adopted a cool air he little felt, making himself recall what he truly wanted, more than anything. What he had almost lost sight of, so caught up in her. It was not Frederica's soft skin or supple lips or the perfect way her body gripped and welcomed his. It was not anything he felt for her. Not stolen kisses or him on his knees, worshipping her as she deserved. It was none of those things.

It was avenging his mother.

The way she had looked that awful day returned to him: bruises on her neck, the broken, awkward splaying of her limbs. He would always wonder how painful her end had been. How many times had she been hurt before the last time? His mother had suffered to give him the best life she could afford, and how was he repaying her? By losing his head over the means by which he could at long last procure vengeance?

Nay. He could not grow weak now. Not with the promise of revenge in clear, beguiling sight.

"I will accomplish splitting open your smug face." Frederica's brother shook her off and stalked forward, nostrils flared, dark eyes almost obsidian. He resembled nothing so much as a bull on the rampage. "That will be enough."

Lord Blanden did not seem the sort who would pull a blade or a pistol from his coat, but one could never be too certain. Duncan had once been shot by a man old enough to be his grandfather whilst at the green baize. He still bore the scar and the memory that anyone—regardless of how harmless he or she may seem—was a danger to him.

Either way, he was not afraid of the marquess and dodged the young lord with ease. "I do not recommend causing harm to my person in any fashion, my lord, as you will not like the consequences. As it is, I already have enough damning information to destroy your sister. I would hate to have to not only reveal everything I know, but to beat you to within an inch of your life as well."

The marquess roared, but Duncan's words did have a staying effect upon him. As did Frederica, who rushed forward once more, placing a calming hand upon her brother's arm. Mere minutes ago, Duncan had been the recipient of that calming touch, and she had stood by his side. Here was a visceral, brutal reminder of the changing of allegiance between them. In this war, he stood on one side, and she would necessarily stand on the other.

"I beg of you, Benedict, stop this madness," she said with quiet persistence. "I alone am at fault for what has transpired here, and I will not have you suffering for my sins."

"Do you not wish to know who the pretender is, my lord?" he forced himself to ask. "Are you not curious about the identity of the other Lord Blanden, the one who has been present here at my club, alone with me? The Lord Blanden I have personally escorted to the scarlet chamber?"

Frederica's gaze swung back to Duncan, and he could not help but note the lone tear that had trickled down her cheek. The cheek he had kissed not long ago. "He is speaking of me, Benedict. I...I found some of your old coats, breeches, and shoes. I disguised myself as a gentleman and pretended to be you so I could gain entrance here."

"Damn it, Frederica!" Blanden's voice cracked like a whip, echoing in the chamber. "Why would you do such a witless thing?"

"I was conducting research for *The Silent Baron*." Her voice sounded small. Laden with regret.

Duncan hated himself more than he ever had.

"Father forbade you from writing that claptrap, Frederica."

The marquess's pronouncement, issued in such a snide, dismissive tone, had Duncan starting forward rethinking his intentions to avoid bloodying the whelp's nose. "You will apologize to the lady, or *I* will take great delight in splitting open *your* face."

Blanden's eyes shot back to Duncan. "You dare to threaten me after you issue threats of ruining my sister and had her cloistered here in your chamber against her will? You have gall Kirkwood. Do you truly think you can ruin the daughter to the Duke of Westlake without repercussions? One word from me, and every last one of your patrons would desert your black hide. Have no fear of that."

Duncan was not frightened of the blustering of one arrogant lord. He took another step forward, challenging Blanden. He grinned. "On the contrary, my lord. One word from you, and everyone will know your sister has lost her innocence to me. Is that what you truly wish?"

Frederica rushed between them, her skirts rustling. The scent of violets assailed him. *Hell*, he could even taste her. She had been so responsive, all silken heat, all for him. He could have her a hundred thousand times and it would never be enough. But Lady Frederica Isling and his inconvenient, irrefutable attraction to her was not what this moment was about.

Rather, this moment was about vengeance.

It was about at long last delivering the death knell to the man whose indifference and cruelty had left Duncan and his mother to the miserable fate awaiting them, nary a backward glance. That was the thing about power and wealth, those who possessed it easily forgot how temporary it was, how quickly they could lose it. One card game. One poor investment. One night of wagers.

He had seen men gain and lose fortunes in hours.

No one knew better than Duncan just how much could be lost in the span of hours, minutes, seconds. Everything. Everything could be lost. He had lost his mother in much the same manner. Sent off for a bun, a pat on the head before he left. Returned to a corpse. Less than half-an-hour between his mother, rosy-cheeked with life and his mother, cold and dead on the floor.

"Please Duncan, do not do whatever it is you are intent upon doing," Frederica implored. Her gaze searched his.

Duncan ground his jaw. "He has yet to offer you his apology."

"You cannot order me about, Kirkwood," the marquess spat.

He opened and closed his fists, testing his knuckles. A great deal of time had passed since he had last engaged in boxing, but he would gladly do so again if it meant getting the apology Frederica deserved. "You will apologize for dismissing Lady Frederica's novel, or I will bloody your nose."

"Do not dare to tell me how to speak, you gutter-born mongrel." The marquess snapped back, fearless.

The stupid sod ought to have known he had arrived at a duel where he would be outgunned and overpowered, left bleeding in the dirt. And yet, he continued on. Ignoring Frederica's wild eyes and flailing hands, he grabbed Blanden's cravat, giving it a threatening yank, uncaring she stood between them, a wide eyed human wall attempting to keep her brother and her lover from decimating each other.

He made certain the marquess was meeting his gaze. "Apologize to your sister, my lord. As it is, I have precious little patience for you, given you are nothing more than a means to a desired end. Test me once more, and I cannot promise you will leave here with all your teeth."

"Duncan, please!" Lady Frederica's soft admonishment roused him from the bloodlust that had begun consuming him. For a moment, he had been thrown back to the days where he had fought and bled for his survival. When it had been an eye for an eye, a tooth for a tooth. "Do not hurt him, I beg you."

What could he do in the face of her gentle pleading on her brother's behalf? She knew he could decimate the marquess just as well as he did. Grinding his jaw, Duncan took a step in retreat, putting some space between himself, Frederica, and Lord Blanden. He had to calm himself, focus on the old prize he sought rather than the new, forbidden one he longed for.

"As you wish, my lady," he conceded. But his eyes remained trained upon her brother. This was not over.

"What do you want, Kirkwood?" Blanden snarled. "You're the greediest bastard in all London, and everyone knows it. What is it you are after? More coin for your purse?"

Ah, here it was. The moment of truth.

He looked back at Frederica's pale face, taking in her pinched lips, betrayed eyes, and undeniable beauty. One last time, to remember her. How could he forget? And then, he flicked his gaze back to her brother before the urge to grovel at her feet and forego all chances of revenge overcame him.

"Your father has something I want very much," he said. "Being a magnanimous man, I am willing to trade him for it —he gives me all the Duke of Amberley's vowels, and in return, I will keep silent about all the nights I spent alone with Lady Frederica, thoroughly debauching her whilst you and the duke and duchess were blissfully unaware." He paused, self-loathing threatening to consume him, before he forced himself to say one last, devastating thing. "I will also promise never to reveal to anyone that I took her innocence this evening in this chamber."

He did not want to look at Frederica after the final word. But how could he not? Silent tears of betrayal ran down her cheeks. Her gaze was riveted upon him. Shocked. Accusatory. Hurt. He told himself he was doing what he must. Men like him had nothing to offer the sheltered daughter of a duke. And what her father held in his possession was priceless. She had gotten what she wished—her night of passion—and he would gain the Duke of Amberley on his knees.

The tradeoff was bitter, but it was all he had. All he could have.

"You are a true bastard," Blanden snarled.

Frederica made a sound, as if a sob were trapped in her throat. A knife in his belly, gutting him, would not have hurt more.

Duncan forced a cool smile to his lips, keeping his eyes trained upon the marquess now, lest he falter. "By nature *and* definition both, my lord. I shall call upon His Grace tomorrow at three o'clock. I trust you will make certain he is prepared to receive me?"

"Go to hell, Kirkwood," the marquess bit out.

"I will interpret that as acquiescence. There is a discreet, rear exit. I will see that Hazlitt escorts you and her ladyship to it, and that your carriage will await you there. Leave this chamber in precisely five minutes and not a moment sooner." Duncan bowed. "Good evening, my lord. My lady."

He fled the chamber to the remembrance of her earlier words, echoing in his mind, mocking him. Haunting him.

You could never hurt me, Duncan.

How wrong she had been. How wrong they had both been.

CHAPTER 14

"What have you done, Frederica?"

She had given herself to a man who had not truly wanted her. That was what she had done. She had fallen in love with a chimera. She had given her heart and her body to him. To a god among men.

And then the god had turned to stone, proving he was a mere mortal after all. Proving he was not at all who she had thought him to be, but that he was instead a heartless sinner.

Had everything between them been a lie? Every word, every touch, every tenderness he had shown her? The pleasure? The things he had done to her...had he even enjoyed it, or had he been so determined to gain the Duke of Amberley's vowels from her father that he had been willing to endure anything?

Even the shameful attentions of a wanton wallflower.

How mortifying. Her heart was broken, and her pride was more battered than a bonnet lost in the street, trampled by dozens of carriages and horses before it was retrieved. The muscle in question gave a great, painful pang. More like one thousand carriages, she acknowledged.

Her pride would heal. Even a trodden bonnet could be restored to rights by a deft hand. But a broken heart? Those were not mended. She had no doubt hers would never be. He had betrayed her, and it was the most painful wound she had ever received. As a girl, she had broken her finger, and that pain had been nothing like this, the awful knowledge he had manipulated and used her to gain what he wanted.

"How did you know where to find me?" she could not resist asking, even if she feared the response.

"Hazlitt found me and informed me." Benedict scowled. "It was all plotted beforehand, of that I have nary a doubt."

Was it?

Duncan had stopped on their way to his chamber, going to Mr. Hazlitt for a hasty, private word. Was that when he had given his instructions? It had to have been. Her heart fell to her feet, and then it fell to the bottom of the deepest pit buried beneath the sea immediately thereafter. It was so far gone, so removed from her body, she would never again be plagued by its disturbing capacity to feel. She was certain of it.

"Frederica? How did you find yourself in such a den of vipers?"

Her brother's angry voice cut through her despondent musings once more. His words unwittingly reflected Leonora's cautious denunciations. Mayhap she should have heeded the warnings of her best friend.

She inhaled deeply, weighing her words and her confession both. "With Father gone to the country, I had a rare freedom of motion. Mother is...Mother. She scarcely notices I am her daughter because I am not a fan or a pretty new gewgaw she can acquire. I found your belongings in a trunk, and they fit well enough. I-it seemed providential."

Dear heavens, how she hated the hitch in her voice. The glaring evidence of the tears she was doing her best to avoid shedding. She would cry, that she knew, and it would be a soul-deep weeping, the ugly, raw sort that would leave her with hiccups, swollen eyes, and a red nose. The sorrow invading her chest like a contagion as they gently swayed through London would not be denied. But neither would she break down in the company of her forbidding brother. She would wait until she was alone and the silence was unbearable, and then she would fill it instead with the bitter sounds of her agony.

"Your discovery of my outgrown, outmoded waistcoats seemed providential?" Benedict thundered. "Damn your foolish hide, Frederica. How did you imagine, even for a moment, that you could enter a gentleman's club dressed as a man—aping *me*, no less—and go undetected? One must pass through three locked doors and a forbidding manservant just to gain entrance. If you had been caught at any step..." his words trailed off as he shuddered.

"But I was caught," she pointed out, swallowing down the knot in her throat this reminder produced. "By Mr. Kirkwood. He knew at once I was a female."

"As would a blind man," her brother snapped. "Of course Kirkwood saw through your flimsy disguise and, swine that he is, instantly cooked up a plot to gain what he desired most, regardless of the cost."

Had he? Cold acceptance settled over her, so visceral and shocking her stomach clenched. It would certainly seem he had. She recalled now the missive she had seen upon Duncan's desk bearing her father's name. Had he already written to her father with his demands then?

But if he had, why would he have orchestrated what had happened between them this evening? And even if he had done, how could he have been so certain she would not only attend his masque but also ask him to ruin her? Nothing made sense. Not the sweetness of his touch and the beauty of

his lovemaking, and certainly not his cold, unflinching countenance afterward as he had laid bare all her secrets without
a care.

"He did not..." she paused, struggling to gather her
rioting thoughts. "Mr. Kirkwood did not plot anything,
Benedict. I had to beg him for future entrée to his club, and
even then, he allowed for no more than three additional
visits."

"I am certain one would have sufficed," her brother
clipped, his tone frigid. "If he allowed more, it was merely to
obtain additional weaponry in his assault against our family.
Weaponry which you amply provided him with this evening,
my lady."

She closed her eyes against the sight of her brother, so icy,
detached, and disgusted with her. Perhaps she deserved his
disgust, his censure. She had knowingly and willingly ruined
herself this evening, and it did not matter if Duncan had
deceived and manipulated her to gain the revenge he sought;
against the man who had fathered him. No one—not a single
person in London—would pardon Frederica's sins. Not even
her own flesh and blood. Especially not them, she realized as
she opened her eyes once more to study her brother's grim
countenance.

He had already judged her. His disgust for her was palpable, permeating the air of the carriage with a familiar sense
of dread. She did not require his approval, but a part of her
nevertheless wished for his understanding, if nothing else.

"You may believe what you wish of me, Benedict." Her
agitated fingers, yet ungloved, twisted in her skirts. "But I
entered into my sins willingly, knowing exactly what I was
doing."

Benedict paled. "It would have been better if he had
ravished you."

His lack of concern for her wellbeing appalled her,

though she knew she ought not to be surprised. She was not cut from the same cloth as her family, and never had that sad truth been more apparent than now. "For whom? Surely you would not wish for your sister to be taken by force."

Her brother's dark gaze glittered, his lips compressing. His tone was cruel, lashing. "I would rather my sister be ravished than know she willingly played the whore for Duncan Kirkwood. You are all but betrothed to the earl. How could you have done something so heedless and selfish?"

She flinched beneath his stinging scorn and the knowledge he would rather her be taken against her will, if it meant preserving his own pride. Had he ever cared for her at all? They had never been close as some siblings were, but neither had she supposed Benedict loathed her as he must.

"I do not wish to marry Lord Willingham," she said baldly. "He is a cold and unctuous man. If anyone were to ravish me, it would be his lordship and not Mr. Kirkwood."

Of that, if nothing else, she was certain. Duncan, at least, had been tender and gentle. He had made her body and her heart sing with his reverent touches and kisses. Willingham made bile climb in her throat. His touch was meant to incite fear rather than pleasure, and he enjoyed the knowledge of the hurt he inflicted. She had seen the malice in his eyes. There was no mistaking it.

"You do not know of what you speak," Benedict said dismissively. "The earl is a gentleman, the legitimate heir to a duchy. Kirkwood is a baseborn bastard with a doxy mother who thinks he can ape his betters and become one. You have allowed your foolishness to distort the manner in which you view him, but allow me to assure you that Duncan Kirkwood is not a gentleman. There is no good in him. He ill uses all the lightskirts at his club. You are no different to him, Frederica. Is that what you would become? Another harlot in dampened skirts, plying her wares for Kirkwood and the lords who line his pockets?"

Her brother's venomous diatribe had its intended effect, piercing sensitive parts of her she would have preferred to remain unscathed. Something inside Frederica toppled and fell. The last thread of hope she'd been clinging to snapped as she thought of Tabitha, the lovely golden goddess who had seemed to wear her heart on her sleeve for Duncan. Had he bedded her as well? Was Frederica one in a sea of so many, each with her purpose, used and then set adrift?

But she refused to reveal her doubts or concerns to her brother. This evening had proven to her, beyond a doubt, where his loyalties lay, and they were most assuredly not with her. Indeed, in that moment, ruined, abandoned, and denounced by her own brother, Frederica could not help but feel no one else in all the world was loyal to her.

Not her brother who detested her.

Not Father or Mother who found her a burden they could not wait to rid themselves of.

Not dear Leonora, who would have her conform to society's strictures.

Not Duncan, who had traded her for the fires of revenge burning bright within him.

No one.

But she still had herself. She had always had herself, and that would suffice. She raised her chin, pinning her brother with a cold stare. "The Earl of Willingham has forced kisses upon me. He has left finger marks upon my arms, along with the promise I shall endure more and learn to enjoy it as his wife. Forgive me, brother, if ruining myself seemed a more preferable option."

Benedict returned her stare. "I know Willingham, Frederica. He would never ill use a woman. I do not believe he hurt you. He is not capable of it. The earl is a prince among men, and a man I am honored to call a friend. You could ask for none better."

None better? Surely he was jesting.

Frederica searched her brother's countenance and his gaze both, and that was when she knew with heart-sinking certainty. Benedict was aware of Willingham's penchant for cruelty. Nothing she had said surprised him in the least. But he would rather her marry a man who would deliver her physical harm than ruin her reputation with a man who had been born a plain mister.

She inhaled deeply, wishing she could not still smell the lingering scent of Duncan upon her, haunting her like a ghost she could not escape. "None better," she repeated bitterly. "If that is what you truly believe, then heaven help you."

"No." Her brother's jaw tensed, harsh and angular and angry. "Heaven help you, dear sister. For you shall need it after this night. I fear not even the intervention of a band of angels would aid you."

She swallowed against a fresh rising tide of bile. It was not a band of angels she wanted as the carriage lumbered homeward, taking her to her fate. It was Duncan Kirkwood's reassuring embrace. His lips on hers. His hands caressing her body. The worship and reverence in his expression.

His apology returned to her.

I am sorry, angel. So very sorry.

Yes, and so was she. So very, very sorry.

The carriage creaked on, carrying her to her fate.

* * *

DUNCAN CALLED upon the Duke of Westlake's residence at three o'clock in the afternoon. He gave his card to a stone-faced butler and waited in the antechamber, his mind flitting to Frederica. Was she somewhere within the same edifice? And then he shook the unwanted question from his mind, for it did not matter whether or not she was. His ties to her would necessarily be severed after this visit to her darling Papa.

His body went cold, a fine sheen of perspiration breaking out on his brow. He told himself it had nothing to do with the notion of cutting her out of his life forever. He told himself he never again needed to see her midnight hair, her pink lips, her lush hips, the petals of her sex…

Bloody, brimming hellfire. Last night, she had given herself to him. He was not proud of his weakness where she was concerned, a vulnerability that seemed to overrule everything. He swallowed. After today, this whirlwind, tumultuous infatuation would be over.

Because today, he would betray her.

For his mother, he reminded himself sternly. And if all went according to plan, Frederica would never be hurt. Her innocence and her reputation would never be called into question. It was small comfort, but all he had to grasp.

Recalling the final sight of her pale, beautiful face, stricken and etched with naked hurt, made his fists clench at his sides and his jaw clamp down so hard his teeth ached. She had seemed so sad and alone, far from the daring minx who had infiltrated his club and kissed him with abandon.

At last, the butler returned, inviting Duncan to follow his lead. Down a hall, past two doors, stopping at the third. A fine thing it was, to be welcomed, albeit reluctantly, in the home of a duke. Whilst he was good friends with the Duke of Whitley, not even Cris had invited Duncan to sup at his table. The butler stood at the threshold, announcing Duncan as if he were the bearer of an august title rather than plain old Mr. Duncan Kirkwood.

He entered the spacious chamber. The door closed with a barely audible click.

Westlake stood, tall, gray-haired, and forbidding. He bore an aura of one who did not appreciate levity, his brows low over his eyes, mouth a thin, tight line of disapproval.

"Kirkwood." He did not bow.

Duncan did, determined to exact his revenge in the most gentlemanly fashion possible. He had no doubt the duke expected him to be a crude, filthy-tongued scoundrel. And though he felt like the lowliest of creatures for the sins he was about to commit against Lady Frederica, he would not be cowed by her father.

His actions had been necessary, he reminded himself, both for the lady and for himself. He had provided the means by which she could avoid a hateful union, and she was the means by which he would finally have his retribution against the soulless bastard who had sired him.

With great effort, he kept his expression carefully composed. "Your Grace. I trust Lord Blanden alerted you of the necessity of this meeting," he said with a coolness he did not feel.

"Indeed, my son has regretfully informed me of your egregious conduct." His lip curled. "I ought to call you out, you ignorant puppy."

He did not flinch, for he had prepared himself for any outcome, and there was not a word Westlake could utter or an action he could take that would surprise Duncan. "Then do so, Your Grace."

"You know I shall not in an effort to salvage what I may of Lady Frederica's reputation." The duke's tone was frigid, his disgust for Duncan palpable.

In that moment, he could not blame him, though he harbored a disgust all his own for a father who would force his daughter to wed any scoundrel with a title so he could be rid of her. But he had come for a purpose, and it was not to berate the Duke of Westlake. It was to get what he had wanted. To hold in his hand the power to lay Amberley low.

If he closed his eyes, he could still see the bruises on his mother's throat, her dead eyes. Yes, he knew what he must do.

"I am prepared to ruin her." He issued the threat with great difficulty.

Westlake's expression pinched. "How much for your silence?"

He did not hesitate, for he had envisioned this confrontation, too. Had practiced what he would say, had known what he would ask for. He was a gambler at heart, and he excelled at bluffing. "Ten thousand pounds and the Duke of Amberley's debts."

"You are mad," Westlake snapped. "That is a fortune and you know it, Kirkwood."

Indeed, it was, which was why it was also his initial offer. He remained calm, raising a brow. "One would think a father would pay a fortune to maintain his daughter's reputation."

"A fortune hunter would think so." Westlake pinned him with an assessing green stare, and though his eyes were the same deep hue as Frederica's, they were cold and hard. "Is that not what you are, Kirkwood? A duke's bastard who has somehow wagered his way into fleecing the finer portion of London?"

"I am a man who has forged his own path in the world," he said calmly, though inside he seethed. He was accustomed to lords looking down their supercilious noses at him. More than accustomed to men who believed in their superiority by the mere virtue of their birth and no other reason. But that did not mean he accepted it or tolerated it well.

"How many other peers' daughters have you ruined, Kirkwood, in your quest for revenge?" Westlake dared to ask.

Duncan's fists clenched, but he took great care to keep his face devoid of any emotion. "None, Your Grace. But then, no other daughters have repeatedly forced their way into my club, dressed as gentlemen, without the knowledge of their families."

He could not resist the last jibe, though after it left his lips, he instantly regretted it, for it would likely only make her father even angrier with Frederica than he already was. Duncan cursed himself for his rashness, his quick temper, his fool tongue. The last thing he wished to do was cause her any hurt or any more trouble.

"You could have turned her away, Kirkwood," Westlake pointed out, his tone biting. "There was no need for you to ruin her, save to gain what you wished."

The duke was correct in his assertion, but he was also wrong. Yes, Duncan could have turned her way. But from the moment he had first seen her, his need for her, his raw, base want had been inevitable and undeniable. However, she had fast become far more to him than the sum of her loveliness and her luscious body's ability to bring him pleasure. Far more than her ability to bring him, quite literally, to his knees.

Could he have gained his revenge, the possession of Amberley's vowels, without ruining Frederica? It was entirely possible. Duncan had been prepared to pay handsomely. He had intended to use the possibility of her ruination as a means of bargaining rather than her actual deflowering. He could take no pride in what he had done. She created a weakness in him, the likes of which he had never known.

He stared down Frederica's father, wishing he could impart what he saw in Frederica. Wishing he could make the man see how vital, rare, and wonderful his daughter was. How she possessed a light that should not be doused.

In the end, he could not say anything he wished, for it would do him no favors in garnering what he wanted. Nor would it benefit Frederica in her efforts to obtain her freedom. But perhaps there was something he could do.

"Seven thousand pounds, Amberley's notes, and your promise that Lady Frederica will not be forced into a marriage that is not of her choosing," he said suddenly.

"I propose instead your silence in exchange for mine," the duke returned bitterly. "You will not speak a word concerning Lady Frederica's lapse of judgment, and in return, I will not let it be known that you are a despoiler of innocents, a villain whose club ought to be avoided at all costs."

Ah, there it was. The threat Duncan had anticipated. "I am afraid such a bargain has nothing to offer me." He strode toward the duke with a mocking air calculated to goad, hands behind his back. "Six thousand pounds, Amberley's debts, and your promise concerning Lady Frederica. That is my final offer."

"Damn you, Kirkwood." Westlake slammed his fists on his desk and unlocked a drawer, extracting a tidy pile of vowels. "Amberley is my friend."

"My sympathy, Your Grace," he said, forcing himself to remain cold and unshakeable. "My final offer stands. Accept it, or I shall leave here and wag my tongue all over town. By this afternoon, all London will know that your darling daughter was bedded by the lowly bastard you sneer at now."

"Very well," Westlake said, capitulating, just as Duncan had suspected he would. "Five thousand pounds, the notes, and my promise Frederica shan't be forced into a marriage that is not of her choosing. Are you happy now, Kirkwood? Was ruining an innocent girl worth it?"

He met the duke's gaze, unflinchingly. "No. It decidedly was not."

Duncan left with all Amberley's debts in his hands, five thousand pounds richer, and assured of Frederica's freedom. He left assured of his vengeance, and it was everything he had ever wanted, the culmination of all the hatred and fury burning in his belly from the time he had been but a lad standing over his dead mother.

But the victory was not a cause for celebration, for he had betrayed Lady Frederica by mere virtue of his visit, and he knew it. *Beelzebub*, he felt sick. Not just in his guts but somewhere deeper. In his chest. In his heart. This was not right. Ruining Frederica was wrong. Hades was not meant to leave Persephone behind. He was meant to take her with him, back to his underworld. Duncan could not resist one final glance at the Mayfair residence of the Duke of Westlake as he left, and as he did, he saw her pale face in a window, watching.

Every instinct inside him screamed to go back inside, to demand Frederica in addition to the vowels tucked inside his coat. But he knew he could not. He was not selfish as Hades had been. He would not consign her to his fate. She deserved better than a man who would use her for his own gain. She deserved better than a duke's bastard, a gaming hell owner who daily tread the line between heaven and hell, a man who was more darkness than light.

And so, he turned his back to her, stalked to his brougham, and stepped inside. As it lumbered onto the street, he refused to allow himself to look back a final time. She was gone from his life forever, as she must be.

The documents he had traded for her innocence burned his chest like a brand. For the entirety of the ride to The Duke's Bastard, he choked down the bile rising in his throat. When he reached his club, he stalked past Hazlitt and a host of others, speaking to no one. Not a damned word.

He went to his chamber, the chamber where he had taken her, where he could still smell violets and the musky perfume of their lovemaking from the night before. With not a moment to spare, he found the chamber pot, dropped to his knees, and retched.

CHAPTER 15

$\mathcal{F}$rederica stepped over the threshold of her father's study, back straight, bearing stiff, prepared to accept her fate. A week had passed since the night she had attended the masque at The Duke's Bastard. A week of forced isolation, during which she had not been permitted to leave her chamber. Her writing implements had been taken, as had the pages of her manuscript.

Mother had visited her once, armed with the spoils of her most recent shopping expedition: a dozen new fans. And she had come with an admonishment as well. *You ought not to have made such a grievous mistake, Frederica. His Grace is settling your future now as he must.*

Though she had begged her for more information, Mother had offered her nothing. She had, however, left Frederica the gift of a fan fashioned of bone and silk, embroidered with roses and embellished with spangles. As if the fan would cure her broken heart or soothe the worry gnawing away at her. She would have far preferred her mother's love and reassurance, perhaps some intervention on her behalf, to the fan.

But her mother had given her all she was capable of giving, and Frederica knew it. She had waited in her chamber, trapped in the purgatory of not knowing what would become of her. She had no funds of her own, and nowhere to go, else she would have attempted to run. Fleeing was not the answer to her woes, but she was hopeful her inevitable banishment would be.

She had no doubt Benedict had related the entire, sordid tale to their father, and even if he had not, Duncan would have. From her window, she had watched him departing, inwardly pleading with him to glance her way. As if he had heard her, he had stopped and looked back. And then he had turned away, climbed into his carriage, and disappeared from her life. She had never known such a sickening sense of finality. The cold burst of grief in her breast. The sinking stone of dread.

She felt both now all over again as she approached her father's desk. She felt every bit the prisoner she was, awaiting the reading of her sentence. She could only hope she would not be forced to become a companion for some gouty curmudgeon in the countryside. Anything, she reminded herself, would be preferable to becoming the Countess of Willingham. If nothing else, Duncan Kirkwood had spared her from that fate, and she would always be grateful for it.

She curtseyed to her father, whose countenance looked as if it had been carved from granite. "Your Grace."

"Lady Frederica," he snapped, his expression grim, his voice bearing the crack of a riding crop. "Seat yourself."

Her relationship with her father had always been tepid at best. He was a man who was not easily pleased. His autocratic temperament made any softening of the heart toward him almost impossible. Frederica supposed it was why her mother attempted to bury her unhappiness beneath a mountain of fans.

"Seat yourself," he ordered again, his voice raising and echoing from the decorated plaster of the ceiling.

She sat, her face going hot. For some reason, regardless of how much she aged, standing before her father awaiting her punishment made her feel like a shameful child who had broken the Sèvres and neglected to eat her dinner. "Forgive me, Your Grace."

"You have much for which you need be forgiven." He was cold. Harsh. As unyielding as he had ever been. "How did you dare, my lady?"

She swallowed, held her head high. "I did not wish to enter a loveless marriage with a man who enjoys the suffering of others. I took the action I felt necessary to avoid such a thing."

"The Earl of Willingham is a gentleman. Any lady would be grateful to take your place and become his countess." His voice vibrated with the passion of his conviction.

But of course. To her father, a man's lineage was the indication of his character. He was a duke, and he had made it clear to her in no uncertain terms that he expected her to become a duchess. Marrying her off to Willingham would have achieved such a feat, upon his inheritance of the Amberley duchy.

"You do not know Lord Willingham as I do," she countered calmly. "He is aggressive with his attentions. There is nothing gentle in his conduct, and I find him repugnant."

Her father slammed his fists down, sending a jolt of shock through her. "You will hold your tongue. You will listen to what I have to say. When I have finished my piece, you will thank me for the mercy I have shown you, and you will never again dare to disgrace this family, my lady. Am I understood?"

He was angrier than she had supposed. The fire in his

eyes was undeniable. She wondered if he truly hated her in that moment. "Yes, Your Grace."

"Her Grace has pampered you," he continued. "She has allowed you to run wild because you are her only daughter. No more, Lady Frederica. Henceforth, you will conduct yourself with the dignity and grace befitting a lady of the house of Isling. You will cease your lowly insistence upon writing a novel. You will marry the gentleman of my choosing. You will lead a quiet, respectable life from this moment forward."

His words fell upon her like the weight of an anvil. *You will marry...*

He could not suppose she would still wed anyone, could he? Why, no man would marry her now, not knowing she had willingly lain with another.

...the gentleman of my choosing.

Of his choosing?

Panic swirled as she searched his inscrutable face, the eyes so like her own, the countenance that had never softened with love or pride when he gazed upon her. "I must be sent away, and I am aware of that, Your Grace. I will accept my fate, whatever you have decided it must be. Please believe that it was never my intent to bring shame upon you. I merely wished to achieve my freedom from a hateful marriage."

"Her Grace allowed you to read too many books," her father barked. "I can see that now. A learned woman will always attempt to usurp her betters, foolishly thinking herself superior. It is a trick of the mind, you understand. The wits of a female cannot hold a candle to that of a man. It is simply a part of the laws of God and man."

Her mother had allowed Frederica to read books because she had been too distracted attempting to fill the emptiness in her life with things. Somehow, she had yet to realize that no trinket or bauble—not even a hundred thousand fans—would be her solace.

"It is my belief that a woman is capable of intelligent thought the same as any man," she dared to dissent, even though she knew it foolhardy to do so in such a moment, and when she was powerless and entirely at her father's mercy.

If indeed he possessed such a thing.

"You are wrong, my lady." His lip curled. "One need only look to your reckless actions for proof of that. Fortunately, however, no one need know about your folly. Kirkwood's silence came at a price, but it was easily bought. No one is aware of your indiscretion aside from your brother, and he will certainly not utter a word to damage your reputation."

Disbelief joined the dread churning inside her. Had she heard her father correctly? "But I am ruined, Your Grace."

He raised a brow. "A lady is only ruined if word of her misdeeds spread. If no one is the wiser, who is to say she is ruined at all?"

The dread grew and grew, until it pressed upon her with such force, she feared she would cast up her accounts before her father. All over his desk. *No. No. No.* This was not right. "Surely a lady's husband will discover such a thing on the wedding night."

The smile curling her father's lips was unkind. Triumphant. "By that time, it shall be too late."

"You cannot mean—"

"I have spoken with Lord Willingham," he interrupted. "He is under the impression you have been ill this past sennight, and he sends his regards along with his wish for a swift recovery. However, he is most eager to make you his bride, and I have accepted his offer on your behalf. The two of you shall be married in two months' time."

"No!" The shout emerged from her before she could squelch it, as if her denial of his words would somehow render them unspoken or any less true.

Fear ran through her, swift and fierce. *Dear God*, her father could not have agreed she would wed Willingham after she had been ruined by the earl's illegitimate half brother, the owner of a gaming hell...it was not possible. But as she searched his features, she realized the ugly, awful truth. She had ruined herself to escape an unwanted marriage, and yet she had been too foolish to make certain everyone knew.

She ought to have attended the masque as herself, shouting her name to anyone who asked. Proclaiming her love for Duncan Kirkwood. Making certain the entire assembly watched as she left hand-in-hand with him, as if they were old lovers. She should not have gone quietly with Benedict, who she had supposed would protect her out of a sense of sibling solidarity. She should not have left that chamber at all.

"Yes, my lady," her father said calmly. "You will be wedded to the Earl of Willingham in two months' time. He will be calling upon you tomorrow to take you for a drive. You will be awaiting him, a welcoming smile on your lips. You have disgraced this family enough, and you will not, by God, do so again."

"If I refuse to leave my chamber, what will you do?" Perhaps she possessed more daring than was wise, for the question had fled her lips before she could rethink the wisdom of it. "If I deny his suit? Refuse to marry him?"

"You will find yourself on the street, forced to live your life as the doxy you have become."

One sentence. A handful of words. And they had the impact of a blade, stabbing her straight in the heart. Here before her was a man who had never cared for her. It was brutally apparent. Little wonder her mother sought solace in shopping.

"You would disown me because I refuse the suitor you have chosen for me?" she asked, her voice trembling with emotion she did not dare release. Not now. Not before him. She would not have him see her weak.

"I am doing what is best for you, my lady," he told her coolly. "One day, when you are the Duchess of Amberley, you will offer me your thanks."

She stood. "That day will never come to pass. I bid you good day, Your Grace."

With another halfhearted attempt at a curtsy, she fled.

His ominous warning followed her. "You will accept Willingham tomorrow, and you will be grateful, biddable, and kind."

Frederica did not answer, intent upon her escape.

It was not until she reached the haven of her chamber that her legs gave way and she collapsed to the floor in a heap of skirts and misery. Duncan Kirkwood had exchanged her entire life—her future, her happiness, her wellbeing, *her heart*—for a handful of gambling notes. For as long as she lived, she would never forgive him.

* * *

DUNCAN DID NOT ORDINARILY DRINK himself to oblivion. In fact, his drink of choice was a warm cup of chocolate spiced with anise and a hint of cinnamon. Entirely innocent. Something more suited to an overindulgent, cosseted wife of a lord, he knew. Not the drink of a man who had clawed his way out of the gutters using nothing but his determination, his fists, and his ruthlessness. But at the moment, none of that mattered.

Indeed, nothing at all mattered, for he was drinking his fine Scottish whisky from the bottle as if it were mother's milk. He swallowed down another burning dram, closing his eyes.

But even with his lids lowered on the familiar opulence of his study, he saw her.

The liquor did not make him forget. Frederica was everywhere.

She haunted him like the most vicious wraith. An entire month had passed since he had last seen her pale face lingering in the window at Westlake House. Since he had kissed her. Touched her. Claimed her. Since he had made her his.

Nay, she was not his.

She would never be his, for he had forfeited that right.

He had traded her for the stack of vowels on the desk before him. He blew out a breath of self-loathing and opened his eyes to the sight of Amberley's scrawl on the documents that would leave the duke destitute. He'd possessed them for a month and had yet to do a damn thing about them.

Because obtaining them had not changed him. It had not left him feeling fulfilled or triumphant. Obtaining the I.O.U,s of his wastrel father did not bring back his mother. It did not ameliorate the senseless horror of her murder. Nor did it assuage the guilt that threatened to swallow him whole.

He had taken Lady Frederica Isling's innocence, and though she had offered it to him, he had done so with avarice, using her as a pawn. Betraying her trust to her father. Leaving her behind, a lamb for the slaughter. He had become the man who sired him, driven by his own selfish wants and needs, willing to commit any sin to gain what he desired.

He drained some more of the bottle. The vowels remained, mocking him. Alongside them, he had all the bits of her he had thieved, two pairs of spectacles, a false mustache, three hair pins, and the page from her manuscript. More than once, he had held the foolscap to his nose, hoping for the fleeting scent of violets.

A knock sounded at his door. Likely a servant attempting to bring him supper, and he wanted none. He preferred whisky as his sustenance. Tipping the bottle back, he ignored the interruption.

Another rap came. "Sir," the muffled voice of his butler, Pretty, arrived not long after, splitting the silence. "His Grace the Duke of Whitley is here to see you. He demands admittance."

Cris.

Beelzebub. He did not wish to see his friend just now. "Tell him I am indisposed."

The door flew open, and the duke strode past the hulking, hideous butler. "He will tell me no such thing, you bounder. Christ, you look terrible, Duncan." He paused, raking Duncan with a gaze that saw far too much, he was sure. "Pretty, fetch your master some hot chocolate and a tray of food."

"Er, yes sir." Pretty executed a half bow. "Your Grace, sir."

Having been born in the stews, he had cut his teeth on the life of a pickpocket. One of many Duncan had plucked from a life of misery, Pretty was loyal, diligent, and somewhat uncertain of proper expectations for his position.

Duncan didn't give a goddamn. He had hired a butler not because he required one but because he had wanted to give Pretty a position at which he excelled. A chance to raise himself above the poverty and misery to which he had been born. The chance Duncan himself had never been given.

Cris waited for Pretty to retreat, closing the door behind him, before crossing the chamber to Duncan's desk. He made a clucking sound with his tongue, one more suited to a governess than a duke. "Such a cruel stroke of fate that a man as bracket-faced as he, ought to bear a surname of Pretty."

Duncan took another swig from the bottle, eyeing his friend. The liquor he had consumed made his tongue loose. "Pretty is not his true name."

Cris lowered himself with negligent grace into the chair opposite Duncan's desk. "Knowing you as I do, I ought not to be surprised. But somehow, I am. Tell me, how it is that your butler bears a sobriquet rather than his surname?"

"He hasn't a surname." Duncan raised his bottle toward his friend in a mock toast before dousing himself with another healthy swallow toward oblivion. He swallowed, smacked his lips. "He was born in the rookeries. Never even knew his mother. He has always answered to 'Pretty,' and so Pretty he shall forever be."

"You are the best man I know, my friend."

Duncan shuddered as he swallowed too much whisky at once. His stomach balked, but he forced it into submission. "Then perhaps you should consider extending your acquaintances, Whitley."

Cris smiled with the confidence only a duke could possess. "I have no wish to extend them, having already discovered all I require in one ill-tempered club owner. Perhaps you know him? Tall fellow, dark-haired, with a sudden penchant for hiding inside his home and drowning himself in drink?"

Fuck.

He lifted the bottle to his lips, tilted it, swallowed. Savored the burn down his gullet. Met his friend's gaze, unwavering. "I know him well."

"I am worried about you, my friend," Cris said then, his tone low, his face devoid of expression.

"Worried? About me? Why?" Duncan attempted to keep his expression blank. A hiccup rose in his throat, and he swallowed it down. Damn, this was growing old. Or he was growing old. Too old for this, surely.

Cris raised both brows, raking him with a telling glance. "Need I answer that question, Duncan? According to Hazlitt, you have not been to your club for a month. Pretty tells me you have hidden yourself away here, refusing most sustenance."

"Hazlitt and Pretty can both go straight to hell," he growled, knowing his two most trusted men were attempting to help him but irritated by their interference nevertheless.

"What the devil is going on, Duncan?" his friend asked. "You gained Amberley's vowels, and from what I understand, you have yet to collect. I expected to return from my honeymoon to find him selling off everything he could in an effort to repay you."

He did not want to talk about it, to relive what he had done. The whisky was just beginning to numb him sufficiently, and discussing the reasons for his self-imposed isolation would only tear open the wounds. "How was your honeymoon, Cris?"

While Duncan was wallowing in his sorrows, Whitley had married the governess who stole his heart. The pair of them were nauseatingly in love. Duncan was happy for his friend, who deserved happiness more than anyone he knew, but he could not stay the stab of envy charging through him whenever he saw the besotted expression on Cris's face at the mentioning of his new wife.

Precisely how he looked just now, grinning in that lovesick fashion so at odds with the hardened rake Duncan had once known him to be.

"I am the most fortunate fellow in the world, Duncan.

The duchess is an angel." Cris gazed off into the distance, still smiling like a fool.

Duncan lifted the bottle back to his lips, misery unfurling along with the envy and self-loathing already poisoning him. "You deserve nothing less, Cris. I am glad for you."

"Thank you, my friend." The duke's smile turned rueful. "Before Jacinda, I thought love was a fiction invented by fools and poets. She has changed everything."

Duncan had known such a woman, one who had left him altered. One he could not forget. One who made his heart seize in his chest whenever he thought of her. A miracle sprung from the dark. His for a fleeting moment and then gone.

He stilled, the bottle halfway to his lips, as a horrible realization settled over him.

He loved her.

He *loved* Lady Frederica Isling. *Bloody fucking hell.*

"Duncan?"

His friend's voice jolted him. He set the bottle down on his desk with a thump. His was a condition that could not be cured. No amount of whisky would right this wrong, though it may dull the insufferable ache. "I have made a grievous mistake."

"I agree." Cris raised a brow. "You ought to have called in Amberley's debts already, but doing so before the wedding will cause an even greater stir, so perhaps all is not lost."

Duncan frowned. "The wedding?"

"Have you not heard? Your beloved half brother Willingham is set to marry the Isling chit."

Four words, and four words alone from the handful Whitley had uttered sank into Duncan's mind.

Willingham.

Marry.

Isling chit.

"Who?" he breathed, fire in his soul. Rancor in his heart. He must have misheard. *Not her. Not her. Please, God, do not let it be her. Not her.*

"Lady Frederica, I believe her name is." Cris paused. "Christ, Duncan. You look as if you've seen a ghost."

He absorbed his friend's words as he would a blow to the face. Or the gut. An act of war. *By God*, this was not meant to be the way of things.

He shook his head, his fists clenching so tightly his knuckles stung. "Damn it, Cris. Are you certain?"

Westlake's promise returned to him, echoing in his mind. *Five thousand pounds, the notes, and my promise Frederica shan't be forced into a marriage that is not of her choosing.* Had the supercilious duke broken his word?

Then an uglier, even more insidious question rose. What if she was not being forced? What if she had chosen Willingham? Worse, what if she had done so to spite him?

"Perhaps the girl's name is Lady Frances. Westlake has but one daughter. I cannot recall now her name for certain now, but it begins with an *f*," Cris said, oblivious to the manner in which Duncan hung on his every word.

"It is Lady Frederica." He shot to his feet, the chamber swirling about him and seeming to tilt. His gut lurched. Why in the hell had he consumed so much of the devil's elixir? He planted his palms flat on the surface, attempting to regain his balance and keep the room from spinning. "I know her name with the same certainty I know my own."

"Christ, Duncan. Shall I have Pretty fetch you a chamber pot in addition to the tray? You look fit to cast up your accounts."

He closed his eyes, but that only made the dizziness worse, so he opened them again, taking a slow, deep breath.

"I don't need a chamber pot, Cris. But I do need your help. Badly."

Cris nodded. "Of course, you shall have it, my friend. Anything you ask."

Duncan dropped back into his chair and told his friend everything.

CHAPTER 16

*B*ecause all London was abuzz with talk of the Duke of Whitley's recent nuptials, the Whitley ball was quite a crush. Frederica sat with Leonora in their customary seats on the periphery of the festivities. She focused on the revelers, hands clasped tightly in her lap, and tried to ignore the ever-growing knot of dread inside her. The knot that said she was running out of time.

A fortnight was all that remained. A mere fourteen days, and then she would become the Countess of Willingham as her father had wanted all along. Whenever she thought of the earl, bile rose in her throat, threatening to choke her. Thankfully, he had not had the opportunity to further press his unwanted, amorous attentions upon her, but her freedom from his punishing, wet mouth and forceful grip was soon at an end.

"You have not heard a word I have said, have you Freddy?" Leonora asked, her soft voice shaking Frederica from her despondent musings.

"Forgive me." She attempted a smile, but she had such little cause for levity in her life that even the act of turning the corners of her mouth up seemed too great a burden to bear. "I have much on my mind."

"I am so sorry your father has forced your hand," her friend said. "After all the effort you went to…"

She had confessed everything to Leonora in the devastated aftermath of what had occurred. No one else knew the truth, save her family. No one else ever would.

Frederica winced. "Yes, after all the effort."

She did not like to speak of Duncan Kirkwood. Six weeks had passed since he had turned his back on her, and yet not a day passed when she did not think of him. When she did not wonder where he was, what he was doing. Who he was kissing. The notion of him with another woman was akin to a knife in her heart, a blade she could only hope would dull with time.

"You could go to those same efforts again." Leonora snapped her fan idly. "Did you ever consider it?"

"I have not seen him in a month and a half." She exhaled slowly, willing away the mountain of hurt lodged inside her. "More importantly, I do not think he truly cared for me at all. I was a means to an end for him. He got what he wanted."

She, on the other hand, had not. Instead, she had lost her heart.

"I did not mean him," Leonora murmured quietly. "You could choose another."

Frederica's cheeks went hot. Of course he had been her first thought. Her *only* thought. Duncan was at the edge of every thought, hovering in each moment, like a splinter lodged deep inside her heart. One she could not remove no matter how she tried.

She fanned herself with one of Mother's castoffs—a bone handle, silk affair embellished with rose embroidery and sequins. "No, I cannot do it, Leonora. Once was enough."

The notion of kissing any other man—of allowing him to

touch her and take liberties—made her ill. She knew if she did not take action soon, she could not be able to avoid such a thing. She would become the Countess of Willingham, the earl's chattel to do with as he wished.

"What shall you do, Freddy?" Leonora's tone was mournful. "You are running out of time."

"I do not know." She attempted to keep the misery from her voice and failed. "I truly thought my father would send me away. I was hoping for my freedom though not depending upon it. I never imagined, however, that he would force me to endure the union regardless of my actions."

These last few sennights had been intolerable. The only slight comfort she found was in the foolscap, ink, and quill she had smuggled into her chamber. She kept them all carefully hidden beneath her bed, writing into the early hours of the morning each night. It was what sustained her, and she nearly had a completed manuscript for her efforts, though she bore purple smudges beneath her eyes as well.

"I wish there was something I could do to assist you." Leonora sighed.

"Thank you for fretting over me, my dear," Frederica said, a rush of affection making her throat go thick. If she had not had her friend during the last month and a half, she did not know what she would have done. "I shall find a way just as I have always done."

Leonora frowned. "I do hope you are right, Freddy."

Before she could respond, the Duchess of Whitley approached, ethereal in a yellow gown with silver net and embroidery. Her flaming hair was artfully styled, and she was undeniably lovely. It was said she and Whitley had a great love match, and watching the duke and duchess earlier, Frederica had been stabbed by a pang of envy.

To love so openly and to be loved in return.

"Lady Frederica, Lady Leonora," the duchess greeted

warmly. "I hope you do not mind if I seat myself here with you both for a moment? My feet are positively aching, and everywhere I turn, someone else is asking me to dance or holding me captive for dialogues and diatribes. Wellington's latest victory is grand to be sure, but I would prefer to discuss it when my heels are not numb."

"Of course not, Your Grace," Frederica said. "You have found just the place to hide. Leonora and I have perfected the art of being wallflowers."

The duchess seated herself with a sigh of contentment, but with rather a lack of grace. The punch she had been holding splashed from her cup and all over Frederica's ivory skirts. "Oh, how dreadful of me! Lady Frederica, I fear I have ruined your dress, and the ball is only just underway. Pray forgive me, my lady."

Frederica looked down at the growing stain, dark and red and ruinous. Rather a metaphor for her life at the moment, she decided. "Do not worry on my account, Your Grace. I shall use this as an excuse to avoid dances." *With my betrothed*, she added silently, for it would not do to air her grievances before a woman she had only just met, regardless of how lovely and modest Her Grace seemed to be.

"I must make amends," the duchess continued, her beautiful countenance pinched with concern. "Come with me, if you please, and I shall fetch my lady's maid. She is a dab hand at removing all manner of stains, and I do believe she will have this problem solved in a trice."

Frederica began to demur, but the duchess was insistent. "I must. I shall feel guilty all evening if you do not grant me this favor, my lady."

She looked to Leonora, who was her usual, amiable self. "Do not worry over me, my dear Freddy. You know how I love to observe. I shall be most entertained."

"Very well," Frederica agreed.

"Splendid." Her Grace rose to her feet. "Follow me. We shall find a discreet exit, and I will have you back in no time at all."

Here, too, was another means of escaping Willingham, at least for the time it took for her stain to be removed. The allure was too tempting to resist. Frederica followed the Duchess of Whitley into the crush.

* * *

DUNCAN WAITED in the hall outside the chamber where the Duchess of Whitley had led Frederica. For the last fortnight, waiting was all he had damn well been doing. Plotting, waiting, biding his time. He was not a patient man, and everything in him now screamed with anticipation.

His body.

His soul.

His heart.

Seeing her tonight—her midnight hair in such stark contrast to her porcelain skin, her lush lips, the elegance of her throat, those curves generously accentuated by her prim gown—had robbed him of breath. She was more beautiful than he remembered. But it wasn't just her fairness of face and form that called to him. It was her. As he watched her slip into the chamber behind the duchess, his heart and his cock had sprung to life in unison.

She was his. And he would be damned before he allowed her to become shackled to the Earl of Willingham, a sadistic bastard he shared half his blood with and none of his proclivities. The earl did not like pleasurable pain. He liked to inflict violence. Duncan had heard the rumors, had spoken with women who had suffered his intolerable cruelty. The notion that Frederica would be subjected to the same as his wife—hell, the notion of her as anyone's wife but his—filled him with a mad frenzy. A need to spill blood.

At last, the door opened, and the duchess emerged alone. She hastened to him, frowning. "Duncan, I will have your promise you will not upset, harm, or ruin her."

He grinned at his friend's wife. She was precisely the woman he would have picked for Cris, had he chosen, the perfect foil for him. "I cannot promise the first, though I most assuredly can the second, and the last has already occurred."

"You understand what I am saying, you vexing man," she warned. "I have done as you asked, playing my part in bringing her here so you may speak with her. But I expect you to behave with honor."

His heart felt lighter than it had since the moment he had whispered his apology to Frederica before opening the door to her brother. "Always, Your Grace."

At least as much honor as he possessed, but he wisely kept that afterthought to himself.

The duchess fixed him with a pointed glare. "Promise, Duncan."

Cris approached them then, his arm sweeping about his wife's waist as he drew her to his side. "He promises, my love. Now allow them their privacy. We have a ball to attend."

Duncan met his friend's gaze, and an understanding passed between them. "Thank you, Cris, Your Grace."

"Jacinda," the duchess corrected softly. "We wish you happy, Duncan. Your lady awaits you."

Yes. She did. But there was one small flaw in the otherwise immaculate fabric of his plans; she was not yet his lady. A flaw which would be repaired soon, he hoped.

He bowed to them both and strode to the chamber, opening the latch and letting himself in quietly. Frederica stood by the hearth where a fire had been lit, holding up her skirts to inspect the damage.

"I think perhaps some boiled milk or a slice of lemon would do," she said, spinning about to face him. Shock froze her for a beat as she took him in, her green eyes blazing into his with the heat of a thousand suns. "You."

Not the welcome he would have hoped for, it was true.

Her beautiful voice fairly vibrated with emotion, anger, outrage, loathing.

He could not blame her. Duncan flicked the lock into place, ensuring there would be no interruptions, and moved toward her, helplessly drawn. "My lady."

"What are you doing in here?" she demanded, gathering her ruined skirts in her hand and retreating, eyes wide. "You must go, Mr. Kirkwood. At any moment, Her Grace will return with her lady's maid, and they will find it strange indeed if the door is locked."

He stopped where he was, a good five paces between them, shaking his head slowly. "No one will be returning. Her Grace spilled her punch on your skirts for my benefit, I am afraid."

Her brows snapped together. "How do you know the duchess?"

"Whitley is my good friend, and Her Grace took pity on me, offering me her assistance for this one instance only, and even then, with great persuasion on my part," he explained gently, his eyes devouring her. He realized it was only the second occasion upon which he had seen her in a gown. She was stunning. Little wonder Willingham wanted her for his own. The reminder sickened him, spurred him on. "Do not think poorly of Her Grace, I beg you. She would not aid me without my repeated promise you would be safe with me."

"But we both know your word is good for nothing, and I

would be safer with a pack of wild, slavering dogs than in your presence," she snapped, her shoulders rigid, chin going high.

"You are safe with me, Frederica." He dared to take another step, hungering to be near her. To breathe her in. To touch her.

Her eyes went even wider. "Do not come any closer to me, sirrah. I shall scream and bring the entire ball upon us."

Her threat was moot, and they both knew it. "No one would hear. We are far enough away from the din, my lady." He had made certain of it.

She skirted a chair and hid behind it, her delicate hands resting on the back. "What do you want, Mr. Kirkwood? What is the purpose of this meeting you have manipulated?"

Beelzebub's blood, he loved her. She was so proud and fierce and glorious, taking her stand against him. He wanted to applaud her. To sink to his knees before her like a supplicant, beg her forgiveness. Kiss her hem. Pledge his loyalty to her forever.

"To see you," he said honestly. "To speak with you. That is all I want."

To make you mine. To marry you. To love you forever. To hope that one day you will love me in return. That you can forgive me for being a blind arse.

But he would not reveal all to her. Not just yet. Not until she was ready and the time was right. If indeed there ever proved such a time.

"What need could you possibly have to speak to me after all this time?" she asked, her voice vibrating with passion. "After what you did?"

"I was wrong," he said simply. Truthfully.

"You were *wrong*," she repeated, her tone one of disbelief. "You planned, from the moment you first realized who I was, to do what you did. You seduced me. Tricked me. You used me to gain Amberley's debts, once you had them, you left me to suffer the consequences. Tell me why I should remain in this chamber, why I should even entertain another word you utter."

"You are marrying my half-brother," he gritted. "I would think that reason enough."

She stiffened, her bearing going rigid. "If that is the sole reason for your interest, you can leave me in peace now, Mr. Kirkwood."

He ground his jaw, stalked closer to her, not stopping until he stood before the chair she was using as a shield against him. Violets, the scent he had hungered for all this time and missed, assailed him in sweet remembrance. "Tell me, my lady. Do you wish to wed him?"

She paled, her nostrils flaring. "Who I marry, and whether or not I wish to marry him, is no concern of yours, Mr. Kirkwood. Indeed, I ceased being a concern of yours the moment you traded me for the vengeance you so desperately longed to obtain."

Guilty.

He had done that. *Yes,* he had. But it had been because he had supposed he had garnered her the freedom she wished. It had been because he had been hopelessly torn between atoning for the past sins of Amberley against his mother and his need for Frederica. Because he had known there wasn't a chance of snow in Hades that her father would ever allow her to wed him.

He had believed he was providing her with the best chance for happiness. That, given the proof of her ruination, her father would send her away, and she would find herself ensconced in some cottage by the sea, happily scratching her pen upon a stack of foolscap, writing *The Silent Baron.*

Foolishness, he realized now. Complete and utter foolishness. There was no simple, happy resolution in life. There had not been for his mother, not for him, not for Frederica. Fighting was a way of life. But he would fight for her. For them. He had gained his revenge, but he had lost something far more important. Her. But from this moment forward, he was willing to do anything to right the grievous wrong he had done her.

"There is something I never told you," he began haltingly. "Something I do not speak of often…my mother was not always a whore. She was a simple country girl. She came to London and was instantly swept into a world of sin. Amberley plucked her from that world and made her his mistress. But when she became with child, he tossed her into the streets. She was forced to sell herself to any man she could, just to keep food in *my* belly."

Her expression softened. "Oh, Duncan."

But he did not want her pity. He wanted her to understand. He needed to explain his actions, if indeed he could. Mere words would not excuse them, but it would be a beginning. "It was Amberley's duty to aid her, to give her some manner of restitution, and yet he cruelly turned his back. Just as it was Amberley's fault, she was killed by one of the men to whom she sold herself, strangled and discarded as if she were no better than an old pair of stockings. I wanted revenge upon the duke for my mother's sake. For the suffering she had, for the life of fear and worry and pain. And I am sorry, endlessly sorry, to have allowed you to become caught up in my need for vengeance."

"I had not realized your mother was murdered, Duncan," she said, her tone gentling with sympathy. With something else, too, but he could not define it.

"I found her," he blurted before he could stop himself. Something about her wide eyes comforted him, something about her lulled him in a way no one else ever had. "She was cold and bruised, and all I could think about was how scared she must have been. I wondered if she thought of me, called out for me. She had sent me off with some coin to gather buns, and when I returned, she was dead."

He relived the horror of that day once more, allowing it to engulf him. Only this time, he had Frederica Isling before him. This time, he did not feel as if he was drowning in an icy sea. Instead, he felt as if he had risen to the surface, as if he could swim to shore at last.

"I understand your desire to gain your revenge," she said. "I always did, even before I knew what you have just revealed to me. But you walked away from me. Left me as if I meant nothing at all to you.

"You meant *everything* to me."

"I wish I believed that." Emotion thickened her husky tones. "Too much time has passed, Duncan. You are far, far too late." Her voice was as pained as her expression, and it slayed him inside.

"Marry me," he said baldly, half demand, half plea.

Also, not what he had planned. He had meant to woo her, to win her. To convince her of the rightness of shackling herself to him, even if he was a social outcast who had taken her innocence and walked away.

But the conviction, the pretty persuasion he would have offered disappeared, instead replaced by two words, and they would not be subdued. Once spoken, they could not be called back, and he could not honestly say he regretted them. He wanted her at his side, as his wife, in his bed. He did not want to abandon her again. To leave her at the mercy of her father and men like his half-brother.

Her lips parted, shock making her eyes go wide. Silence hung in the chamber seething with condemnation. It was not long before she found her voice. "Marry you? How dare you use me in another attempt at gaining your revenge upon Amberley?"

"Marrying you would be my honor," he said and he meant it, though he could not blame her for doubting him. He had provided her no reason to give him her trust. "I do not deserve you, and I know it. But taking you as my wife would have nothing to do with vengeance and everything to do with protecting you as I ought to have done from the moment I took you to my bed. Before that, even. From the moment I first kissed you."

She stared at him, tears shimmering in her eyes. "I asked you to kiss me that day, just as I asked you to ruin me. I am to blame for the straits in which I now find myself, and I have made peace with my mistakes, Mr. Kirkwood. I will not be your duty any more than I will be your vengeance."

Damn it, he was making a muck of this. He wanted to skirt the chair, remove the obstacle between them, and take her in his arms. But he was also aware he must do his penance. He needed to earn her. "I am not worthy of you, this I know. Regardless of how much wealth and power I amass, I will always be the bastard son, born on the wrong side of the blanket. I will never be a lord, nor do I aspire to be one. You will not one day become the Duchess of Amberley if you wed me. But I...I care for you, Frederica. I care as I have never cared for another. From the moment I first saw you in my club, disguised as a gentleman, I was drawn to you. My time away from you did not diminish that fierce spark within me. It only enhanced it."

He spoke from the heart. Truer sentiments could not be found inside himself. He wished he had taken a different path on the day of the masque, that he had proclaimed to her brother and anyone who would listen that she was his. That he was keeping her, like Hades and Persephone. That they would rule his underworld together. Forever.

Her gloved hands gripped the back of the chair in a tight clench. "Why now? It has been six weeks."

Had she, too, been counting? He took one more step, approaching her as he would a spooked horse. "Six weeks of agony," he said. "I had convinced myself I had procured us both what we wanted the most. For me, it was revenge. For you, your freedom."

A tear slid down her cheek at last. "You got your revenge, did you not? But in the end, I was denied my freedom. And you did not care. I saw you the day you came to see my father. You left with what you wanted most. If you had truly wanted me…if you had cared for me, as you now claim, you would have taken me with you then, when I was free."

"Christ knows I should have," he agreed. "I am so sorry I did not. I am sorry for every day, every hour, and every minute I have spent without you."

She shook her head, another tear glittering as it fell. "You are too late now. The damage has been done. I am promised to the earl."

Damn it. This was not what he wished to hear. One more step closer, and he was almost around the chair now. So near, he saw the clear delineation of the teardrops studding her dark lashes like spangles.

"Tell me something, Frederica," he said, his voice raw. Hoarse. "Is Willingham the suitor you spoke of? Is he the one who forced his kisses upon you?"

"What do you care?" she lashed out angrily. "It is all settled now. Nothing will change it."

"Because I know what manner of man he is," he bit out, giving in to his instincts at last and closing the distance. Two more steps round the chair, and they stood face to face, chest to chest. He allowed himself the pleasure of touching her then, framing her face with his hands. An innocent gesture that belied all the emotion, want, and need warring within him. "He will hurt you, Frederica. He will cause you pain, and he will enjoy it, and there will be nothing you can do to stop him."

She bit her lip, saying nothing, and ice-cold fear replaced all else.

"Has he already hurt you, angel?" he asked with soft menace.

"Not recently, no. With the preparations, he has not been alone with me," she whispered.

Duncan's mind was made. He was going to kill Willingham. He was going to hunt him down, and he was going to beat him until his knuckles split and he heard the sickening crunch of the other man's bones. "What has he done?"

"Nothing."

She was lying, and he knew it. "Tell me, Frederica."

"He…has forced kisses upon me. He…grips me with so much force I bear bruises later." A shuddering breath emerged from her. "He told me I would grow accustomed to it, that he would teach me."

The hell he would.

"You cannot marry him," he told her, inwardly furious. Furious at the cowardly fop who had been given everything his entire life and yet still needed to inflict pain upon those weaker than him. Furious that Willingham had touched his woman. Had forced unwanted advances upon her. Furious at her father for breaking his word to Duncan and promising Frederica not just to a man she did not wish to marry, but to a man who would crush her beneath his boot.

"I must." Her gloved hands settled over his. "I am betrothed to him."

His gut curdled at the word, at its meaning. No part of him could fathom that he was in love with Lady Frederica Isling, and she was going to marry his half-brother. Indeed, every part of him refused to consider her anything other than *his*.

"I have a plan," he said, searching her eyes. "Do you trust me?"

"No," she answered without hesitation.

Well, Beelzebub's brimstone. At least she was honest.

CHAPTER 17

*H*e had a plan, he said.
     He cared for her, he said.
He wanted to marry her, he said.

Frederica stared into Duncan Kirkwood's impossibly blue gaze, and in those inscrutable depths, she found hope for the first time in six interminable weeks. She did not dare trust him. He preyed upon the weaknesses of men for his living. Indeed, he had made a fortune from it. He had intended to use her as a pawn to gain his revenge upon his erstwhile father from the moment he had first discovered who she was.

He was beautiful.

Debonair.

Dark and dangerous.

He was the man who had taken her innocence and then cast her off with nothing more than an apology and one last glance back at her from the street. He was the half-brother of the man who took pleasure in bruising her tender flesh. Everything about what he proposed was wrong.

And yet, everything was right.

Too right.

Because Duncan Kirkwood's delicious scent had invaded her senses, and his large, warm body was all but flush against hers, and they were alone in a bedchamber of all places, and his hands were upon her. And because she knew how delicious his kisses were and how talented his hands and mouth could be. Because she remembered how it felt to have him inside her, stretching her, marking her as his. She remembered how she had been so full, full of Duncan, full of life, full of love.

His plan could not possibly work. She swallowed, forced herself to return from the clouds. "Why would Willingham agree to your proposal?" she asked him, doing her best to remain strong against the devastating onslaught that was Duncan Kirkwood.

"Because I shall make him," Duncan ground out, his jaw clenched.

Oh dear.

"I do not wish for violence."

"No one deserves violence more, my lady," he growled.

So protective, so fierce, Mr. Duncan Kirkwood. He was indisputably a man of hot passions and unapologetic convictions. When he spoke, he meant it. But where had he been? Why had he taken six merciless weeks to decide he wanted her in his life? Frederica closed her eyes, attempting to regain herself.

"No violence," she repeated, her resolve weakening.

He was touching her. So near to her. And God help her, she wanted him more than she ever had. *You can have him*, her heart whispered, that cunning thing. *Forever.* How potent a lure was the notion of taking Duncan Kirkwood as her husband? Of kissing that sensual mouth whenever she wished, of learning his body and his desires, of allowing him to teach her the art of pleasure? More potent than the promise of immortality, she feared. Perhaps just as false.

"I will promise you anything but that, angel," he said with such tenderness one would have supposed he was courting her with gentle wooing rather than threatening to beat the Earl of Willingham. "He hurt you, and I will hurt him in turn. We shall see how he likes to be the recipient of pain."

"Duncan." She frowned. "You must not. Not on my account."

"It is a long time coming for him, angel," he said, caressing her cheek with his thumb. His hands were ungloved, and his bare skin upon hers was like the charge of gunpowder. Explosive. "On your account and on account of every other female he has ever so injured without her consent. In my world, we believe it must be an eye for an eye, a tooth for a tooth. He hurt my woman, and now he will know the same hurt."

My woman.

How she liked the sound of that on his supple lips. She liked it too much.

"I am not yours," she reminded him, for he had not earned the right to claim her. Nor was she certain he could, given the hopelessness of their disparate situations. "And I do not—"

His mouth was upon hers then, swift and unexpected, warm and wonderful, and tasting of Duncan and the forbidden, of sin and redemption, too, and—unless she was mistaken—chocolate. He tasted good enough to eat, and she had missed him. Had ached for him. Six long weeks of alternately yearning for him and hating him crashed upon her in that moment. She became desperate. Her arms wound around his neck, and she rose on her toes, kissing him back with as much unskilled urgency as she could manage without swallowing him whole.

Their tongues tangled. His hands were on her waist, drawing her against him and the unmistakable outline of his cock, full and thick. They kissed and kissed until she was making soft sounds of urgency and he was eating them up. Until his palms were planted upon her arse—yes, she knew the meaning of the word at last—cupping her, lifting her, and grinding her body against his. Her legs parted, her skirts having been gathered to her waist by his clever hands, and then her core made contact with his breeches.

She was bare, her swollen flesh impaled upon the stiff fabric. Upon the delicious ridge of him. *Oh.* How sinful. How wonderful. This was what she had missed. Duncan. His body. His knowing wickedness. Simply *him.*

He caught her in his arms, guiding her legs around his waist, and walked them several paces until her back met a wall. Deftly, he used his strength to pin her there, off the floor, pressed between plaster and his hard body. His mouth slanted over hers, at once gentle and possessive. Knowing and ruthless. Wicked and wonderful.

She was on fire, coming back to life. Everything she had felt the night he had made love to her returned, only this time stronger. More forceful. This time, she understood what the sensations meant. She knew what friction and pressure Duncan would grant her.

And she wanted it.

She wanted to come undone for him. Because of him.

For so long, she had dreamt of him, had lain awake in her bed, miserable and isolated, thinking of him. Imagining him and his knowing hands and lips and tongue. She had touched herself, had worked her flesh in the same manner as he had, and she had experienced small tremors of satisfaction. But nothing she had dared try thus far compared to Duncan's body against hers, his mouth voracious on hers, his tongue, his fingers, his…

He thrust against her, the hard line of his cock glancing over the sensitive bud he knew how to pleasure so well. She moaned into his mouth, ravenous for him. She wanted more. Wanted everything. Her hands were in his hair, on his broad shoulders, down the solid plane of his back, finding his bottom. His was well-shaped, perfect handfuls, tight and firm. He angled himself against her more fully, driving against her in steady, rhythmic thrusts that mimicked love-making. Each pass of his cloth-covered cock over her bare flesh stoked the fires rising within her.

Her mind ceased to function. Instead, she was taken over by the sensory; Duncan's masculine scent in her nose, his taste in her mouth, the burgeoning shape of him pressing into her most sensitive flesh. He drove against her, his mouth taking hers as his body once more led her to the oblivion of full and complete bliss.

She was desperate for him, needing more, raking her nails all over his body, offering herself to him as if he had never walked away from her. Because she belonged to him, just as he belonged to her. Because she needed more. She needed something she had not even imagined, something she had not fathomed, a mere hour before.

She needed contact. Friction. More of him. *Starving.* She was so starved for this man. For his flesh, for the sweet weight of his body atop hers, for his large hands, his mouth. His tongue. *Good heavens*, his tongue, long and willful and persuasive.

He settled himself more firmly between her thighs with ease, setting his lips to her throat. His pulsing cock was seated against her cunny. A sharp stab of need pulsed through her. She wanted him inside her, and her body knew it before her mind did, her hips arching in desperation, seeking to accept that which had yet to be offered. Except, even in that motion, she found minor comfort.

And so she did it again, dragging herself over his hard cock, longing for it to be buried inside her. Now that she had experienced such wild fulfillment, she had no wish to settle for anything less. But this...he jerked his hips into her, thrusting...*oh,* this, too, could make her lose control.

"I promised I would not ruin you," he muttered against her mouth. "That I would not dishonor you. I want you so damn much, Frederica Isling. More than you will ever know."

She was close, so close, to reaching her pinnacle thanks to the full swell of his manhood and need humming through her wet, aching flesh. "You have already ruined me," she said, kissing him once more with an abandon she would worry about regretting later.

He tore his mouth from hers on a groan. "If I don't touch you right now, I'll go mad."

"Yes," she agreed. Right now, her body demanded the pleasure only he could give her. She needed his touch, too. "Touch me, Duncan."

His fingers found her, parting her folds, deftly flicking over the swollen bud. He lovingly stroked her, giving her what she needed, until she was straining against him, breathless, the knot inside her tightening. "That's it, angel. Come for me."

She could stand no more. The furious rush was upon her, sudden and hard. Her body seized, rocked by dozens of delicious tremors. He stayed with her, increasing his pace and pressure, milking the last of her response until she was drained and limp, sagging against him, her face pressed to his throat above his cravat. She could not speak, so she held tight to him, breathing him in, feeling the heavy thudding of his heart against her.

After a time, he released her slowly to the floor, gently righting her skirts. He kissed her slowly, sweetly, and then he broke away, staring down at her with an intensity that shook her. "I will take care of you from this moment forward, angel. I promise you."

And perhaps she was a fool, because she wanted to believe him.

* * *

FOR THE SECOND time in as many months, Duncan awaited a duke. But this time, he had summoned Amberley to him. And the duke had come. Finally, after a lifetime of being turned away and ignored. Of being treated akin to a pile of horse dung in the street, he had not only received a reply—terse though it may have been—but he had been graced with the duke's presence.

He was struck for a moment as the duke stepped over the threshold of his office by the absurdity of it, that he should have had to go to such lengths to obtain an audience with the man who had sired him. That he now held locked in his desk the papers containing the duke's future. He nodded to, Hazlitt who bowed silently and left the chamber, closing the door behind him.

Just that easily, Duncan and the duke were alone.

"Your Grace," he greeted with a nonchalance he did not feel, bowing.

Amberley shuffled forward with the aid of a walking stick; his large frame hunched over as if each step he took pained him. But though his body had been broken by age and a dissolute life, his eyes—the same as Duncan's—were clear.

As was the sharpness of his hatred, sparkling in the depths like a knife. "Kirkwood. What is the meaning of this?"

Duncan ignored the ill-mannered demand, strolling to the sideboard and fetching himself two fingers of whisky.

"Would you care for some Scottish whisky, Amberley? It is the finest illegal swill money can buy."

The duke, well-known for his endless thirst for both liquor and cunny, licked his lips, hesitating. "Yes."

He wondered how much the admission had cost the old bastard. Whatever it was, it was not enough. Nothing would be. Taking everything from the Duke of Amberley would not right the wrongs that had been done to Duncan's mother. He poured some whisky for his unlikely guest, grinding his jaw to keep the temptation to spit into it at bay.

In silence, he handed the duke his glass. "Seat yourself, if you please, Your Grace."

The duke's hand gripped the head of his walking stick as if it were a claw, his arm trembling. "I do not intend to remain long."

"You will remain as long as I require you to remain," he said softly, but with enough dark determination for the hardness within him to show.

"Why have you lured me here with the promise of your aid in getting my vowels returned to me?" he bit out.

"Because I alone can assist you with such a feat." Duncan took a sip of his whisky, savoring its familiar burn. Not as hedonistic as chocolate, but it would suffice. "I am in possession of all your I.O.U.s, Your Grace. A tidy fortune, too."

"Westlake," the duke growled with such virulence he broke into a cough. The fit had him doubled over, his whisky sloshing over his hand. "He would never betray me by selling them to you."

"Ah, but I'm afraid he did." Duncan walked calmly to his desk, unlocking the drawer and box where he kept all things of value in the club. He produced the neat stack of vowels in question. A staggering sum, all told, not just a tidy fortune as he had indicated. And it was all his for the taking.

But he had found the one thing in life worth more to him

than his club, the money he amassed, the power he wielded, and the revenge he could inflict upon the man he would forever blame for his mother's death. And it was the woman he loved. For her, he would surrender anything. Everything.

"Would you beggar me now, Kirkwood?" The man who had fathered him demanded.

Duncan considered him, amazed at love's capacity to heal. He did not feel the angry sting of rancor in his chest when he looked upon the duke now. If anything, he pitied the man. He had squandered his fortune and his health, turned his back on a woman and child who were his responsibility, and his only legitimate offspring liked to force himself upon the powerless.

"Tell me something. Did you rape my mother, or is ravishment a crime only your son, the earl, aspires to?"

"How dare you malign Lord Willingham?" the duke spat. "Your mother was a whore who spread her legs for half of London. You could have been anyone's son."

Duncan stalked toward him. "You will apologize for insulting my mother."

"I don't care if you call in all my debts, you insolent puppy," the duke blustered. "I'll not apologize for speaking truth. Nor will I claim you as mine. I have one son only. If you think I shall change my mind and acknowledge you, you are deadly wrong. I will lose everything I have first."

He smiled without mirth. He had dreamt of this meeting, and he had always known how it would proceed. A man who had turned away a begging child would not become a saint as he aged.

"I want you to know one thing, Amberley." He moved closer, crowding the old man with his larger, more muscled frame. "My mother was a good woman, forced by the ways of the world to earn her bread at the mercy of men like you. She died the same way, some fancy cove's hands around her throat, squeezing the life from her. Her death is on your soul, and you will answer for it, one way or another."

"Is that what this is about?" the duke's lip curled into a sneer. "What would you have me do, Kirkwood? Kiss her tombstone to make amends? The world had one less whore on the day she died, and that is the truth. If she had lived, she would have made more like you, vile, greedy, insolent curs attempting to raise themselves from the gutter by any means. Name your price for my vowels, and you shall have it."

"My price has just increased, I am afraid." He tossed back the contents of his whisky and stalked away before he did something foolish, like slamming his fist into the duke's face. "First, I demand an apology for the manner in which you spoke of my mother just now. Second, I demand Lord Willingham cry off his betrothal to Lady Frederica Isling."

There was another price, but he would extract that directly from Willingham himself. With pleasure.

The duke's eyes narrowed. "What else?"

"I want Willingham to cry off the betrothal today. Within the next hour." *The sooner the goddamn better.* Every minute Frederica was promised to Willingham was like a blade in his gut. Waiting to make his move until Cris's ball had nearly killed him, but he had known it was the best way to reach her. And he would gladly wait an eternity for the chance to call her his. "Carry out these requirements, and I will return all your vowels to you, unencumbered. Your debts will be canceled, and you will be saved from ruin."

Amberley raised his glass to his lips at last, gulping the contents with practiced ease. "And if I do not?"

"I will call in all your debts immediately, of course. You will be beggared." He smiled again, and this time it was with true elation, the unparalleled jauntiness of knowing he had bested his foe. "It may also interest you to know that I have recently acquired a press. One of my ladies here intends to write her memoirs, with a special section dedicated to the cruelty of one Lord W., and a great deal of details, all of which would prove quite shocking and damning to gentle society. I will be more than happy to publish this volume and see it distributed heavily throughout London."

He had bought the press, it was true, but he had bought it for Frederica. A little bluffing never did a gambler wrong, however.

The duke paled.

It was all the proof Duncan needed that the elder man was aware of his other son's proclivities. His gut tightened. To think Frederica would have been gifted to such a monster...it made him want to rage and rend.

"Will I need to take such drastic measures, Your Grace?" he prodded, for he needed his answer. And he needed it now. He had to have the promise Frederica would be freed. That she would be his.

"No," spat the duke, flinging his empty glass to the carpet. It landed with a hollow thud but did not break. "I shall do as you demand, and I shall also see to it that Willingham does as well. But first, I will have your written acknowledgment of the exchange."

Duncan strode to his desk and put his quill to foolscap, scratching out the agreement and signing his name with a flourish. Before it had even dried, he offered it to Amberley. "Yours, Your Grace."

The duke took it in his gnarled fingers, but Duncan held firm. "Oh, dear me. There is one more stipulation I neglected to mention." This one was for his own benefit, purely and simply. For his mother's, too. "I require you to sink to your knees and kiss my shoes."

"Never!" came the outraged bellow, almost instantly.

Duncan was not surprised. The desire to see the duke so

humbled before him was strong. He made a motion as if to tear the paper. "Very well, Your Grace. If you wish—"

"No, damn you," the duke bit out, cutting him off. "I will do it."

Duncan nodded. "You may proceed."

And as he watched, the Duke of Amberley lowered to his knees and kissed the tip of first his left, then his right shoe. *That was for you, Mother.* Unmoved, he watched as Amberley rose once more, slowly, grimacing, obviously in pain. His heart was unmoved, so, too, his pity.

Lady Frederica, however, is for me. All for me.

He relinquished the foolscap to the duke.

"Within the hour," he repeated coolly as the man who had sired him—the man who would never acknowledge him—retreated from his office. Time had changed them both, and circumstances had been reversed. But in that moment, the only joy he could cling to was the realization that Frederica would soon be free.

CHAPTER 18

The Earl of Willingham handed Frederica into his curricle, seating himself beside her. The day had dawned cool and gray, a slight mist descending with occasional persistence. Not the sort of weather for a drive, it was true.

She settled her skirts into place, wishing herself anywhere but where she was. What a grim, unwanted situation. Had it been only yesterday that she had been back in Duncan's arms, his mouth on hers, his body pinning her to the wall, his fingers working their magic upon her, bringing her to shuddering submission?

His words returned to her as she watched Willingham slide into his seat, taking up the reins.

I will take care of you from this moment forward, angel. I promise you.

I have a plan. Do you trust me?

She had. Lord help her, she had trusted Duncan Kirkwood once again without having one reason for doing so. But his promises seemed dreadfully far away by the light of day, with her unwanted betrothed at her side.

How could she free herself from this untenable mess? Moreover, how could *he*?

"You are looking well rested, my lady," the earl said, an undercurrent she could not quite define sharpening his tone.

"Thank you," she said.

In truth, she had scarcely slept, tossing and turning amidst thoughts of Duncan. His reappearance in her life had been unexpected. Incredible, wonderful, all she had wished for, but frightening just the same. He owned her heart, but he had betrayed her and turned his back on her before. What would stop him from doing so again?

"My lady?" the earl prompted, his tone piercing her musing with his vehemence. It was a jolt to her senses. Unwanted. Jarring.

"Forgive me, I was woolgathering."

Anger creased his expression as he took up the reins and set them into motion. "From this moment forward, you will listen to me when I speak, my lady. As your husband, I demand both your attention and your obedience, along with your loyalty."

She inhaled slowly. Her *obedience*. Marrying this man was insupportable. "I am not a child, my lord. You need not speak to me as if I am one."

I will take care of you from this moment forward, angel.

She thought of Duncan's words once more. But where was he? And why was she once again suffering the attentions of the earl? They were running out of time. In less than a fortnight, she would become the Countess of Willingham.

"Women are simple-minded as children," he said coldly. "And when you are disobedient, you will be punished like one. Is there anything you wish to tell me, Lady Frederica?"

A cold tendril of fear unleashed itself within her. "What are you implying, my lord?"

"That I saw my betrothed in the company of another man

at the Whitley ball last night." His tone vibrated with anger. "Oddly enough, that same scurrilous mongrel has demanded I break our betrothal. You would not know anything of such distressing matters, would you?"

Dawning realization turned the fear to horror. They were not heading in the direction of the park. She had been too distracted by her thoughts to notice. Where did he intend to take her?

She had to be brazen, to convince him to abandon whatever evil he had plotted. "I know nothing of anything you have just said, my lord," she lied with a calm she did not feel. "If you wish to break our betrothal yourself, you need only say as much. It is not necessary to suggest someone has forced you to do it."

"Do not lie," he barked, slanting her a look so rife with fury it bordered on maniacal.

There was the face of the man who enjoyed inflicting pain. Who found pleasure in force. Her mouth went dry, but she forced herself to continue their conversation. Perhaps if she could distract him…strike him over the head and take the reins…scream…leap from the curricle before they reached their destination…

"I-I am not lying, my lord," she said. "Please, I beg of you, return me to my home. I am feeling unwell."

"You will be begging soon, Lady Frederica," he warned, his voice dark and menacing, sending a chill straight through her. "On your knees."

Desperation made her act, attempting to scramble from her seat. Before she could manage to open the curricle door, however, a hand fisted in her hair, hauling her back in a tight hold so painful her hair felt as if it were being ripped from the root.

"You cannot escape," he growled. "I saw the two of you leave the same chamber separately. Did you truly think no one would notice your absence? That no one would question where you had gone?"

He must have followed her at a discreet distance, hiding out of view. She had been so shaken in the aftermath of Duncan's fierce passion that she would not have noticed the sun had it suddenly dropped at her feet.

"I was repairing a stain on my gown with the help of the Duchess of Whitley," she insisted.

"Liar," he charged, yanking on her hair. "You were allowing him to put his dirty, swindling peasant hands upon you, and I will make you pay for it. You belong to me. I will take great pleasure in knowing I have taken what he wants. I will so ill use you that he will never be capable of even looking upon you afterwards. You will be so thoroughly ruined your father will have no choice but to sanction our nuptials, and then you will spend the rest of your days regretting the night you played the whore for a worthless bastard like Kirkwood."

"No," she cried out, held captive by her hair as they drove down an alleyway, slipping into a part of town that was unfamiliar to her. "Please, my lord. You must release me. You cannot abuse the daughter of the Duke of Westlake and think to escape punishment."

"Your father is so desperate to be rid of your unwanted burden that he all but begged me to marry you. When I tell him what I have done to you, he will have no choice but to ensure our wedding continues as planned." His lips grazed her ear. "I will put a babe in you today, my lady."

His tongue on her ear made her want to retch. She jerked away, but his grip on her hair would not relent, and the force of her attempt at escape sent a hot rush of tears to her eyes. "Do not do this, Lord Willingham," she begged. "Release me or I shall scream."

He continued to navigate the curricle one-handedly,

releasing a bitter chuckle. "Do not try anything clever, my lady. I have a pistol in my pocket, and I am not afraid to use it upon you if I must. Moreover, we are fast heading into a place where no one would care if I bent you over and ravaged you on this bench."

She forced back her fear. "I will fight you."

He released her hair, shoving her back into her seat with abrupt force that sent her toppling. "I hope you do. In the end, I will only enjoy it more and use you harder."

She choked down bile at his vicious words. Somehow, by some means, she had to escape him. It was the only choice she had.

* * *

WITH HAZLITT and two other guards at his side, Duncan stormed through the reeking halls of the grim East End tavern where Willingham had taken Frederica. If any harm befell her, Duncan was not just going to thrash Willingham to a bloody carcass; he was going to damn well kill him.

Thank Christ his instincts had made him have one of his men stand guard over her after he had issued the warnings to Amberley. He had not trusted the earl's reaction to the news Amberley would bring him, and something inside Duncan, some niggling understanding, had protested urgently that selfish, vainglorious bastards like Willingham did not simply relinquish what they wanted and walk away.

Men who took by force did not like to be bested.

As he reached the chamber where they had been told Frederica had been taken—Duncan had far more coin to grease the palms of the tavern keeper than Willingham did, and in the end, greed won—a scream tore through the air. The scream belonged to Frederica.

Every thought fled, and he was mindless. A weapon. He

threw himself into the door, shoulder first, determined to get to her. To tear Willingham apart with his bare hands if he must. On the second attempt, the door splintered open, and he crashed into the chamber with a warrior's cry, his pistol raised.

The earl had been grappling with Frederica, but upon Duncan's forced entry, he spun, holding her against him in a tight grip, pointing a pistol to her temple. Her dress had been torn to the waist, revealing her shift. Her hair was in wild disarray, her eyes wide and fearful, sobs making her chest rise and fall in jerky motions, tears on her cheeks.

"Release Lady Frederica," he ordered Willingham with a bravado he little felt, given the gun pressing into Frederica's skull and the finger of a demented scoundrel upon the trigger.

"Take one step closer, and I will end her," the earl warned, his tone one of deadly intent.

"If any harm comes to her, this day will be your last," Duncan warned. He had a pistol in his hand, and three armed men at his side—including Hazlitt, who was a madman when the situation warranted it—and he was not going to allow the soft-palmed lecher before him to hurt Frederica.

Lords did not strike him with awe as they once had, before he had been wise and world-weary enough to know better.

Men of honor, men who upheld their words and promises, who were honest, loyal, and steadfast in their actions and promises, those men impressed him. Men like Willingham? They were not men at all.

He just needed time. Distraction.

"You are too late, *brother*," Willingham taunted. "I already had her."

The earl's claim hit him like a blow. He stiffened, absorbing the shock, the denial. For a moment, his gaze searched Frederica's frantically. My God, had he been too late?

He stepped forward, spurred by the need to protect Frederica and the need to decimate Willingham. "If you have hurt her, I will kill you myself. Slowly."

Holding Duncan's gaze, the earl grabbed a fistful of Frederica's shift and tore, revealing her breasts. And then he palmed one roughly, squeezing until she cried out in pain and her creamy skin reddened with the force of his violence. "She likes it rough. I've heard you like to watch, Kirkwood. Perhaps I ought to fuck her again in front of you. Will that be evidence enough that she is damaged goods? My seed is already inside her, but I will show you once more if it would convince you to leave what is mine alone."

Frederica's eyes were closed, her nostrils flared. The sight of her being hurt before him was pure torture. Bloodlust rose within him, pure and true, and he vowed the earl would pay for this. He made to take another step forward, but Hazlitt halted him with a hand on his arm and a meaningful look. There was a reason Hazlitt was his right hand.

"She is not yours," he told Willingham flatly. "You cannot fathom her father would willingly give her hand to you after you have abducted her and abused her. Your game is at an end. Release her now, and we will allow you to walk away with impunity."

"She is mine, and I will do what I want to her." To emphasize his proclamation, the earl roughly twisted Frederica's nipple, pinching it, pulling it.

Frederica's eyes shot open, luminous and shockingly green, the greenest he had ever seen them. "I love you, Duncan," she said.

"And I love you." The words left him of necessity, without thought, without restraint. He loved her more than he had even imagined possible, and he regretted deeply telling her for the first time whilst she was being held captive by a lunatic.

And then he realized, in the next horrifying instant, that she meant to sacrifice herself.

Everything unfolded in a mad jumble. With a roar, he leapt forward. Frederica jammed her elbow into Willingham's midsection. Pistols fired. His. Another's. Plaster rained. A scream rent the air. A hoarse cry echoed. Duncan fell to his knees. A body dropped to the floor with a sickening thud. Blood rushed over the dirty floorboards, filling in the gaps between planks with their dark red abundance.

CHAPTER 19

*H*usband.

It was a new word for Frederica.

A beloved word. She wanted to say it over and over. Aloud. In her mind. She wanted to write it on foolscap a hundred times and then simply stare at it, absorbing the breathtaking beauty contained in seven simple letters.

"Will there be anything else this evening, my lady?" asked her new lady's maid after giving a final stroke of her brush through Frederica's unbound locks.

She looked at her reflection in the glass, scarcely recognizing herself. A cloud of dark hair rained down her shoulders. Her eyes were wide and vibrant, her skin pale in contrast to the robe she had chosen with her husband in mind. It was midnight-black silk, soft and wicked, just as he was.

"Mrs. Kirkwood, if you please," she said with a smile. "And no thank you, Verity. That will be all."

"Of course, Mrs. Kirkwood." Verity curtseyed, and then hastily took her leave.

"Husband," Frederica repeated to herself, her smile deepening.

At long last, Duncan was hers, and she was his. The wound on her arm, caused by the Earl of Willingham's pistol, had almost entirely healed. Thankfully, in the melee which had ensued following her elbow to his midsection, his pistol had been sufficiently dislodged so that it had fired into the ceiling, merely glancing off the tender flesh of her upper arm in the process.

Two bullets—one belonging to Duncan and one belonging to Mr. Hazlitt—had found their mark in the earl. A shudder passed through her as she thought of that horrible day and all its terror and pain. In the end, the earl had found his absolution, dying on the floor of the tavern where he had spirited her, choking on his own life source. *Penance,* Duncan had told her calmly that day, and he had been right. *He can never hurt another woman again now.*

It was her only solace that day, along with knowing he could have hurt her far worse than he had. He had manhandled her, groped her, and torn her gown, and she thanked the Lord every day that Willingham had not forced himself upon her as he had intended. He had run out of time, thanks to Duncan's swift arrival.

Not long afterward, she had learned the full truth from Duncan, that he had given up his revenge to wed her. Even after Willingham's death, he had still returned the vowels to Amberley. *I do not need revenge any longer,* he had told her. *You are all I need.*

In the month following the tumult at the tavern, Duncan had convinced her father to allow them to marry. The scandal of Willingham's death had created quite an outcry, and though Duncan had made every effort to keep her name from the scandal sheets, she remained the betrothed of a man who had died in salacious fashion, shot to death—as the story went—by his lover's husband. Creating a new diversion —the love match between the gaming hell owner and the duke's wallflower daughter—had proved a boon.

Suddenly, Frederica had found herself in the scandal sheets, depicted as a tiny maiden slung over the shoulder of an enormous beast of a man who carried dice in one hand and a bag of coins in the other. She did her best to ignore the intentionally hurtful caricatures. Some people relished being mean spirited and unkind, and ignoring them was the most effective ammunition against such miscreants.

If ever there was a time to push such trifles from her mind, it was tonight.

Her wedding night.

She awaited Duncan in her new bedchamber, an immense and luxuriously appointed room he had decorated with her in mind. From the elegant Aubusson to the exquisitely carved bookshelves and matching writing desk—complete with a plentiful supply of writing implements and foolscap— the chamber had taken her breath from the moment she had first crossed the threshold. Mother had given her hundreds of baubles and trinkets, but never had she received a gift that was so perfect for her. A knock sounded at the door adjoining her chamber to his.

Except for the man himself. He was the most perfect gift of all. The only one she would ever need for the rest of her days.

She smiled. "Enter."

And there he stood, her husband. Mr. Duncan Kirkwood, notorious gaming hell owner, unrepentant sinner with a surprisingly gentle heart, and a thoroughly beautiful man. He, too, wore black, a banyan belted at the waist, and she drank in the sight of him, tall and lean and strong and hers.

Only hers.

Their eyes met from across the chamber, and a grin

curved his lips, so wide his dimples appeared in a rare show. He made a full, elegant bow that should have seemed silly given his bare calves and feet peeping from beneath his robe. But Duncan could do anything, and with his singular, debonair grace, he never failed to make heat blossom inside her.

"My lady," he said, still grinning as he ended his bow and strode over the handsome Aubusson to where she stood.

"Mrs. Kirkwood," she corrected for the second time that evening, smiling back at him.

"Mrs. Kirkwood." His large hands splayed on her waist, drawing her against him.

"I like the sound of that, Mr. Kirkwood." Their betrothal —in spite of all the wagging of tongues it had produced—had been exceedingly proper. Her father had insisted upon it, and her mother had spent many a frustrating hour as an impediment to their time alone, detailing the spoils of her shopping expeditions in unwanted detail. Frederica had not even been alone with Duncan until today.

Twining her arms around his neck was a privilege she had been denied for far too long, and she did it now, her soft curves seeking out the unforgiving, masculine planes of his body. He radiated heat, his delicious scent of musk, amber, and lemon sending a trill of want to settle between her thighs.

"As do I, my angel." Reverently, he settled his lips over hers.

He kissed her sweetly, coaxing her mouth open, his tongue dipping inside. He tasted of chocolate, sweet and bitter and exotic. And of Duncan, of everything her heart yearned for. His hand roamed from her waist to cup her face, and he withdrew, looking down at her, devouring her with his brilliant gaze.

"Thank you," he breathed.

Her lips tingled with his kiss, and she wanted more. "For what?"

He kissed the tip of her nose, his eyes never straying from hers. "For trusting in me when I did not deserve it. For marrying me when I am not worthy of you. I know this is not the life you ever envisioned for yourself, that I am not who you would have chosen, given different circumstances. But I will do everything within my power to make you happy, Frederica. From this day until my last, and even beyond if I can help it."

She traced her fingers over the slash of his cheekbone, the divot in his chin. "This is precisely the life I have always wanted, and you are the only man I would ever choose. I love you, Duncan, with all my heart, with everything that is in me."

"That day in my office, you told me you wanted to wed a paragon, and Christ knows I am far more sinner than I could ever be saint."

He had remembered. It was a day she would never forget. Thinking of it still made her cheeks go hot and a pulsing ache throb between her thighs. "I told you I wanted someone who is caring, who is kind. Someone who will not frown upon my writing. A man who will champion me rather than attempt to silence and stifle me. A man who is bold and adventurous of spirit. That is what I said that day, and the man I described is you, my love. It has always been you."

His expression turned fierce. "I love you so damned much, Mrs. Kirkwood." His thumb swiped gently over her lower lip. "But you have some of it wrong, I am afraid. I am not kind. Nor am I particularly adventurous, though I shall gratefully rectify that as long as you are willing to help me and a bed is nearby."

"You are wicked, too. I do think I neglected to mention that trait, also quite dear to me." She ran her fingers through his thick, golden hair, allowing the silken strand to sift gently back to his scalp. "But you are kind indeed, and I have always known it. Mr. Hazlitt told me about the foundling house you built, and of all the funds you have given to women and children in need."

His jaw tensed, a flush rising on his high cheek bones. "Hazlitt bloody well should have held his tongue."

"I am grateful he told me." She kissed him, a quick though fervent peck. How could he see himself as anything but the good, honorable man he was? "It makes me love you more. You may dress in black, but your heart is pure as snow."

"I do not know about that." His lips met hers again. "My heart wants to do some wicked and depraved things to you tonight."

Anticipation coiled within her. "Then perhaps you should, husband."

"With pleasure." Before she realized what he was about, he scooped her into his arms, and turned, carrying her toward his chamber. "Tonight, I want you in my bed, where you belong."

She buried her face against the strong cords of his throat, pressing a kiss there, where the throb of his pulse reminded her of how vital, alive, and necessary he was. How beloved. "I love you."

He set her gently on her feet alongside his bed, and then his mouth was upon hers, fierce and hungry. Their hands traveled over each other's bodies, tugging open knots, discarding silk, until there remained no more impediments between them. And then he lifted her onto his bed.

She had a moment to feast on the glorious sight of him naked—his long legs and thick thighs, broad shoulders and sculpted chest, the lean plane of his abdomen, and the long, beautiful jut of his cock—before he joined her, settling between her thighs. "You are mine, angel," he said, dropping a kiss on her knee. "Here." Higher, trailing delectable nibbles over her thigh. "Here." Over her belly, worshiping one puckered nipple and then the other. "Here, too." Back down her body he traveled, setting her aflame as he went. He kissed her mound. "Especially here."

Words fled her as he suckled the hidden bud, drawing a taut burst of exquisite pleasure through her. His finger slid through her folds, probing gently at her entrance as he sucked and laved and nipped, working her into a frenzy. More. She needed more. Him inside her.

She twisted her hips off the bed, and he gave her what she wanted, his finger sliding wetly to the hilt. But it was not enough. He seemed to sense her building need, adding a second finger, gently using his teeth. Her core contracted instantly, a series of breathtaking spasms rocking through her as she spent.

He kissed his way up her body once more, over her ribs, across her breasts. He kissed above her madly beating heart. "And most importantly, here," he murmured against her skin.

She caressed him everywhere she could. His shoulders, his chest, and then she grew daring enough to reach between them, taking him in her hand. He was hot and firm, the skin surprisingly silken. Touching his rigid manhood made a fresh ache pulse within her, a new onslaught of need.

The breath hissed from him, fluttering over her flesh. "Bloody hell, angel."

"Do you like this?" she whispered.

"Yes." He took her hand in his and showed her how to pleasure him.

He kissed her throat, kissed a path to her ear, nibbling at it until she shivered. His large body was atop hers, a welcome weight pressing her to the bed. She slid her hand over him, up and down, relishing her ability to make him groan and rock against her.

"I love you," he said as he trailed his lips across her jaw.

They met in a kiss, open-mouthed and voracious, tongues tangling. She tasted herself on his tongue, mingling with his chocolate. Frederica sucked on his tongue, body angling against his, seeking more. Seeking everything. She wanted to consume him and to be consumed by him all at once.

He broke the kiss, pressing his forehead to hers. "Put me inside you."

His sinful command sent a trickle of wetness between her thighs. Feeling bold, she guided him to where she ached. As one, they moved. His cock glided inside her. One thrust of his hips, and he was buried inside her as deep as he could go. She was full of him, stretched, and this time, there was no nip of pain, only the sweet rush of boundless pleasure.

He sealed their mouths again, and it was the kiss of possession. The kiss that said she was his and he was hers. It was the kiss that said they had both finally found their home in each other.

Duncan flexed his hips, beginning a rhythm that was torturously slow at first, allowing her body to accommodate his size. As she arched against him, demanding more, faster, he obeyed, thrusting in and out. They were one, mindless together. His fingers plucked at the sensitive bud he had already so thoroughly pleasured, and it was all she needed.

She cried out her release, clenching on him, bringing him deeper. He sank inside her faster, harder, riding out the ripples of her pleasure, until he reached his release. He came with a hot rush inside her, and she clung to him, their hearts pounding together.

"I love you," she said when she had at last caught her breath.

He kissed her slowly. "I love you, my angel. You are a miracle. *My* miracle, and I'll never stop loving you."

* * *

FREDERICA LOOKED at the Duke of Amberley, and she could only feel one emotion: pity. Before her sat a man in the sunset of his life, a man who had no one and nothing left. He had shuffled into her drawing room with his walking stick and his pronounced limp, as if the weight of the world had settled upon him and he found himself struggling against it. He looked far older than his years, a man who had lived a life of iniquity and now paid the price.

It was late afternoon, and Duncan was not yet due to return from his club. When the duke had initially sent word he wished to meet with her, she had been stunned. Her initial reaction had been to deny him, but she had relented against her better judgment, wondering why he had requested an audience so long after what had transpired with Willingham.

"Thank you for seeing me, my lady." His tone was formal and stilted.

"Mrs. Kirkwood," she was quick to correct. A habit, it would seem.

"Mrs. Kirkwood," he acknowledged, the name sounding even more awkward than his greeting. As if he disliked the taste of it on his tongue.

How odd to think he was the father of the man she loved and yet wished nothing to do with him. She would never understand how the duke could have so cruelly refused to help his own son. But then, his treatment of Duncan had made him the man he was, formidable, determined, and strong. The best man she knew. "I admit I am curious as to why you would seek me out, sir."

"As you can imagine, it concerns your husband."

Her lips compressed. Just what she had feared. If this man thought to hurt Duncan in any manner, he was deadly

279

wrong. She would protect him at all costs. "Mr. Kirkwood is not at home."

"I did not expect him to be. Indeed, if he were, I would not imagine he would see me." The duke paused, seeming to gather his thoughts. "I have written him, and he refuses to answer."

Either the man before her had no notion of how deeply he had hurt her husband or he was utterly lacking in empathy. "I am sure he feels there is nothing left to be said between the two of you."

"That is precisely what he feels," came a deep voice she knew and loved so well.

With a start, she turned to find Duncan striding over the threshold of the chamber. He delivered a perfunctory bow to the duke and then another to her before standing at her side. She stood, wanting to throw her arms about him in a protective embrace but settling for silently demonstrating her support.

Amberley struggled to regain his feet. "Kirkwood."

Duncan's hand sought hers, their fingers tangling. Tension radiated from him, and she absorbed just how tightly he was wound through their joined hands. "Amberley. What reason have you to importune my wife and trespass at my home?"

"You will not answer me, and there is a matter of great import I wish settled."

"You have your vowels back," Duncan bit out. "As promised. What more could you want from me?"

"Nothing." The duke's expression changed, softening somehow, making him seem more world weary and less frigid. "There is something I wish to give you."

Duncan stiffened at her side. "I do not want anything from you, Amberley."

"It belonged to your mother." The duke reached inside his

coat and extracted a ring, holding it out to Duncan. A large ruby winked from an elegant gold setting. "It was a gift from me to her, and when I ended our arrangement, she left it, too proud to take anything from me. I…I thought it fitting for you to have."

Duncan did not move to take the ring, so Frederica accepted it in his stead, knowing it was a piece of his mother he would wish to keep, regardless of who it had come from. He had nothing else left of her save his memories. Here, in this ring, he would have something she had worn on her finger.

"Why now?" Duncan asked coldly.

"Because it is long overdue, and I have regrets. More regrets than you can imagine." Amberley seemed sincere. Almost regretful.

But her husband was not convinced. "Do you require funds?"

"No."

"Then why?" Duncan growled.

She squeezed his fingers with hers, aching for him. He still bore so much pain from his past, and now he was once again being forced to confront it. His grip on her tightened, as if he drew strength from her.

"Because I will die soon, and I wish to make amends," Amberley snapped. "My heart is ailing, my body betraying me, and I…I am responsible for Willingham. For what he became. I am also bequeathing everything that is not part of the entail to you and your heirs."

Frederica gasped.

Duncan's reaction was equally swift and strong. "I have built my own fortune, and I do not want or need anything from you, old man."

"You will have it whether you want it or not." Amberley paused. "Regardless, you are my son."

There it was. The acknowledgment Duncan had been longing for.

Years and a lifetime of heartache too late.

Frederica ached for him.

"There was a time when I would have given anything to hear you say those words, Amberley," he said, "but that time is long gone."

Amberley inclined his head. "Fair enough, Mr. Kirkwood. But you shall be hearing from my solicitor, whether you like it or not." He offered a stiff bow. "Good day Mrs. Kirkwood. *Son.*"

And then, he turned on his heel, and with achingly slow steps and the clack of his walking stick on the polished floor, he made his exit. When he had gone, Frederica drew Duncan into her embrace, still clutching his mother's ring tightly in her hand. He buried his face in her neck, inhaling, his arms wrapping around her waist.

"I dreamt of this day as a lad," he whispered. "The day he would say I was his. The day he would call me son."

"Oh, my love," she said softly, stroking his back, kissing his cheek. "I am sorry it took all this for you to have that day."

"I am not." He pressed a kiss to her throat and then raised his head, gazing down at her with so much tenderness she trembled. "For if I had not experienced every day of my life that led me to you, I never would have found you. I would not now be holding you in my arms. I found my happiness in loving you, Frederica. I do not need the Duke of Amberley or the mantle of *son* or a moldering heap of stones for that. All I need is you."

"And all I need is you, my darling man." She could not resist rising on her toes and sealing her mouth with his.

EPILOGUE

*F*rederica sat in the yellow salon, a cheerful room she had transformed into her daytime writing office. It boasted another large, beautifully carved desk like the one in her chamber, floor-to-ceiling windows that over-looked the charming little garden, and golden walls dotted with paintings she had chosen herself.

Sunlight splashed everywhere, particularly in the after-noons, and she adored the brightness. After so many nights scrawling her work with nothing but a lone candle for accompaniment in the evening, so much light was most welcome, and being within the space never failed to fill her with a sense of gratitude.

She dropped her quill back into its inkwell and surveyed her desk. Her latest manuscript was neatly stacked, complete with all its corrections and deletions. Her foul copy was often scarcely legible, and she knew it. But at least her next book was well underway, and not a moment too soon as the book she had retitled *The Silent Duke* was due to be printed any day now.

Even so, as thrilled as she was that Duncan's publishing

company was about to make her novel come to life, there was another reason for the happiness bubbling up within her. Indeed, she could scarcely concentrate upon the scene she had been attempting to write.

It was incredible. Frightening. Thrilling.

It was everything, all at once, but she ought not to be surprised, because she had married Duncan Kirkwood, and each day with him was an adventure of the best sort.

A knock sounded on her door, and she rose from her chair, needing to stretch. She had been writing away for at least three hours, and her knees were protesting, growing stiff. "You may enter," she called out.

Their hulking butler Pretty entered the chamber, bearing some parcels. Another of Duncan's good deeds, the butler was still growing accustomed to his position, but he was nevertheless progressing nicely. "Good day, my lady. We have received another delivery from Her Grace."

Dear heavens. She certainly hoped her mother had not bought her more inkwells. Frederica strode to the servant, accepting the packages. "Thank you, Pretty. That will be all."

He bowed and left once more. Frederica opened the first package and found a sterling silver inkwell, along with a note from her mother. It was engraved with a rose motif and inlaid with mother-of-pearl. Quite lovely, and dear, too, she was sure. Before she could inspect the other parcels, the door opened once more.

And there stood her husband, so handsome he made her ache. She could not wait to tell him her news. "Duncan, you are home."

"Hazlitt is running the club for me today as I have more important matters to attend to. Namely, my wife, who is looking utterly fetching in this sunlight."

He moved to her and she to him, and they met in the middle of the chamber. They kissed with the frantic urgency of lovers who had been parted for a decade rather than a man and woman who had last kissed mere hours before. But that was the way of it with them, always had been and always would be. Frederica had been so caught up in his arrival she had neglected to relinquish her latest inkwell, and it pressed between their chests as their lips devoured each other's.

Duncan broke away first, caressing her cheek, his gaze trailing over her with so much heat she swore she would turn into a smoking heap of ruins at his feet. He looked down at the inkwell her mother had sent, already forgotten.

"What have you there?" He dropped a kiss on her cheek.

"Another inkwell from my mother, I am afraid," she said. Much had changed for her since she had become Duncan's wife, but some things would never alter, and her family was one of the latter. Her mother still spent most of her days engrossed in shopping, her father remained a disapproving jackanape who insisted she could have avoided a mésalliance with Duncan, and Benedict sided with Father, though he had warmed to Duncan in gradually increasing increments.

"It is a miracle there are any inkwells left to be had in the city." Duncan raised a golden brow. "She sent you five only yesterday."

Yes, she had, in addition to the three dozen or so she had already gifted upon Frederica. Tall inkwells, short ones, porcelain, glass, sterling silver... Mother had found, purchased, and given them all to Frederica. She rather fancied it was her mother's way of apologizing for her lack of tender emotion toward her. But perhaps it was simply that Mother was running out of space for her acquisitions at Westlake House and needed a new location of storage. Frederica could not be sure.

"This one is quite lovely, adorned with roses and mother-of-pearl," she said blandly. "And you must admit, the inkwells are, if nothing else, a far more appropriate gift than the fans."

"Naturally," he agreed, grinning down at her. "But who needs a hundred of the damned things all at once?"

She smiled back and shook her head ruefully. "No one."

He framed her face then, gazing at her in that way of his, seemingly as if he could never tire of committing her face to memory. As if he could look a thousand times and it would still never be enough. "I have a gift of my own for you, my love."

"You do?" She could not resist drawing him to her for another kiss.

She teased the seam of his lips, and with a growl, he opened for her, his tongue sliding against hers in a decadent caress. She could kiss this man forever and never grow weary of it. But she had news to share, and that news would not be contained. It rose within her, buoyant and miraculous, like an ascension balloon.

She broke the kiss, gazing up at him with her heart in her eyes. "I have a gift for you as well."

"Do tell, Mrs. Kirkwood." His gaze darkened with wicked intent. "I hope it involves you, naked, seated at your writing desk and me on my knees before you."

Heat shot straight to her core at his words. "I should like nothing better, but that is not the gift I had in mind."

"My gift to you first, because I am selfish and I cannot wait another moment for you to have it." He reached into his coat and extracted a handsome leather-bound volume, holding it out to her. "An even exchange. Give me the bloody inkwell."

Her book, in print, at last.

Awed, Frederica handed off the inkwell and accepted *The Silent Duke*, running her fingers over the cover, tracing the embossed gilt of her name. "Oh, Duncan. It's beautiful! I love it so."

"It is the first copy, and I wanted you to have it."

"Thank you." She hugged it to her. "Thank you, my love."

"The hard work was all yours." He drew her to him for another kiss.

When she was breathless, she tore her lips away once more, heart bursting with love and happiness. "Now for your gift." She took his hand—the one that wasn't holding the inkwell—and brought it to her stomach.

His eyes widened, and he stilled, an expression of adorable befuddlement on his face. "Frederica?"

"A babe," she whispered, smiling as tears welled in her eyes.

"Are you certain?" his tone was hushed, reverent.

She nodded. "Do you like your gift, my love?"

He caught her to him in a crushing embrace, burying his face in her hair. "It is the best gift I have ever received aside from you, angel."

* * *

SOMETIME JUST BEFORE the sun began its daily sojourn into the sky, Duncan sat in his study and turned the final page of *The Silent Duke*. Tears burned his eyes as he stared at the cover of the leather-bound volume. *F. Kirkwood*, it read. She had chosen to use her own name rather than a pseudonym as most ladies in her position would have done.

He was glad now, pride in her burning through him, for the novel he had just read was a masterpiece. It was all Frederica, imaginative, vibrant, bold, and determined. Her sentences flowed, her characters drew him in as he read, until he had desperately awaited the next paragraph, the next page, and he had read all night long, replacing his candles thrice until the story reached its completion.

His heart pounding, he extinguished the lights and found his way to his wife, holding her book clutched in his fingers all the way. They had sold all the initial copies they had run, some one thousand of them, and he expected they would do another run within the month.

He was happy for her.

Grateful for her.

Humbled to be privileged enough to call the gorgeous, talented creature that was Frederica Kirkwood his wife. Finding his way to her through the dark, he climbed stairs, stalked a hall, let himself into her chamber where he was greeted by the soft sounds of her breathing into the night. Shrugging out of his garments, he slipped beneath the bedclothes and alongside her.

With a sweet sound, she reached for him, her hand landing upon his bare chest. He caught it in his and raised it to his lips for a worshipful kiss. "I finished your novel, Frederica."

She stirred awake, shifting closer to him. "Mmm. Duncan, I love you."

"And I love you, my darling wife." His hands were upon her now, because he could not help himself, and she was naked as he had left her beneath the coverlets, so smooth, so silken, and warm. His goddess. The deliciously rounded arse he had so admired on the day he had first seen her nestled against his groin. "You told my mother's story."

"Someone had to, my love," she said softly, burrowing herself deeper into his arms.

He smiled into the darkness, his hands moving to the gentle swell of her belly where the new life they had created together grew. Happiness settled into the marrow of his bones, deep and contented and exquisite.

"Thank you, angel." He kissed the top of her head. "Your novel is beautiful. I loved every moment of it. And I am heartily glad the duke loses his ability to speak."

Though his father had attempted to establish a truce,

much time and healing would be required before Duncan could ever forgive him for his ill treatment of his mother.

"It is not a fitting enough punishment." Her hands covered his, warm and small and beloved. "But I could not have his manhood fall off, could I?"

Duncan could not contain his laughter at her question, for it was so very Frederica, the essence of the sensual, intelligent, eccentric, bold woman who owned his heart. "Have I told you I love you recently?"

"Two minutes ago, or so, but you may say it again if you like." She turned in his arms and pressed her mouth to his.

Duncan had never stood a chance against the persistence of one midnight-haired lady who had taken his world and his club by storm one day. Smiling against her lips, he kissed her back.

She was, without a doubt, the best gamble he had ever made.

"I love you," he told her again, and then he rolled her onto her back and made love to her as the sun rose over London.

THANK you for reading Duncan and Frederica's happily ever after! I hope you loved their story! If you're looking for Morgan's story, *Marquess of Mayhem* do read on for a sneak peek or find it here. If you're looking for more deliciously wicked Regency romance from me, check out some of my latest series, *The Sinful Suttons and The Wicked Winters*.

Please consider leaving an honest review. Reviews are greatly appreciated! If you'd like to keep up to date with my latest releases and series news, sign up for my newsletter here or follow me on Amazon or BookBub. Join my reader's group on Facebook for bonus content, early excerpts, giveaways, and more.

* * *

Marquess of Mayhem
Sins and Scoundrels Book 3

FROM THE MOMENT MORGAN, Marquess of Searle, discovered the true identity of the Spanish guerrillero responsible for his capture by French troops, he had made three objectives.

Objective one: sell out his commission and return to England before the Spaniard. *Accomplished.*

Objective two: ruin the bastard's sister so she would be forced to wed him. *In medias res.*

Objective three: make the rest of the Spaniard's life a living hell until he ended it on the field of honor. *A promise.*

Retribution was the sole thing on his mind when Morgan first saw Lady Leonora Forsythe. She was seated on the periphery of the ballroom, attended by a turban-wearing dowd with a wan complexion. He could only assume the turban was the lady's mother.

He had been told Lady Leonora suffered an unfortunate limp, which precluded her from dancing. He had not been told she possessed the breathtaking beauty of an angel. The former did not deter him. He could easily guide her into a darkened alcove or an empty hall. Nor did the latter. Even angels were meant to fall.

Watching her, he sipped from his glass of punch. The stuff was sickening and sweet and its only saving grace was in the bite of the spirits lacing it. When he imbibed, he preferred unsullied spirits. The sort that made him forget, if only for an evening. Sadly, not even a drop of illicit Scottish whisky was to be had at the Kirkwood ball.

The man owned a gaming hell that served the best liquor in the land. Morgan would have expected better, but he supposed anything less than proper ballroom fare would have been frowned upon by the tittering lords and ladies who had assembled here this evening. Kirkwood's wife was a duke's daughter, and it would seem the festivities were his attempt to blur the boundaries between his world and the quality.

Morgan didn't give a damn for balls. He also didn't give a damn about the punch he was drinking or the room in which he stood or the fact he was not imprisoned and being tortured by French soldiers who wanted answers he refused to give. His body, beneath the trappings of his evening finery, was marked with scars and burns, all testaments to his inability to ever give a damn about anything again.

Anything except making the Spaniard suffer, that was.

El Corazón Oscuro, the Dark Heart. Also known as the Earl of Rayne, half-brother to Lady Leonora. It was almost impossible to believe as he flicked his gaze over her, marveling at her white-blonde hair and skin pale enough to rival cream. But it was true. The blackest-hearted devil he had ever known and the lovely woman in the diaphanous silver gown shared blood.

And soon they would share one more connection.

Morgan's wrath.

But first, he needed an introduction.

Want more? Get *Marquess of Mayhem* now!

DON'T MISS SCARLETT'S OTHER ROMANCES!

Complete Book List
HISTORICAL ROMANCE

Heart's Temptation
A Mad Passion (Book One)
Rebel Love (Book Two)
Reckless Need (Book Three)
Sweet Scandal (Book Four)
Restless Rake (Book Five)
Darling Duke (Book Six)
The Night Before Scandal (Book Seven)

Wicked Husbands
Her Errant Earl (Book One)
Her Lovestruck Lord (Book Two)
Her Reformed Rake (Book Three)
Her Deceptive Duke (Book Four)
Her Missing Marquess (Book Five)
Her Virtuous Viscount (Book Six)

League of Dukes
Nobody's Duke (Book One)
Heartless Duke (Book Two)
Dangerous Duke (Book Three)
Shameless Duke (Book Four)
Scandalous Duke (Book Five)
Fearless Duke (Book Six)

Notorious Ladies of London
Lady Ruthless (Book One)
Lady Wallflower (Book Two)
Lady Reckless (Book Three)
Lady Wicked (Book Four)
Lady Lawless (Book Five)
Lady Brazen (Book 6)

Unexpected Lords
The Detective Duke (Book One)
The Playboy Peer (Book Two)

The Wicked Winters
Wicked in Winter (Book One)
Wedded in Winter (Book Two)
Wanton in Winter (Book Three)
Wishes in Winter (Book 3.5)
Willful in Winter (Book Four)
Wagered in Winter (Book Five)
Wild in Winter (Book Six)
Wooed in Winter (Book Seven)
Winter's Wallflower (Book Eight)
Winter's Woman (Book Nine)
Winter's Whispers (Book Ten)
Winter's Waltz (Book Eleven)
Winter's Widow (Book Twelve)

Winter's Warrior (Book Thirteen)

The Sinful Suttons
Sutton's Spinster (Book One)
Sutton's Sins (Book Two)
Sutton's Surrender (Book Three)

Sins and Scoundrels
Duke of Depravity
Prince of Persuasion
Marquess of Mayhem
Sarah
Earl of Every Sin
Duke of Debauchery

Second Chance Manor
The Matchmaker and the Marquess by Scarlett Scott
The Angel and the Aristocrat *by Merry Farmer*
The Scholar and the Scot *by Caroline Lee*
The Venus and the Viscount by Scarlett Scott
The Buccaneer and the Bastard *by Merry Farmer*
The Doxy and the Duke *by Caroline Lee*

Stand-alone Novella
Lord of Pirates

CONTEMPORARY ROMANCE
Love's Second Chance
Reprieve (Book One)
Perfect Persuasion (Book Two)
Win My Love (Book Three)

Coastal Heat
Loved Up (Book One)

ABOUT THE AUTHOR

USA Today and Amazon bestselling author Scarlett Scott writes steamy Victorian and Regency romance with strong, intelligent heroines and sexy alpha heroes. She lives in Pennsylvania and Maryland with her Canadian husband, adorable identical twins, and two dogs.

A self-professed literary junkie and nerd, she loves reading anything, but especially romance novels, poetry, and Middle English verse. Catch up with her on her website http://www.scarlettscottauthor.com/. Hearing from readers never fails to make her day.

Scarlett's complete book list and information about upcoming releases can be found at http://www.scarlettscottauthor.com/.

Connect with Scarlett! You can find her here:
Join Scarlett Scott's reader group on Facebook for early excerpts, giveaways, and a whole lot of fun!
Sign up for her newsletter here
https://www.tiktok.com/@authorscarlettscott

facebook.com/AuthorScarlettScott

twitter.com/scarscoromance

instagram.com/scarlettscottauthor

bookbub.com/authors/scarlett-scott

amazon.com/Scarlett-Scott/e/B004NW8N2I

pinterest.com/scarlettscott

Printed in Great Britain
by Amazon

26383155R00172